Mary E. Pearce, a Londoner by birth, now lives in the relative peace of Gloucestershire. She tackled various jobs – shop assistant, filing clerk, waitress, usherette – before settling down to write seriously in the 1960s. Her career began with the appearance of short stories in magazines and has led to the publication of nine highly successful novels which have been translated into Dutch, French, German, Italian, Japanese, Norwegian and Portuguese, as well as being bestsellers in America.

'An author with a rare feel for country life and speech' *Sunday Telegraph*

'Warm and vivid' *Publishers Weekly*

'About the human nature of people which is Mary Pearce's secret ... The dialogue both convinces and entertains' *Manchester Evening News*

'All the characters are drawn with warm understanding and humour' *Eastern Daily Press*

Also by Mary E. Pearce:

The Apple Tree Saga
APPLE TREE LEAN DOWN
JACK MERCYBRIGHT
THE SORROWING WIND
SEEDTIME AND HARVEST

CAST A LONG SHADOW
POLSINNEY HARBOUR
THE TWO FARMS
THE OLD HOUSE AT RAILES

MARY E. PEARCE

The Land Endures

WARNER BOOKS

A *Warner* Book

First published in Great Britain in 1978
by Macdonald and Jane's Publishers Ltd
Published in 1986 by Macdonald & Co
This edition published by Warner Books in 1994
Reprinted 1996

A CIP catalogue record for this book is
available from the British Library.

ISBN 0 7515 0905 1

Printed in England by Clays Ltd, St Ives plc

Warner Books
A Division of
Little, Brown and Company (UK)
Brettenham House
Lancaster Place
London WC2E 7EN

For
Kathleen and Eric

Chapter 1

The farmhouse welcomed them from the beginning. They felt they belonged there, all of them, as though the place cast a spell on them. Stephen had had his doubts, of course, and sometimes Gwen had shared in them, for the purchase had not been an easy one, and the outgoing farmer, Mr Gould, had driven a hard bargain over the valuation of the standing crops. But that was behind them; a thing of the past. Holland Farm was now theirs, even if it did have a mortgage on it, and when they clip-clopped into the yard and saw the old, quiet house waiting for them, they knew they had made the right decision.

The house was not quiet for long. As Stephen and Gwen stood in the hall, waiting the arrival of the furniture van, the children ran from room to room, making their own discoveries. After the tiny house at Springs, the space of the farmhouse delighted them. Their voices rang out, echoing, and their feet pounded the bare boards.

"Is it possible," Stephen said, "that four children can make so much noise?"

"Does it distress you?" Gwen asked. She followed him into the big kitchen. She still worried about him, ceaselessly, for the war had left its mark on him, and even now, more than a year after his discharge, his nerves were still badly frayed. "Shall I tell them to be quiet?"

"God, no! Let them yell. They never had the chance in Prior's Walk."

And yell the children certainly did. It seemed they meant to make up for the past.

"Chris! Come and look! This bedroom is vast!"

"Never mind the bedroom. You come up here. There's a secret cupboard in this wall."

"I can see the cattle from up here. *Our* cattle. And some

1

sheep. Yoo-hoo, Joanna, why don't you come?"

"Where's Jamesy calling from?"

"He's up in the attic. So's little Emma."

"The furniture's coming!" Jamesy shrieked. "I've seen the van coming up the track."

"It's miles away yet," Joanna said, glancing out of the nearest window. "It'll take all day, the rate it's going."

But downstairs they ran, in search of their parents, and found them in the kitchen-cum-living room, where three casement windows looked out on the yard and where, in the big blackleaded iron range, the wood ashes were still warm, although the Goulds had been gone two days. There was a bundle of sticks in the hearth, together with a heap of logs: a gesture of Mr Gould's goodwill. Stephen threw the sticks into the stove and blew on the ashes until they caught. Soon he had the split logs alight, and the children's faces were lit by the flames.

"The furniture's coming," Chris said.

"Is it?" said Stephen. He looked at his watch. "Two o'clock. Bang on the nail."

"As soon as they've unpacked the kettle," said Gwen, "make sure they bring it to me."

It was cold for early October. They would all be glad of a cup of tea.

Gradually, as the carpets were laid and the furniture was carried in, the house became more and more their own, beginning with the kitchen-cum-living-room, the most important room in the house. Wing-chair; book case; old sagging couch; the Monet print and the oval mirror: all these soon had a place and looked as though they had been there for years; but some disagreement arose as to where the dining-table and chairs should stand, and the carved mahogany sideboard, and the desk that had come from Stephen's office. The removal men had their own ideas and the foreman especially argued with passion.

"Oh, well!" Gwen said. "I can always alter things afterwards."

But when, on leaving, the men came into the kitchen again, to receive Stephen's tip, the foreman looked round at their handiwork and touched Gwen's arm.

2

"You won't better that!" he said to her. "Not if you try for a hundred years!"

And he was right, as Gwen afterwards had to admit, for even when spring-cleaning time came round and the furniture had to be shifted about, she found herself putting it back again, item by item, as before. Holland Farm was like that. It was not a place that invited change.

The weather was wet the day they moved in and remained wet throughout the weekend, but the four children were perfectly happy, poking into cupboards, attics, cellars, till the house had yielded all its secrets. Under a floorboard in the attic they found a broken china mug, a spinning-top, and a small wooden doll.

"The Goulds had no children," Stephen said, "and they lived in this house nearly fifty years."

"Visitors' children, perhaps," said Gwen.

But there were other discoveries: drawings of animals on the walls, revealed when the wallpaper was removed; a girl's name, Rosina Lane, entwined in a pattern of vine-leaves; and, under another loose floorboard, a bunch of herbs in a sealed jar that bore a label and these faded words: "Gathered by me on Midsummer's Eve: Cicely Lane, aged eleven; year of grace, 1860."

The two sisters, if sisters they were, would now be old ladies of seventy or more, but to the Wayman children, coming to the house in 1919, Cicely and Rosina Lane were still two children like themselves, held up as models to one another or used to excuse some fall from grace. "Cicely would never have bitten her nails," Joanna said to little Emma, and Jamesy, having borrowed something without permission, said scornfully: "Rosina would never have made such a fuss about a rotten box of paints!"

* * * * *

After the house, there were the farm buildings to be explored: stables, cowsheds, cartsheds, barns; and all around lay the meadows and fields, almost two hundred and fifty acres, spreading their slopes to the south-west, and running down to the Derrent brook. The freedom of it

3

went to their heads; released from school at the weekends, they ran wild from dawn to dusk; clattered into the house for meals, and bundled out again in a rush, the instant they were given leave.

"Look after Emma!" Gwen would call, but they would be gone like mad things, helter-skelter across the yard, with Emma trotting along behind.

"No doubt what *they* think of Holland Farm," Stephen said. "How did we manage to keep all that energy pent up close in the house at Springs?" And sometimes he would say to his wife: "What do *you* feel, now we're here?"

"Ask me in a few years' time!"

It was only a joke, and they both knew it. Leaving Springs and buying the farm was the best thing they had ever done. There were no regrets on either side. They wondered why they had waited so long.

It was the war that had made up their minds, by showing them where their values lay. Stephen had been gassed in 1918, and the doctor's advice had been very blunt.

"Get out of doors as much as you can. It's the only thing for lungs like yours. If you go back to your damned office, you'll be asking for trouble, no doubt of that!"

So Stephen sold his partnership in the legal firm of Hallam and Dobbs and worked for a year on a farm near Springs, helping an ex-Army man like himself, and learning something about the land. He had always had a hankering to farm, and Gwen was a Worcestershire farmer's daughter. They had no one to consider but themselves and their children, for Gwen's parents were both dead and so were Stephen's, and the only relations they had left in the world were his two cousins, who lived in India. Land prices were high just then, but he had the money from his partnership and a small gratuity from the Army, and, after raising a mortgage, he was able to buy Holland Farm. His own house and his own land! What better investment could there be for the future of his family? But he worried sometimes, nevertheless.

"I *must* make a go of it," he said. "I can't afford to make mistakes."

"Of course we shall make a go of it! Why shouldn't we?"

4

Gwen said.

Why not indeed? Farm prices were pretty good, having risen throughout the war, and there were government guarantees. But Stephen knew that the good times would probably not last forever. He therefore went cautiously and was always ready to take advice, either from the neighbouring farmers or from the men who worked for him. These men were there when he took the farm. He made no changes but hoped for the best.

"They're not a bad bunch," Gould had said. "There's only one you've got to watch and you'll soon find out which one that is. He belongs to the union. You'll soon hear from *him*!"

Stephen thought this was prejudice. He was inclined to be amused.

"Is there only one union man among them?"

"One's enough!" Gould had said.

The man in question was Morton George. He had a watchful, suspicious manner, but never looked you in the eye. Stephen decided to reserve judgment. Of the eight men there, he found he liked Bob Tupper best. The others, when they gave advice, made a mystery of the reasons behind it, but Bob Tupper gave it straight.

"I shouldn't plough the Home Field yet, 'cos that'll still be workable later on, even when it's wet. I'd start with the Freelands and the Goose Ground – they're dry enough now but they won't be for long."

It was the same when buying stock. Bob would go with him to the sales and, with a few quiet words in his ear, tell him what to guard against.

"Not only in the cow," as Stephen, laughing, said to Gwen, "but in the farmer who's selling her!"

Bob knew the district inside out; he was an expert in everything; and Stephen was thankful to have such a man. Bob was in his early forties. Except for two years away in the war, he had been at Holland Farm since the age of eleven, thirty-two years in all, longer than any other man there.

"You should be foreman by rights," Stephen said.

"Mr Gould didn't hold with that, setting one man above the rest. He didn't hold with paying the extra wages neither."

"I'm not Mr Gould," Stephen said.

Most of the other men were pleased when Bob's new status became known. Their jibes were friendly, good-humoured, broad.

"Twopence to speak to you now, is it, Bob?"

"Shouldn't you wear a bowler hat?"

"Will the news be printed in *The Gazette*?"

Billy Rye said the promotion made little difference that he could see.

"Bob's been telling us what to do for donkey's years. It's just been made official, that's all."

Only Morton George seemed less than pleased. He lounged in the office doorway, nibbling a straw.

"I suppose it's on account of the war."

"What do you mean?" Stephen asked.

"Well, you're both old soldiers, you and him."

"That's got nothing to do with it. Bob is the senior man here. It's only right to recognize that."

"We should've voted among ourselves. That's the proper way to get a foreman."

"Now look here –" Stephen began, but was interrupted by Billy Rye.

"If we *had've* voted," Billy said, "Bob would be foreman just the same cos he's the best man for the job and we all know it." And then, to make light of it all, Billy gave Bob Tupper a nudge. "If I don't get a drink outa you after that, I shall want to know the reason why!"

Bob Tupper was not the only war veteran at Holland Farm. Nate Hopson was another. On November the eleventh, Armistice Day, these two men arrived for work wearing sprigs of evergreen in their caps, and later on that same morning, carting muck from the muck-bury, they stopped work at eleven o'clock and, removing their caps, stood bare-headed in the rain, remembering their fallen comrades.

It was not true that Stephen favoured these veterans, but it was inevitable that he should feel some kinship with them. The war had left its stamp on him and them, as on all those men who had gone to the edge of the pit and looked in, and that stamp could be recognized at a glance. Tupper and

6

Hopson saw at once that Stephen had been out at the Front. They heard the huskiness in his voice and knew he had suffered poisoning by gas. They noticed the three crooked fingers of his right hand and the deep scar running up his arm, and they recognized it as a shrapnel wound. And they, although they bore no visible scars, were just as easily known to him. They had a certain look in their eyes, as though they marvelled at everything they saw and yet were weary in their souls.

They gave themselves away, too, in their habits of speech and the jokes they made, as when Bob referred to his sandwiches as "wads" or gave the time as "thirteen-fifteen." Once, when the cattle were being driven up an unfenced track between two fields and kept straying out over the ploughland on one side, Tupper, walking behind the plough, shouted to Hopson, in charge of the herd: "Watch your dressing by the right there!"

Stephen would smile on hearing these things, even while he shrank inside. Neither he nor they ever talked of the war. They tried to put it out of their minds, though they couldn't of course, and would never be able to, all their lives. Still, something was salvaged from the waste: the kinship was there, and it made him smile.

As for Morton George, who sneered behind Stephen's back, it was partly because he felt left out.

"What do you talk about, you and him? All about how you beat the Hun?"

"The trouble with Mort is, he's jealous," said Nate.

"He should've said so before," said Bob. "He could've had my place out there if only he'd asked me in 1916."

"He was too busy running the union."

"Oh, you can laugh!" George exclaimed. "Who got your wages up to forty-eight-and-six a week?"

"I shall have to do something about that union of yours."

"Join it, d'you mean?"

"I shall have to remember it in my prayers!"

* * * * *

Stephen was determined from the beginning that Gwen

7

should have help in the house, and it happened that there were two women already there, who had worked for Mr and Mrs Gould and were now willing to work for the Waymans. Gwen had been ill with 'flu the previous winter, and the illness had pulled her down badly. She herself would never admit it; she liked to think she was as strong as a horse; but Stephen was concerned for her, and tried to save her all he could.

The duties of a farmer's wife overflowed the house itself. The dairy claimed a lot of her time, and there were the chickens, the turkeys, the geese. There were sickly lambs to hand-rear and often a calf that had to be weaned, and later on, at harvest times, she would be needed in the fields. It was useless for Stephen to say that Gwen must not do all these things: she wanted to do everything; it was therefore a comfort to him when Mrs Bessemer agreed to stay on, for she was a cheerful Amazon, with mighty arms and enormous hands, who would surely make nothing of the household chores.

But Gwen and he soon perceived that although Mrs Bessemer would polish fanatically at the tops of tables, she had a dislike of bending her back, and it was in fact Agnes Mayle, short and dumpy and quick-tempered, who worked the hardest and got things done. Agnes would scold Mrs Bessemer, who spent a whole morning cleaning the silver, and would chivvy her from place to place, thrusting a bucket and mop into her hands and doing her best to make her ashamed.

"How can you sit there, rub-rub-rub, when Mrs Wayman's slaving away, scrubbing and scouring for all she's worth? Get into that dairy and give her a hand!"

There were ding-dong battles between these two, and Agnes Mayle's rough tongue often prevailed where Gwen's civil entreaties failed. But on one score at least the two women were in accord, and that was in their devotion to the children. Agnes was an excellent cook, and during the school holidays, the children would sneak in repeatedly, sure of being given a tart or a rock-cake each, still warm from the oven. And Mrs Bessemer, not to be outdone, was a specialist in providing drinks. On cold winter days it was hot cocoa or beef-tea, and in summer-time, when the hot days came, it was ice-cold gingerade, the recipe for which was a jealously guarded secret.

"That's my Bert's favourite drink. He'd drink it all day, given a chance. He says nobody makes gingerade like me."

"It's not the only thing your Bert drinks," Agnes muttered, under her breath.

Mrs Bessemer's husband, Bert, was invoked every day at Holland Farm. His word was law, and it seemed he held very strong ideas.

"My Bert don't like me peeling onions. We never have them at home ourselves. He don't like me cleaning your silver by rights, on account of it spoiling my hands, and that's why I have to wear them gloves. He don't like me spoiling my hands. They're a woman's best feature, he always says."

Gwen wondered about this fastidious man.

"What does your Bert do?" she asked, and before Mrs Bessemer could reply, Agnes gave a snort and said: "He's a cowman at Outlands, same as my dad!"

"*Second* cowman," Mrs Bessemer said.

Gwen was careful not to smile.

"How is it that you both work here, instead of at Outlands, then?" she asked. "I've heard Mr Challoner say more than once that he needs someone to help in the house."

"My Bert wouldn't like me working there. Mr Challoner's a widower, as you know, and must be sixty if he's a day, but he's got a sweet tooth as the saying is. It'd never do, my going there. Agnes will tell you. She knows what he is."

Agnes, by her silence, seemed to concur, but Gwen, to avoid further gossip concerning a neighbour, began to talk of other things. She mentioned it to Stephen, however, later that day, and he was not in the least surprised.

"Challoner ought to marry again. The trouble is, he's gone up in the world, now that farming is prospering, and there's no woman in the district worthy of the honour he could bestow."

"I thought you liked him," Gwen said.

"He's been a good neighbour to me so far. I've got no

9

reason to complain. But as for the people who work for him, that's a different matter, I'm afraid. He talks of his men as though they were dirt."

"I'm disappointed," Gwen said. "I thought he was rather a nice man."

But, as Stephen said, he himself got on well enough with Challoner, and that was something to be thankful for.

At its central point, for a hundred yards or so, Challoner's land ran with Stephen's; but a lane came down from Puppet Hill, passed through the yard at Outlands Farm, and continued on down to the village; so for two thirds of the way down, the two farms were thus divided. This in itself brought problems sometimes, especially at harvest time, when a loaded waggon from Holland Farm, going down, might meet an empty one from Outlands coming up. But a friendly agreement already existed between the two farms when Stephen arrived, and, by talking things over beforehand, it was easy to avoid serious trouble.

When the men from Outlands did meet the men from Holland Farm, there was a great deal of swearing and argument between them, before one or the other gave way. But it was only a ritual and was much enjoyed on both sides. There were two tractors at Outlands; there were only horses at Holland Farm; and this meant a certain rivalry.

"When are you going to get mechanized?" Johnny Marsh would ask, jeering, and Bob Tupper as often would say: "When that there tractor drops a foal!"

Challoner himself often chaffed Stephen on this score.

"Even old Gould had a tractor, you know, and you're a young man of thirty-five. I'd have thought you'd be bang up to date, making us older ones open our eyes."

"I can't afford to buy tractors yet," Stephen said. "I want to get my mortgage paid. And I'm happy enough, using horses."

There were eight mares at Holland Farm; he meant to breed from them if he could; and one of the first things he did was to buy a Shire stallion at Capleton Mop. There were no good stallions in the neighbourhood, so it seemed a good idea to keep his own, even if it was something of an extravagance.

"Besides which," as he said to Gwen, "I've already had a few enquiries from farmers round about, who've got brood mares, so Lucifer will not only be earning his keep but making a profit on the side."

When the stallion arrived and Bob Tupper inspected him, he remained silent a long time. It looked as though he disapproved. The stallion's face was light grey: "white as moonlight," Gwen had said: but his neck and body were dappled and dark, and his hind quarters were iron-black.

"Well?" Stephen said, impatiently.

"Strikes me he's a different horse in front from what he is behind," said Bob.

"But what do you think of him?" Stephen asked.

"I suppose he'll do," Bob said.

He was not much in favour of keeping a stallion on the farm. It meant a lot of extra work, and who had time for coddling a horse that ate its head off, day in, day out, got the odd mare into trouble now and then, and never did a hand's turn in front of the plough?

"If that's all that's worrying you," Stephen said, "I'm quite happy to look after Lucifer myself."

But that was not right, either, and Bob gave a series of little grunts.

"I daresay I'll manage to fit it in."

And manage it he did, for Lucifer was always in tip-top condition, beautiful in every respect, and he soon had an excellent reputation with farmers who bred from their own mares. When the stud fees came in they were kept in a cashbox of their own, and every six months or so Stephen would give half the money to Bob Tupper, for him to divide among the men.

"Have a few drinks at The Rose and Crown – Lucifer's paying!" he used to say.

* * * * *

Stephen and Challoner both kept sheep and it was the custom, already established many years, for the two farms to share their shearing, both flocks being done at Outlands one year, Holland Farm the next.

11

That year it was Challoner's turn, and on a fine morning in May, the flocks were herded together at Outlands, and shearing platforms were set up in the big barn. The doors at both sides were open wide and a warm wind blew gustily through, bringing, now and then, a skitter of rain. One doorway had a row of hurdles across it, made to open like a gate; the ewes were let in, a few at a time, delivered into the hands of the shearers, and let out naked the other side, to join their bleating lambs in the fold. Stephen's shepherd, Henry Goodshaw, got on well with the Outlands shepherd, Arthur Thorne, and to see these two experts handling their clippers, sending the fleeces rippling back, was something that made the children stare. Chris, especially, watched by the hour, and Challoner's younger son, Gerald, older than Chris by eighteen months, brought him a ewe and some clippers to try.

"Go on, I'll hold her. Try your hand."

Chris wanted to try but he was afraid. Supposing he were to cut the ewe? Reluctantly he shook his head and watched as Gerald displayed his skill.

"Nothing to it!" Gerald said. "Any fool can shear a sheep!"

The two boys went to the same school, King Edward's in Chepsworth, but they were at home for Whitsuntide. All the children were on holiday and ran to and fro among the shearers. The older ones helped to tie up the fleeces, and little Emma pottered about, gathering up stray wisps of wool or stirring the warm tar in its pot.

"Come out of that!" said Morton George. "D'you want to get it on your pinny?"

Emma stared at him in surprise. Nobody ever spoke to her like that. She turned away without a word and walked to the far end of the barn, to swing on a rope that hung from the rafters. But after a while, feeling herself no longer observed, she slipped away out of the barn, into the house in search of her mother.

Gwen and Mrs Bessemer were busy in the kitchen with Kitty Cox, preparing luncheon for the shearers. Kitty was the stockman's wife and worked in the house six days a week. She was strong, cheerful, sturdy and rough, and stood no nonsense from anyone. She put a biscuit into Emma's hand and sent her out to the garden to play.

Gwen was surprised, knowing John Challoner's passion for improvements on the farm, to find they did not extend to the house. Admittedly there were carpets in the best rooms and velvet curtains at the windows, but there was no piped water supply and no adequate sanitation. Water for the house came from a hand-pump outside the door, and the privy was merely a filthy latrine in a tumbledown shed next to the dairy. The kitchen range was very old and the stovepipe so rusted that it constantly smoked, yet Kitty was expected to produce a feast for the hungry shearers, and by some miracle, produce it she did.

Baked ham, boiled beef, and three pressed ox-tongues were carried out to the smaller barn and set on the trestle table there. Pork pies, mutton pasties, and jellied brawn, with bowls of potatoes, beans, and green peas, were carried out and set down there. Spotted dick puddings, apple tarts, jam turnovers and egg custards: all these were carried out; and, last but not least, a whole cheese was set on the board.

"I wish their damned union could see them now!" Challoner remarked to Gwen. "Stuffing themselves at my expense!"

They were a merry party at the table that day. The two groups of workmen got on well and the barrel of beer loosened their tongues. They returned to work in high good humour and as the shearing recommenced the jokes were still flying from mouth to mouth.

"I ent got room for a ewe in my lap. My belly's too full with all that good food."

"It's the Chepsworth ale that's done *me* in. This ewe of mine has got six legs!"

"Anybody want a trim?" Tupper asked. His clippers went snip-snip in the air. "Short back and sides? Or maybe a bob?"

"Bobbed by Bob," said Billy Rye, and there was laughter all round as the men settled down to work again.

Later, however, towards the end, a quarrel blew up suddenly between Morton George on the one hand and an Outlands man named Jack Mercybright on the other.

13

"Call that shearing?" Mercybright said. "The moths could do a better job than that!"

Indeed the ewe was a sorry sight. She tottered away from Morton George with ridges of wool left on her sides and blood seeping from three or four cuts.

"It's these damned clippers, that's what it is! I never used such duddy things!"

"It's a bad workman that blames his tools."

"Supposing we swap, then, you and me? You take my clippers and I'll take yours."

"Supposing you deal with that ewe of yours before the flies get wind of her?"

"Don't you tell me what to do!"

George snatched up the pot of tar and angrily dabbed at the ewe's wounds. He sent her, with a kick, to join the rest. The two shepherds, Goodshaw and Thorne, watched and listened while they worked, but neither of them spoke a word. The other shearers were silent too. Mercybright was an elderly man with thick grey hair and a grey beard, and was tall enough, when he stood erect, to look down his nose at Morton George.

"Now what? You gone on strike?"

"Maybe I have. I've a good cause. Shearing ent my proper work. Why should I shear the bloody sheep?"

"It's everyone's work when it's there to be done."

"It's shepherd's work. It ent mine. Why should we help to do their work?"

"They help in the fields at harvest time. What's the odds for God's sake?"

"The shepherd gets a lot more pay. Lambing money, for a start. Ask them two just what they earn!"

Outside in the yard, loading fleeces into a cart, Stephen and Challoner heard most of this. Challoner swore and leapt down. Stephen followed him into the barn.

"What's going on?" Challoner bawled, but the two participants turned away, each seizing a ewe from the man at the gate and stooping to the work in hand. Challoner, after a glance round, led the way outside again.

"You need to watch that fellow George. He's a union man, he stirs things up. I've got three of them here, you

14

know, and the first chance I get they'll be out on their necks."

"I agree with what you say about George. The man's a slacker, I know that. But why shouldn't they belong to a union? *We* belong to the N.F.U.".

"That's different," Challoner said, but was unable to explain why.

That evening, when the shearing was done, Stephen and Gwen and the four children walked back home across the fields. The pockets of Emma's pinafore were stuffed with bits of sheep's wool and she carried a lamb's tail in her hand. Her small legs were soon tired, and Stephen offered her a pick-a-back ride.

"*I'll* carry her," Chris said. He crouched for his sister to climb on his back. Gwen had told her eldest son that his father must be saved from exertion whenever possible, owing to the pains in his chest and side, and Chris had taken the lesson to heart. "Hold tight, Emma! We're off!" he cried, and galloped across the fields towards home, leaving the others well behind.

"My hands are all soft with handling the fleeces," Joanna said, marvelling.

"So are mine," Stephen said.

"And mine! Have a feel!" Jamesy said, and they all had to feel one another's hands, to marvel at the softness of their skin.

"It's the lanolin," Stephen said.

"What's lanolin?" Jamesy asked.

"It's the natural grease in sheep's wool. It's used in the making of ointments for our skin."

"Is it good for freckles?" Joanna asked.

"It won't rub them out, if that's what you mean."

"What a pity. I wish it would."

"Silly thing," Jamesy said.

Over their heads, their parents smiled. The business of watching their children grow up was a strange thing full of queer little quirks. They knew each one so intimately; the physical bond was so very close, every thought and feeling could be divined; yet what could they know of the people these children would one day become? Each one so different, moved by an unknown force within, yet all bearing a common likeness. Not just the likeness of face and form, but the affinity created by small daily experiences shared, stored up as though in a bank, from which they could draw at will.

The four children would grow apart. As adults they might be scattered about the world. But the memory of this particular day, for instance, would always be shared by all of them, and however briefly they might meet, a word would be enough to bring it back. The warm gusty day with its little showers; the smells of sheep muck and wool and tar; the magical softness of their hands: the day would be one they would remember always, in future times, when they were old; and the sharing of such memories was a thing they could only experience together, as members of the same family.

"It's a queer thing, being a parent," Stephen said, and Gwen, laughing, took his arm, knowing how much he had left unsaid.

They walked on with Jamesy and Joanna, and soon saw that Chris, arriving first, had already been at work. Smoke rose from the kitchen chimney. The kettle would be on for tea.

* * * * *

It was a wet summer that year. Haymaking spun itself out and was not finished until late July. Stephen had other worries, too, for the government was regretting its policy on corn prices and was threatening to remove the guarantee. His harvest that year was good enough, considering the wet season, but in November, when he sold his corn, prices were already beginning to fall, giving warning of what was to come.

Just before Christmas Morton George came to him and asked for a rise of ten shillings.

"Don't be ridiculous," Stephen said. "You know what the present situation is."

"Yes, and I'm putting in now, before it gets worse. The union's behind me in asking for this rise. They gave it out at

16

the meeting last night."

"The union needs to face facts."

"I've seen the corn prices in *The Gazette*. The farmers ent all that badly hit."

"I've got to look ahead," Stephen said. "The good days for farming are petering out. We've all got to face that fact and pull in our horns."

"You don't need to tell *me!*" George exclaimed. "It's what our speaker said last night. There's dark days in front of us, I know that, and who's going to suffer? – Men like me!"

Stephen knew that it was true.

Chapter 2

Just after Christmas that year, the mare, Nancy, gave birth to Lucifer's first foal. Emma, the youngest of the Wayman children, was allowed to choose the foal's name, and the name she chose was Phoebe.

"I bet you can't spell it!" Jamesy said, and all three older children rocked with mirth.

"Emma's quite good at spelling," said Gwen. "Miss Protheroe is pleased with her."

Emma, being only five, went to Miss Protheroe's "Little School", in the cathedral close in Chepsworth. It was the older children's task to call and collect her at four o'clock every day, and because of its tiny tables and chairs they scornfully called it the "Dolly School."

"Phoebe's a good name," Stephen said. "Emma has chosen very well."

Later, in March, at the Mare and Foal Show in Chepsworth, Nancy and Phoebe won first prize. Stephen lifted Emma up so that she could pin the red rosette on Nancy's headstall. Then Emma was put onto Nancy's back and with Stephen leading her by the rein, and with Chris leading the foal nearby, the whole family walked back home.

"My! But you must be tired!" Mrs Bessemer said to them. "You must be nearly ready to drop."

"I'm not tired," Emma said.

"You've been riding," Joanna said.

The spring was a dry and sunny one; the driest, it was said, for sixty-three years; and yet the nights were bitterly cold. Often during the Easter holidays, the children awoke to a world white with frost, and yet the days were bright and warm.

They were never at a loss how to fill their time. The

farm's secrets were known to them now, and they went in a kind of ritual from one marvel to the next, willing to share them with one another but guarding them fiercely from outside eyes. There were crabapple trees out in blossom along the hedges in Long Gains, and the moorhen had chicks on Copsey Pond, but few people were allowed to know. Cowslip places and bluebell places; squirrels' nests and foxes' earths; catkin bushes and wild cherry trees and the thrush that built in the pony's stall: only their parents and Agnes Mayle were allowed to know about these things; everyone else was kept in the dark.

And of course there was always the work of the fields. They watched the men ploughing and drilling; they watched the shepherd delivering lambs; and they poked their noses into the sheds, eager to know what was going on.

"What do *you* want?" said Morton George.

"Nothing much," Chris said.

"Take it and go, then, and shut the door!"

But the other men were friendly enough: Tupper and Hopson, especially, and the younger men, like Jenkins and Rye: the children were always welcome with them; and Chris, the eldest, now thirteen, was sometimes allowed to take the handles of Tupper's plough or ride on the step behind the drill, keeping the grain on the move in the box and calling out when it ran low.

Stephen's health was improving a lot. The tightness in his chest and the pain in his side, legacies of the poison gas, rarely troubled him these days. He was doing more and more on the farm: milking every morning and evening; hoeing the rootcrops, digging the drains; ploughing his quota with the men.

Sometimes the whole family were out in the field at the same time: working together in the sun and the wind; resting together, eating their food; returning home in the fading light, with the jingle of horse-chains and the rumble of wheels. They, as a family, were self-complete. They wanted no one but themselves.

"You live in a world of your own up there," John Challoner used to say. "Aren't you ever coming down?"

This was because Stephen never wanted to go to the

village whist drives; never joined the Crayle Hunt; never spent an evening at The Rose and Crown; never attended the N.F.U. "social evenings". Challoner liked to do all these things. He sometimes called Stephen a dull dog.

But Stephen did take some part in local affairs. Challoner had got him onto the parish council and the vicar, Mr Netherton, had voted him onto the board of managers of the village school. Stephen at first was against this. He felt it would be presumptuous of him to sit on the board of the village school when he sent his own children to schools in Chepsworth. But he was persuaded to change his mind. He already had a certain interest, for the school playground abutted on to his land, and he had agreed to the vicar's request that the little meadow of three acres, just behind the school, might be used by the pupils for their summer games. And Stephen, as the vicar pointed out, was a useful man on any board because of his knowledge of the law.

Nevertheless, Stephen felt some embarrassment when he met Miss Izzard, the mistress-in-charge. "I feel an intruder, poking into your school's affairs when I've only lived here eighteen months." But she said, in a straightforward way he liked, "You let us use your meadow, Mr Wayman. That's passport enough as far as I'm concerned."

There was much news in the papers at that time of the hardships suffered by the coal-miners of England and Wales, who had been on strike for three months. Early in May, at a meeting of the school managers, the vicar reported that Miss Izzard wanted to hold a concert in the school, to raise funds for the miners' children. The vicar, who was in his early fifties, was a man anxious to move with the times but always uncertain how far he should go. He tended to lean on younger men, especially those who knew their own minds.

"I don't know that I approve of this scheme. It could well be argued that we were encouraging men to strike. But Miss Izzard, as you know, is an obstinate young woman, and she insisted that I put it before the board."

One or two of the managers shared the vicar's uncertainty, but Stephen took a firm stand.

"The miners are striking for a fair living wage. That's not

much to ask, it seems to me. Whatever the rights and wrongs of it, that's no reason why their wives and children should starve!"

So the concert was held and raised the sum of twenty pounds. Stephen took all his family, and Joanna was so much impressed by the young lady pianist from Cheltenham, who wore a long dress with net sleeves and played two pieces by Mendelssohn, that she went home filled with a new resolve to practise her scales before school every morning.

"When's your recital?" Jamesy asked, putting his hands over his ears. "If I buy a ticket, can I stay away?"

Joanna's ambitions, musically, were apt to alter with the wind. The spirit was willing but the flesh was weak, and her piano practice soon became as intermittent as it had been before.

* * * * *

The dry spring gave way to a dry summer. The days began to be very hot, and the children gloried in the sun. They shed their school clothes the instant they got home and ran about in cotton shorts until, as Henry Goodshaw said, they were "brown as eggs, the lot of them."

Often it was difficult to get the three older ones into bed, for the evenings never really grew dark. But there came a moment eventually when peace descended on the house, and Stephen and Gwen would walk out into the fields, glad to see the sun go down, after its fierceness during the day, and thankful for the coolness of the falling dew.

One evening it rained, a rain so light it was almost unreal, falling softly and silently from clouds so high they could not be seen. Stephen and Gwen walked out in this rain and stood with their faces upturned to it. They held out their arms and spread their hands and asked for the rain to soak the earth. The scent of it as it touched the grass; touched the hot surface of the soil; was a miracle of coolness and sweetness, and they drank it in through nostrils and mouth, greedily, with a kind of lust.

Gwen went forward into the rain, and her dark hair, with

21

its loose fronds, caught and held the droplets of light. Her eyebrows and lashes were speckled with them; her face, her throat, her naked arms, shone with the wetness of the rain; and her white cotton dress clung to her, showing the long shape of her thighs. She spun around and her wet skirts flared out. Then, suddenly, she was still.

"Why are you looking at me like that?"

"Can't I look at my own wife?"

"Only if you tell me what you're thinking."

"I was wondering what the children would say if they could see you twirling about."

"You think it's unseemly at my age?"

"It's my thoughts that are unseemly," Stephen said.

During the course of a busy day, Gwen was many things to him: a voice calling him in to his meals; a pair of eyes that saw things he missed; a pair of hands outstretched to help; mother of his children and mistress of his house. But at moments like this she was none of these things. He had time now to look at her; to rediscover the girl in her; to rediscover himself as a lover.

"You look even younger than when I married you. You might be eighteen, standing there."

"The light is fading, that's why."

But there was enough daylight left for her to see the look in his eyes, and for him to see the hint of warmth kindling under her clear skin.

"Whatever's the matter with us?" she said.

"It must be the rain," Stephen said. "It's making us drunk." Then, later, walking home: "It won't do much good, a sprinkle like this. What we need is a thorough soak."

"You don't think we'll get it?" Gwen asked.

"Not a chance," Stephen said.

In a few minutes more, the rain had stopped, a teasing promise unfulfilled. The next day was as hot as ever.

Hay harvest that year was all over within a week, but the hay was poor stuff, very light and dry, The aftermath of grass in the fields, instead of growing fresh and green, remained as it was, just short pallid stalks, with all its goodness burnt away. People began to speak of a drought.

During the summer of 1921, the newspapers made sorry reading. Famine in Russia; riots in Egypt; and in Germany terrible bitterness at the severity of the war reparations being exacted by the Allies. Republican atrocities in Ireland; continuing strife in industry at home; a decline in prosperity on the land. The threatened repeal of the Corn Act became reality in June, and John Challoner, along with every other farmer in England, felt that he had been betrayed.

"The same old story! We might have known! The farmer was a hero during the war. Now he can go and hang himself! Don't you mention Lloyd George to me!"

But Challoner found some crumb of comfort in the fact that the Wages Board was to be abolished, together with the power of the county council to enforce their own rules on cultivation.

"At least we can damn well *grow* what we please! And decide for ourselves what to pay a man when he's finished work at the end of the week. I shall have something to say to them, especially those union tykes, when we've finished with harvest this back-end!"

Stephen, however, was sick at heart. "We may be able to grow what we please, but shall be be able to sell it?" he said. And, walking with Gwen in the cornfields, with their bright illusion of riches to come, for the first time he began to have doubts of his wisdom in buying Holland Farm.

"It won't be too bad this harvest, I suppose, with the government paying compensation. But as for next year! — My God! What then?"

"Oh, we shall manage!" Gwen said. "We'll have to cut down a bit, that's all."

·"Maybe you're right," Stephen said, but he was more vexed than comforted by the cheerful way she brushed it aside. "Maybe you're right. Let's hope you are."

"Did you sell those weaners today?"

"Sell them? I practically *gave* them away! The market's glutted with pigs just now. You've read the papers, haven't you?"

"There's no need to bite my head off."

"Sorry!" he said, in a loud voice. But what in God's name,

he thought, did she expect?

The hot weather was getting him down. The drought, according to the national press, was "serious but not yet grave." Stephen fretfully disagreed.

"They should see Holland Farm!" he said to Gwen.

Water was low in ponds and wells, and the pastures were badly burnt up. The cows were sickly, swallowing so much dust as they grazed, and the heat was affecting their milk-yield. Turnip seed and mangold seed, three times sown in the Twelve Acres, had each time failed to germinate, and peas and beans in the Goose Ground were all shrivelled in their pods.

Even in the meadows, like Long Gains and Gicks, the ground had opened in terrible fissures, and Stephen gave orders that a close watch be kept on the cattle in case they should stumble into the cracks., Such an accident had happened at Lucketts, a farm on the other side of the brook, and the cow in question, having broken her leg, had had to be destroyed.

Everywhere it was the same, the parched land crying out for rain, sheep and cattle suffering, and in places the early slaughter of beasts because there was not enough food for them. On a farm near Peggleton, a man had been gored to death by a bull, never before known to be vicious. The heat, it seemed, had maddened it. On the railway at Bounds, sparks from an engine had set fire to the grass and broom on the bank, and the fire had spread into cornfields nearby, destroying thirty acres of oats. Fires broke out repeatedly on Springs Hill and the Burlows beyond, and when the fires had been put out, the burnt patches could be seen, like great black scars, as though the smooth green flanks of the hills had been branded by an enormous iron.

Fire was Stephen's constant dread. He kept a close watch on his men, for they were smokers, one and all. And sure enough, in the stackyard one day, a sudden whoomphing assault of flame! Bob Tupper was at work with his prong, clearing the yard of old hay and straw, ready for the building of the new cornstacks. The fire shot up from the loose hay as he was forking it into a cart. It leapt at him like an angry dog, and the searing heat, sucked quickly in as he caught his breath, burnt his mouth and throat and lungs.

He ran to the nearest drinking-trough, put his head into the water, and doused the rest of himself with a splash. Then he turned to deal with the fire. By that time Stephen and most of the other men were there and the flames were douted in a trice. Bob, much blackened about the face, with a sore throat and singed eyebrows, now gave vent to some choice language, and it seemed he knew where to lay the blame, for Jimmy Jenkins had passed through the yard a few minutes before, smoking a hand-rolled cigarette.

"Supposing the kids had been playing here?" Bob Tupper said to him, and Jimmy, who was only seventeen, looked at him in horror.

"I'll never smoke another bloody fag," he said, "until we've had some bloody rain!"

"If you break that promise," Stephen said, "I swear I'll sack you on the spot!"

* * * * *

Harvest was going to be early that year, but all the corn crops were woefully poor. Oats in the One-and-Twenty Field were so thin and light in the grain, they were not worth cutting after all, and Stephen folded the cattle there to eat the oat-crop as it stood.

The water shortage became acute. In the house there was strict rationing; every drop must be saved for the stock; but there was some slight relief when Stephen, poking about in the Bratch, where an old cottage had once stood, found a well full of brackish water and piped it to the pastures below. Most of the ponds had dried up, and even the deep dark Copsey Pond, shaded by surrounding trees, had been reduced to a mere puddle, six feet or so below its banks. Because of the steepness of these banks, and the low level of the pond, the sheep who came from the meadows to drink were in danger of toppling in and drowning, so Stephen gave orders to Bob Tupper that someone should be sent to fence it round.

Bob sent Morton George and Jimmy Jenkins. They put a roll of wire netting into a barrow, together with their tools and a bundle of stakes, and threw their luncheon-bags on top. This was a day in early July, a day as hot as any that summer so far, and the two men sweated in the heat. The pond had dried up completely now. The bottom was merely a black morass, and out of it stuck an old waggon-wheel, a few dead boughs from the trees around, and the grey skeleton of a pig. In one of the meadows next to the pond, sheep, grazing the stalky grass, stopped eating and stared at the men, ears twitching at the noise they made as they hammered the stakes into the ground.

Two thirds of the way round, their roll of netting came to an end. They would have to go back to the farm for more.

"It's almost dinner-time now," George said. "I'm just about dying of flaming thirst, so how about going up to the pub? We'll finish this when we get back."

They took their satchels from the barrow and tramped, melting, across the fields to where, on the edge of Huntlip Common, stood a small public house called The Black Ram. The landlord gave them his paper to read. They talked about Dempsey and the big fight. The pub, with its sunken stone-flagged floor, was cool. They stayed there, drinking, until it closed.

When they got back to Copsey Pond, Jimmy, the younger of the two, offered to go for the netting alone.

"Oh, sod the netting!" George said. "Seems to me it's a waste of time. No sheep is going to drown in *there*. How can they when the water's gone? If Tupper asks me about this job, I shall say it's a bloody waste of time."

He threw his satchel into the barrow and began trundling it away. Jimmy shrugged and followed him. Behind them, under the willow trees, one third of the pond remained unfenced. A moorhen emerged from her nest in the bank and picked her way across the mud. A wagtail perched on the broken wheel.

In the farmyard, when George and Jenkins returned, they were called upon to take a turn at the pump, with orders to fill the water-cart. The electric motor had broken down; the water had to be pumped by hand. Stephen was in the cartshed, overhauling the reaper-and-binder. He stopped work and called to George.

"Did you put that fence round Copsey Pond?"

"We ran out of wire," George said. "But the water's all dried away now. No sheep's going to drown itself in there. There's no need to worry until we've had rain."

Stephen gave an impatient sigh. The men had been gone since eleven o'clock. Now it was almost half past three.

"Oh, very well!" he exclaimed. "You'd better leave it for today. Get a move on, filling that water-cart. The troughs are empty in the top pastures."

He went back to work on the reaper-and-binder, feeling fretted and annoyed. The two men had wasted half a day, just when time was becoming precious, for Nate Hopson had broken his leg and was going to be laid up for some time, and harvest was getting under way. The fence round the pond would have to wait.

* * * * *

They started cutting in the Oak Field and then went on to the Eighteen Acre, and every day as they toiled in the heat, they were choked by the everlasting dust that rose and enveloped them like a cloud. Stirred up by the horses' hooves and the blades of the reaper going round, the dust seemed to blast itself into their skin. Their eyes were on fire with it; bloodshot, inflamed; and their throats ached intolerably.

"Oh for some rain!" groaned Billy Rye, and nobody there upbraided him for a prayer so strange at harvest-time. "God be good and send some rain!"

But no rain came. There was no relief. The pillar of dust towered above them, and all day long they followed it, toiling and suffering in their sweat. The sun was a tyrant over them, and their day of deliverance was not yet come.

Sometimes, in the distance, thunder could be heard, but the promise of a storm remained unfulfilled. The hot sky pressed on the earth. There was no breath of air between the two. There was only the weight of heat pressing down and the throbbing current of heat rising up, visible in its shimmering waves. And out of the heavy, sagging sky the tiny black thrips or thunder-bugs descended on all living

27

things to crawl, minute but maddening, and add their torment to suffering skin.

Emma came running into the house, weeping because of the tiny thrips that crawled on her face, her scalp, her arms, and were clustered, black, on the front of her frock.

"Horrible dirty things!" she cried. "Mummy! Make them go away!"

Gwen removed them as best she could and rubbed the child's skin with lemon-scented oil, but the thrips came on her just the same, and Emma, gradually growing calm, would sit on the garden-seat by the hour, unable to think of anything but the tiny insects that plagued her skin.

"No," she would say, again and again. "No. No. I tell you *no*." And at each vehement syllable, one smaller finger would descend to rub out another of the tiny, creeping, hateful things that had dared to settle on her person. "No. No. I tell you *no*."

Often when Gwen had finished in the house and the dairy, she would join the men in the harvest-field. They were cutting a crop of dredge-corn now: oats and barley, winter sown; the best crop of the harvest so far. There were no delays in this weather. Long before the last sheaves were stooked, the waggons were lumbering to and fro, and a new stack was rising in the stackyard. Gwen helped to set up the stooks and then took a fork to help with the pitching. Stephen worked at the next waggon. He gave her a smile but said nothing. There were few words wasted by the harvesters toiling in the heat that year.

Gwen was wearing a printed frock, the pattern of which, in the course of that summer, had faded from a rich dark blue to a pale and ghostly shade of grey. On her head she wore a straw hat with a curving brim down over her eyes, and on her feet an old pair of sandals without any straps.

Stephen was aware of her constantly, without directly looking at her. They were so close in their intimacy, and knew each other in such a way, that whenever she took a sheaf on her fork and raised it aloft to the man on the load, it was like a movement of his own body. Knowing her lissomeness as he did; the grip of her hands and the curve of her arms; the shape of her shoulders, breasts, and thighs:

he felt her movements in himself and knew that she in turn felt his. He knew when she turned to fork a sheaf; knew when she lifted it overhead; and knew how, at the very last, she danced a little on her toes, reaching up as high as she could to deliver the sheaf to the man on the load.

She, as a girl on her father's farm, had been bred to this work. It was in her bones. He would never have the knack of it so well as she, digging into the sheaf just so, raising the fork and turning it, all in one motion, scarcely seen, yet so exactly right each time that the sheaf could be taken from the curve of the prongs without danger, without delay. He liked to see her out in the fields. It was another bond between them, that they worked together, side by side.

And yet he was anxious about her too. He felt that she asked too much of herself; went beyond her woman's strength. Today, for instance, as the load grew higher in the waggon, he wished she would stop and take a rest. With every layer of sheaves on the load, she had to reach higher and higher still, and he sensed the tremulous weariness in every movement of her arms. He could see the strain of it in her face, shaded though it was by her broad-brimmed hat, and could hear the shortness of her breath.

"Don't overdo it, will you?" he said. "It's most unwise, in this heat. I think it's time you went back to the house."

"But I've only just come out," she said. "Would you shut me indoors again?"

Gwen could be obstinate when she chose.

* * * * *

Mrs Bessemer came to the farm only in the mornings nowadays. She could only work two hours a day. The prolonged hot weather was making her ill.

"What about us?" said Agnes Mayle. "Ent we supposed to feel the heat?"

But Mrs Bessemer's illness was perfectly genuine. The heat reduced her in a terrible way, and sometimes she fell to the floor in a faint, eyes wide open and face pale as death. She stayed at home in the afternoons, and Gwen and Agnes managed alone.

"Shall I get another woman in?" Stephen asked.

"Good gracious no!" Gwen exclaimed. "Surely this weather will break some time?"

"Sometimes I wonder," Stephen said.

The heat was a burden on them all. Even the children, when they came home from school, sought whatever shade could be found and sat engaged in quiet games. The heat was a strain even on them.

And everywhere it was the same. The earth and everything that lived craved rain, but no rain came. The grass in the leys was so pale and dry that grassland and stubble looked alike. Even in the meadows the grass was brown. There was no greenness anywhere. The fruits of the earth were withering; the tiny apples fell from the trees; and the brown crinkled leaves were everywhere, crackling dead and dry underfoot.

"You know what I think?" Mrs Bessemmer said. "I reckon it's the end of the world."

"Don't talk daft!" Agnes said.

But Gwen, as she went about the farm, observing the suffering of the animals, sometimes shared Mrs Bessemer's fears. The earth was dying in the heat. Only a miracle, she felt, could ever bring it to life again.

In Huntlip church, as in churches throughout the country, prayers were offered up for rain. But still no rain came. The sky pressed closer upon the earth, and the beasts of the field were borne down, panting open-mouthed in the heat.

* * * * *

It was a day in mid-July, and Gwen was all alone in the house. Agnes had finished her day's work and had left early, to take some milk to Nate Hopson, still laid up with his leg in plaster. Stephen was with the other men, cutting thirty acres of wheat on the far side of Woody Holl.

Gwen went out into the garden to fill a basket with lettuces, radishes, and spring onions, ready for the children's tea. There was thunder in the air. The sky was yellow and deep mauve, mottled like an angry bruise. She was on her way back to the house when she heard the faint sound of a sheep bleating, and noted it as an unusual thing, for the sheep had been quiet all through the drought. Perhaps, today, the storm would break.

The air was so close she could scarcely breathe. She set her basket on the step and went across to the stable yard, to look in over the door of the shed, where an in-calf heifer lay in the straw, somewhat sickly and near her time. Having seen that the heifer was all right she stood for a moment, listening, and heard the sheep bleating again. The sound was remote, indistinct, but there was a querulous note in it, and a certain persistence that worried her.

She went through the gate into the Home Field and walked slowly across the stubble. She was wearing her sandals, without any straps, and the stubble scratched her naked feet. The sandals were soon full of dust and seeds and the needle-sharp barbs from the oat-flights that worked their way painfully into the skin. She stopped for a moment to empty them, then went on across the slope.

The sheep was no longer crying now. Gwen stood listening, but there was no sound. She put up her hand to shade her eyes and gazed out over the empty fields. The stubble lands were bleached and bare. Between the stalks, on the snuff-dry earth, the pimpernels were open wide. She was thinking of turning back towards home when the sheep began bleating again, and this time she heard in the drawn-out cry the unmistakable note of distress. She walked across the next two fields and down to the meadows in the dip, and so came to the dried-up pond with its incomplete fence and its circle of trees, and its waggon-wheel sticking out of the mud.

The flock was in the meadow called Gicks, and a ewe had gone down the bank of the pond for the sake of the coolness of the mud at the bottom. She had probably lain there, cool, for some time, and now, when she wanted to come out, her hindquarters were stuck in the mud. She was heaving about in it, clumsily, and her efforts had gouged out a deep rounded pit, in which the last of the moisture gathered, making a loud sucking noise as her haunches scrabbled and sank back.

The mud at the outer edge of the pond was dry, and had opened in fissures six inches wide. Gwen climbed over the wire netting and picked her way down towards the ewe. When she had gone five or six yards, the mud grew soft and covered her feet above the ankles. She trod carefully, slock-slock, and held her skirts above her knees.

When the ewe saw her coming, it made another frantic heave, trying to hump itself out of the pit. But it only sank back again as before. Gwen now let go of her skirts and they hung trailing in the mud. She leant forward, facing the ewe, and seized it at either side of its neck, gripping wool and flesh together. But when she leant backwards, using all her strength, the ewe began to turn away, heaving sideways instead of forwards, and Gwen was pulled to her knees in the mud.

"Stupid animal!" she said. "Can't you see I'm trying to help?"

She let go of the ewe and flung out her arms to keep her balance, struggling onto her feet in the mud and trying to climb onto firmer ground. But the ewe, on finding itself released, scrabbled about sideways and backwards, and Gwen was suddenly sucked down, into the centre of the pit. The mud yielded under her and in an instant was up to her waist, closing between herself and the ewe but dragging them both down together.

Suddenly she became afraid. There was a wellspring beneath her feet; she could hear it bubbling and could feel its surge; but surely the bottom of the pond could not be so deep as to suck her down? She gave a little scornful laugh. With her arms outstretched, she tried to move. Her feet trod the softness down below, seeking firmness; expecting it.

There was no firmess. Only liquid mud. And she was sinking all the time. She reached up to the willow trees; she reached out to the broken wheel; but branches and wheel were too far away. Only the ewe was close to her, unmoving now, supine in the mud. Gwen again took hold of it and tried to lift it out of the pit. If with her help it could clamber out, its momentum in turn would help her. But her strength was nothing. The animal's weight was mountainous. And the weight of the thick black viscous mud was pressing on her, squeezing her flesh, numbing her body from the waist down.

Her only chance was help from elsewhere. The essential thing was to keep calm. She opened her mouth and gave a loud cry. She put all her strength into her voice, and the cry travelled out across the fields, a long-drawn *hallooo* of desperate appeal.

But who was to hear her when she called? Agnes had gone to Rayner's Lane. The children were not yet home from school. Stephen and the men were harvesting in a field on the other side of the farm. There was no one to hear her when she called but the flock grazing in the meadow nearby, and the ewe beside her in the mud.

Her cry was a shock to the terrified ewe. It reared itself up in the mud beside her and began a violent scrabbling. Its two front feet came down on her, and the sharp cloven hooves scrabbled madly, cutting her face and tearing her frock, marking her flesh in several bright weals from her throat and shoulders down to her breasts. When she sought to protect herself, her hands and arms met the scrabbling hooves and were lacerated most dreadfully. And now, when she cried aloud for help, the cry was full of pain and fear.

"Surely not!" she said, sobbing. "Surely I'm not going to die like this? Please, God, make somebody hear!"

Panic got her by the throat. She cried out for help again and again, but nobody heard her, nobody came. And the ewe, with its marbled yellow eyes, its black nostrils streaming mucus, its heavy body against hers, was bearing her downwards all the time. It was leaning on her. It was taking her strength. Whenever she uttered her cry for help, it reared up and trampled her. When she was silent, it was still. But even then, very gradually, she was sinking lower into the pit.

In the heat the mud had a terrible stench. The ewe also stank, because of its fear. Gwen, breathing with painfulness, thought of it as the smell of death. Why had she tried to help the ewe instead of going to fetch the shepherd? What would Stephen say to her? And, thinking of Stephen, she began to cry, turning her face away from the ewe and yielding, exhausted, to the pull of the mud.

Then her fighting spirit revived. She tried yet again to struggle free. Her mind was clarified, sharpened by fear. She knew she was struggling for her life.

* * * * *

The children came home to an empty house. They sought out their father in the harvest field. He was surprised that Gwen was nowhere to be found, but he thought she would very soon turn up, He told them to get their own tea and to bring something up to the field for him.

While he ate, with the other men, the three older children set up some sheaves, and Emma sat in the shade of the hedge, plaiting a bracelet of cornstalks. They stayed with him until six o'clock and then, when three of the men went down to see to the evening milking, he sent the children back to the house. If their mother was not yet back, Joanna was to put Emma to bed, and when she and the others had done their school prep they were to go to bed themselves.

Stephen and the men worked until dusk. Most of the men then went straight home, but two of them returned with him, leading the horses, Boxer and Beau, with one loaded waggon which they put in the barn.

The house was in darkness, upstairs and down. Plainly Gwen had still not come home. Stephen could not understand it at all, and he was more than a little annoyed, for the in-calf heifer, placed in Gwen's care, was lowing distressfully from the shed.

"Where the devil's my wife, I wonder? I shall have to see into this!"

At that moment Henry Goodshaw came into the yard, having been the rounds of his flock in the meadows. He stood for a while deep in thought, and his look and manner were very strange. He asked to speak to Stephen alone. He had found Gwen's body in the mud of the pond. The ewe, by its bleating, had drawn him there. The ewe had trampled her to death.

Chapter 3

The silence that settled over the farm was something that had to be broken down. The men would stop talking when he came by, and would listen to him, when he gave his orders, with a kind of considerate gentleness that was almost more than he could bear. They would answer him in quiet voices, doing their best to be natural, but failing because of what they knew; because the knowledge filled their minds.

One day he came upon three of them in the field of barley at Long End. They were trying the grain in the palms of their hands, rubbing it till it broke from the husks. They had been talking until he came. Now they were silent, avoiding his glance. The field was not far from Copsey Pond.

"Well?" he said. "What do you think?"

"I think we should cut," Tupper said.

"Then for God's sake get started!" Stephen said. "Why stand about wasting time?"

Nobody blamed him for lashing out. They felt they deserved it, the three of them, because their lives were still intact, and their womenfolk were safe at home. They put themselves in Stephen's place. "If that was me – " Bob Tupper said. He had no need to say more.

They knew they ought to talk to him, but there was danger in every remark, and they wanted to spare him their clumsiness. And Stephen himself was unable to talk. The silence, though a burden, was refuge too. He could give his orders on the farm; conduct his business on market day; speak to Agnes about the children, and speak to the children when need be. But each of these was a separate task, and he came to each task with his mind prepared. Whenever one overlapped another, he felt as though he would go to pieces. How did men manage, who lost their wives? He could face only one thing at one time. When he gave himself up to the farm, and the children came to him with their worries, he felt he could hardly bear to look at them. And when, at certain allotted times, he gave himself up to his children completely, the work of the farm did not exist.

Only Agnes Mayle, taking charge of household affairs, had the courage to mention his dead wife's name.

"Mrs Wayman used to pay us on Fridays," she said, when Stephen mentioned the matter of wages; and always, whatever queries arose, she answered in the same forthright way: "Mrs Wayman dealt with the eggs," or "Mrs Wayman's poultry book is up on that shelf, behind the clock."

He got through those early days somehow: the nightmare of breaking the news to the children; the coroner's inquest; the burial; the reporters calling at the house; the sympathy and the good advice. "You must think of your children," the vicar said, and Stephen angrily turned away. "I don't need *you*," he said in his mind," to tell me what I have to do."

* * * * *

He got his children through those days: saw them off to school in the morning; made sure he was always there to meet them when they came home in the afternoon; set time aside to talk to them, and tried to wrap them round in love.

But soon the holidays would begin, and the prospect filled him with secret dread. He took the three older ones aside and told himself they were almost grown up: Chris thirteen; Joanna twelve; Jamesy eleven in two months' time.

"I'm worried about little Emma," he said. "She's only five and she's young for her age. Now that the holidays are nearly here, I want you to take great care of her, and see that she's never left alone. Will you promise me you'll look after her?"

Solemnly they gave their word, but when the three of them were alone, they looked at each other helplessly, eyes questioning, doubtful, afraid.

"What are we supposed to do?" Chris said. "Dad doesn't tell us what to *do*!"

Looking out through the kitchen window, they could see little Emma in the garden, following Agnes as she hung out the clothes, handing her the pegs from the raffia bag.

"Emma's all right," muttered Chris. "*She's* too young to understand."

* * * * *

A new stack, at the edge of the stackyard, was leaning dangerously to one side. Poles were needed to shore it up. Morton George was given the job and Bob Tupper said to him, "See that you do the thing properly! – *This* time!" George did the job and the stack was shored up safely enough. He went to Stephen, alone in the byre.

"I reckon you'd better give me my cards."

"Why now, suddenly?"

"It's all these remarks!" George said. "It's the way the others look at me. D'you think I don't know you hold me to blame?"

Stephen could never bring himself to look at George. He hated to see him about the farm. But the burden of blame could not be carried by this one man alone. It was too much for any man.

"You were at the inquest," he said. "You heard what the coroner had to say."

An element of negligence had been involved. That was what the coroner had said. But no single person could be blamed, and Mrs Wayman had met her death through a series of tragic circumstances, and because, in her concern for a helpless animal in distress, she had taken no thought for her own safety.

"I know what *he* said!" George exclaimed. "But it's what the chaps've got to say!"

"Do you *want* me to give you your cards?"

"If I've got to put up with all these remarks –"

"That's something you've got to sort out with them."

"And what about you, Mr Wayman, sir? I reckon *you*

blame me right enough!"

"Get back to work," Stephen said.

* * * * *

The holidays came; long hours to be filled; and once again
Agnes took charge. She chivvied the children about the
house until some order prevailed there each day, and she
found them a great many things to do.

"I can't do everything myself! Mrs Bessemer's having one
of her turns. So just you get busy and show some vim!"

There were chickens to feed and eggs to collect; there
were pans in the dairy to be scoured out, and the dairy floor
to be sluiced down and scrubbed; potatoes to be dug from
the garden for lunch, peas to be shelled and mint to be
chopped, and the carving-knife to be sharpened and
cleaned. And when the household chores were done she
would issue forth with them out of doors to help with the
harvest in the fields. She would make a game of it, ordering
them about, and they would work to some elaborate plan,
seizing the sheaves and setting them up and arranging the
stooks in such a way that they made a pattern across the
field.

"Damn and butter!" Agnes would say. "I ent got enough
to finish this star!"

The way she scowled and pursed her lips, and the way she
clumped across the stubble to snatch two sheaves from
Trennam's hands, made the children laugh aloud. They
ran about after her, snatching up sheaves from one place
and setting them down again in another, until the stooks on
the slope of the field formed an enormous six-pointed star.
And Stephen, seeing them at their game, hearing their
voices across the field, gave thanks for Agnes and such as
she, who kept things going and knew what to do.

"When is your cousin coming, daddy?" the children
asked almost every day.

"Not just yet," Stephen said. "It's a long journey from
India, you know."

He had cabled his cousin, Dorothy Skeine, telling her of
Gwen's death, and Dorothy had answered by return that

she would come at once to England, to keep house for him and look after his children.

"What's she like?" the children asked. "Is she young? Is she pretty? Is she nice?"

"I haven't seen her for fifteen years, but no, she's not young, not exactly," he said. He wondered himself what she was like. Fifteen years was a long time. "You'll see for yourselves in due course."

"Why can't Agnes live with us?"

"Agnes has got her father and brothers to look after, as you well know. She's working too hard as it is."

Their father's cousin was on her way. She was coming to England in a ship. They tried to picture her but failed.

"I wish she'd *come*," Joanna said.

"I'm not so sure," Jamesy said. "Supposing we don't care for her?"

"Supposing she doesn't care for *us!*" said Chris.

They were silent, sunk in thought.

* * * * *

Sometimes at night while the children slept, Stephen walked in the empty fields. Harvest was almost over now, the earliest harvest in many years. They would begin ploughing soon, if the plough could cut through the hard-baked earth.

"God! The ploughing!" he said to himself.

His mind veered away from it, rejecting it, unable to think. Yet he knew the ploughing would be done; the seed would be sown, the green blades would come; and the earth would tilt away from the sun, taking its quarterly season of rest.

How was it that he could work by day, as though he cared about what he did? How was it that he could walk the earth; could eat and drink and go to sleep; talk to people; put on his clothes; when he was filled with such a rage? Even on the night of Gwen's death, he had helped to deliver a new calf. The thing was hateful, unspeakable, and yet he did it just the same. Was this the way it would always be?

One night he walked in the harvest field, and there was a

moon very nearly full. The cornsheaves stood, leaning together in the stooks, and each stook had its long shadow, slanting towards him across the stubble. The air was hot and perfectly still but suddenly, as he walked in the field, there was a little flaw of wind that blew on the ground among the stubble and spiralled upwards into the sky, carrying with it dust and chaff and little bits of pale-glinting straw.

The play of the wind, and its rustling noise, were like a presence among the sheaves, and he came to a sudden startled halt. The earth had been so perfectly still that the wind touched him and took his breath. The rustling awoke something fearful in him. It seemed like the spirit of the earth, that moved on heedlessly, down the years, knowing nothing of the emptiness that death created in human hearts. The earth spirit would keep him alive even though he was dead within, and the knowledge of this made him afraid.

Two miles away, beyond Blagg, a motor car ground up the steep road and changed gear about half way. Its headlamps came swinging over the hill, marked the course of the road for a while, and vanished again down into the dip that held the village. This brief intrusion from the outside world seemed to leave a greater silence behind. The aloneness and emptiness were everywhere. And he asked himself yet again: What in God's name did a man do, who had had so much and then lost it all?

On his way homeward, down the field, his foot kicked something on the ground. It was a single sheaf of wheat, dropped by a careless harvester, and it lay on the ground, having burst from its bond. Stooping, he gathered the loose sheaf, and tied it securely together again. The cornstalks rustled and so did the ears, and the bunch of straws that made up the bond were dry and brittle between his fingers, breaking into tiny splinters that pricked and penetrated his skin. He took the rustling sheaf in his hands, carried it with him a few paces, and set it upright against a stook. The moon watched him from overhead as he followed his shadow down the slope.

* * * * *

40

One day when Stephen walked into the garden, he found his children close in a group, and in their midst, fawning, soft-eyed, a spaniel puppy three weeks old.

"Mr Challoner sent it to us. Gerald brought it, it's ours to keep. We *can* keep it, can't we, dad?"

"Yes, of course," Stephen said. "Have you decided on his name?"

"We're calling him Sam," Jamesy said.

The puppy was everything to them. They took it with them everywhere. It gave some meaning to their lives. And Stephen felt a twinge of shame, because he had not thought of giving them a puppy, and John Challoner had.

People were really very good. Mrs Bessemer, although still suffering from the heat, had them to tea once or twice a week and allowed them into Bert's pigeon-loft, to see the pigeons and stroke their breasts. The children always had plenty to do. Everybody saw to that. Bob Tupper, in his dinner-hour, cut them each a pair of stilts, and they stumped about, up in the air, able to see over hedges and walls and to rat-tat-tat on the dairy window, making poor Agnes jump out of her skin.

Gerald Challoner came over sometimes, driving one of his father's tractors, and Chris was allowed to take the controls. Nate Hopson came over, with his leg in plaster, and challenged Joanna to a race, he on his crutches and she on her stilts, and the prize for Joanna when she won was Nate's old Army cap-badge, which she wore with great pride, clipped to her blouse.

But there were times, inevitably, when no one could fill the space in their lives. One day during piano practice, Joanna completed an exercise without any faults or hesitations, and swung round in triumph at the end, having heard someone come in at the door.

"Did you hear that, mummy?" she exclaimed, and of course it was Agnes standing there. The moment of triumph was splintered into bits. Joanna stared through hot surging tears. "Why did mummy have to die?"

"She didn't *have* to! She just did!" Agnes marched across to a chair and punched a cushion into shape. "As to the why of it, don't ask me! The why is always followed by zed, and

41

zed is the end of it, that's what I say!"

Agnes would do anything in the world for the four children, but she had no comfort to offer them. Death was death. It took the best. There was no rhyme nor reason in the world, and her attitude rubbed off on them.

The vicar called at Holland Farm, and, waiting for Stephen to come in from the fields, sat with the children in the garden.

"You must miss your mother very much."

"Of course," said Chris, in a curt tone. "She happens to be dead."

The vicar was shocked. He himself never spoke of death. He felt he had a duty to these four children facing him.

"Don't you know where your mother is?" he asked, eyeing each of them in turn. "Surely, now, you can tell me that?"

Chris and Joanna looked away. The vicar's question embarrassed them. They knew what he wanted them to say, but they had no use for the life hereafter, even if its existence could be proved. He turned his gaze on Jamesy instead.

"What about you, young man? Can you tell me where your mother is?"

"Yes," said Jamesy, "she's in her grave."

When Stephen came, the vicar stood up. He would not stay more than a moment, he said. He knew how busy farmers were.

"I came to see if I could help. With a young family like yours, I know what problems there must be, and if there's anything I or my wife can do –"

"You're very kind," Stephen said. "But my cousin, Miss Skeine, is coming back from India soon. She's going to make her home here, and look after us all, my children and me."

"So glad, so glad," the vicar said.

Stephen went with him to the gate.

"I wish she'd come, this cousin of dad's, *if* she's coming," Jamesy said. "How much longer is she going to be?"

* * * * *

42

The day came when cousin Dorothy was expected. Stephen went in the pony and trap to meet her train at Chepsworth station, and the four children remained at home, under orders to be on hand ready to welcome her on her arrival.

When their father returned and drove into the stable yard, the children were at the kitchen window, where they could get the earliest glimpse. Emma stood on the kitchen stool. She was wearing her best blue cotton frock. Agnes, discreetly, was upstairs, but no doubt had her look-out post. The house was as clean as a new pin.

The woman who descended from the trap was thin and loose-boned. She wore a grey silk blouse and a grey worsted skirt that reached to the tops of her old-fashioned boots. Her brown-skinned face was narrow and long, with strong cheekbones and strong-jutting chin, and eyes set deep under bristling eyebrows. She had already taken off her hat, and her grey hair, cropped amazingly short, covered her head in a close frizz, tough and tight-curled, like steel wool. When she descended from the trap, it was with a little ungainly leap, revealing stockings of dark grey lisle, gathered in wrinkles about her knees; and as she stood in the stable yard, gazing at the house and the farm buildings, she flung out her long ungainly arms in a wild gesture of ecstasy.

"England!" she said, in a powerful voice that rang round the yard. "England again! Oh it does smell so good!"

At the kitchen window, the children watched.

"Is that *her* ?" Joanna breathed.

They eyed one another in dismay.

"I do think dad might have warned us," said Chris, lifting Emma down from the stool, and Jamesy said, resentfully, "Why do we have to have her here? We didn't ask her. She asked herself."

When cousin Dorothy came indoors, the children stood in a formal row. Their father introduced them to her, and she shook hands with each of them, vigorously, squeezing their palms. She treated each child to a long, hard look, and her eyes were unexpectedly blue, looking out keenly from under her brows.

"You needn't think you are strangers to me, just because

43

we've never met. I've seen your photographs, over the years, and had news of you now and then, *when* your father remembered to write. I know a lot about you, never fear, and what I don't know I shall soon find out!"

The three older children stood like posts. Looking at her, they were struck dumb. Only little Emma spoke and that was because, leaning towards cousin Dorothy, she was counting the tiny round black buttons sewn close together, dozens of them, down the front of the grey silk blouse. Stephen warningly cleared his throat, and Chris, with reluctance, began to speak. Sometimes he wished he was not the eldest of the four. All sorts of duties fell on him. He fixed cousin Dorothy with his scowl.

"It's very kind of you to come all the way from India. We hope you'll be very happy here."

"What a beautiful speech," cousin Dorothy said. "I shall be happy, I promise you."

"We've certainly got a lot to thank cousin Dorothy for," Stephen said, pointedly. "She's made a considerable sacrifice, leaving India to come here."

"Oh, don't tell them that, for goodness' sake! Do you want them to hate me from the start? Anyway, it isn't true. I was glad to leave India. Very glad." Once again she threw out her arms, striding about the big kitchen, looking around her with rapturous eyes. "Oh, to be in England now that April's there!" she said in her powerful, loud-thrilling voice.

Jamesy looked at her with scorn.

"It isn't April, it's August," he said, and, turning stiffly towards his father, he asked: "Can we go out now? We *did* wait in."

"Very well," Stephen said. "No doubt cousin Dorothy will be glad to excuse you."

In another moment the children were gone, the puppy yapping at their heels.

"I apologize for my children's lack of grace. I hope you will bear with them for a bit."

Dorothy raised a brown-skinned hand.

"They are the ones who must bear with me."

"It's very good of you to come. What did Hugh say to

your leaving him?"

"Oh, never mind Hugh!" Dorothy said. Her brother was dismissed in a single wave. "He's well established out there. Plenty of servants to run round after him. You need me more than he does now."

There was a pause. Dorothy stopped striding about and stood with her hands on the back of a chair. She began to speak of Gwen's death.

"Tell me about it," she said to him.

* * * * *

He realized, for the first time, that he had not fully faced the facts of Gwen's death. The manner of it. The horror, the pain. The fear she had suffered, perhaps for hours. In keeping the details from his children, he had succeeded in keeping them from himself. Even at the inquest he had not really faced up to these things: the need for control had shut them out; and in the weeks that had passed since then, his mind had sheered away from them.

He had faced the meaning of Gwen's loss: what it meant to him and his family; but not the agony of her dying. That he had pushed deep into his mind; into some dark forgetfulness; and now, as he talked to Dorothy, the horror was still too great to bear. It threatened him, deep in his soul. Even the war had not prepared him for such a death as Gwen's had been.

"And all for the sake of a damned ewe! The stupid brute lived, did I tell you that? It trampled my wife to death in the mud, and Goodshaw found her, all bleeding and torn!"

In his rage, he flung away. Dorothy watched him. She gave him time.

"Is he still employed here, the man who didn't finish the fence?"

"Yes," Stephen said, "he's still here."

"I hope I don't meet him, then, that's all."

"He's no more to blame than I am myself."

"You're talking nonsense, my dear boy."

"It's Gwen herself I blame!" he said. Again his anger overflowed. "She had no *right* to go down there, being so

45

careless with her life! Why didn't she fetch one of us? We were just up there, in the harvest field. We were less than half a mile away!" After a while, controlled, he said, "I wish we'd never come to this farm. If we'd stayed in Springs she'd still be alive."

Hands clenched in his breeches pockets, he stood in front of the open window. Out in the yard, under the elms, the children sat in the stationary trap. Chris had the ribbons in his hands, and Joanna was nursing the puppy, Sam. Jamesy, frowning, patient, intent, was removing a cleg from Emma's hair. Huddled together in the trap they looked forlorn the four of them, their faces wistful but lacking hope.

"My poor children!" Stephen said, but Dorothy Skeine, looking at him, knew that he would take longer to recover from the loss than they.

* * * * *

At first there was some uncertainty as to what the children should call her. They resolved it themselves and called her aunt Doe. Whether or not there was an element of derision in the name, as Stephen suspected, she accepted it without demur.

"I see you're looking at my hair, Joanna. Does it strike you as strange?"

"It's so short," Joanna said.

"Six months ago I had no hair at all. It's only recently begun to grow. Shall I tell you what made it fall out?"

The children said nothing. They merely stared. But she needed little response from them.

"Kala-azar! That's what it was. It's a nasty disease you get out there. India's a terrible place for diseases, you know. It's a terrible place for many things."

"Then why go there?" Joanna asked.

"Why indeed!" aunt Doe exclaimed.

Dorothy Skeine had a great sense of duty. Because of it she had gone to India in 1907 with her bachelor brother, a clergyman, and had helped him to run a mission school in a village outside Ranjiloor. Now duty had brought her home

46

again, but this time there was no hardship involved, and she made that clear right from the start. To be back in England was reward enough. She felt as though she had been reborn. Everything enchanted her. So that when Stephen talked to his children of the debt they owed to their aunt Doe, and the need for showing some gratitude, they were quite unmoved.

"Nobody asked her to come here. She came because she wanted to. She says so twenty times a day."

"It's very good of her all the same."

When aunt Doe's tin trunk arrived at the farm, there were presents for them from Ranjiloor: a soapstone model of the Taj Mahal; a pair of slippers with upcurled toes; a sandalwood box with a secret compartment; and a wood-wind pipe such as snake-charmers used when charming snakes in the market-place.

"No snakes, I'm afraid!" she said to them. "They would never have survived the journey to England."

The children thanked her with formal politeness, and carried their gifts away with them, up to their playroom in the attic. They examined them, but without any joy. Somehow the gifts were rather bizarre. They came from India, a place unknown, and there was a certain shoddiness about them. The soapstone model was chipped and cracked; the gilding on the slippers was flaking off; and the secret compartment of the sandalwood box kept springing open by itself. As for the snake-charmer's wooden pipe, it proved extremely difficult to blow.

"Here, you have a go," Jamesy said, pushing the pipe towards Joanna. "You're the one that's supposed to be musical."

After trying for ten minutes, all Joanna ever achieved was a few squeaks of piercing shrillness and an ache in the glands below her chin.

"Let me try," Emma said, and her efforts were so unexpectedly successful that the other children fled from her, leaving her alone in the attic, where she remained until supper-time.

"Where's Emma?" their father asked.

"She's up in the attic, charming snakes! Can't you hear

her?" Joanna said.

The children were bored by aunt Doe's stories of India. They listened with perfectly blank faces and changed the conversation as soon as they could.

"Who on earth cares," Joanna said to Chris one day, "how many annas make a rupee?"

"The mysterious east can remain mysterious as far as I'm concerned," said Chris.

But when she tried to talk to them about the farm, the fields and the woods and the district around, they were equally unresponsive.

"I'm hoping you'll take me for some walks. I thought we might go blackberrying."

"They're not worth picking, after the drought. And anyway, it's still too hot."

* * * * *

Aunt Doe took over the running of the household, and Agnes was glad to hand it over to her. She and Agnes got on well. They worked together as a team. And in dealing with Mrs Bessemer, still suffering from the heat, aunt Doe was brusque but sympathetic.

"It's hotter than this in Ranjiloor. But it's just as well for you to take care. Heatstroke can be a terrible thing."

The children resented the changes she made. When she wanted to wash their hair, Joanna led an open revolt.

"Agnes always washes our hair."

"Not any more, now that I'm here. Agnes has got enough to do."

"We're old enough to do it ourselves."

"I don't think Emma is old enough."

"*I'll* see to Emma's," Joanna said.

"Very well. It's just as you please. So long as you're clean, that's all I ask."

"We always *were* clean, before you came," Joanna muttered, under her breath. "*We* never suffered from kala-azar!"

Stephen, a witness of this behaviour, was worried by their hostility. He liked his cousin well enough. She had been a

48

good friend to him during his youth. But she had altered in the past fifteen years, and sometimes, seeing her through his children's eyes, he had to admit that she made a ridiculous spectacle, with her outlandish clothes, much mended and patched, the hem of her skirt often hanging down or else fastened up with a safety pin, and her habit of groping inside her blouse, twisting herself into dreadful contortions as she searched for an errant handkerchief.

Her voice and her manner embarrassed them, especially when outsiders were present. They were barely civil to her face, and behind her back they mimicked her.

"Not *Skeine* as in *wool*," Chris would say, catching her intonation precisely, and the manner in which she used her hands, "but *Skeine* as *though* to *rhyme* with *bean!*"

Sometimes Stephen was on the point of breaking out angrily at them. Aunt Doe saw it and restrained him.

"If it doesn't work, my being here, I shall have to go," she said.

"They have no right to behave like this, when you've come all this way for their sake."

"They want their mother back again, and no one else will do," she said. "We must make allowances."

To the three older children she was a fool. They avoided her whenever they could. If they had any problems to be resolved, they went to Agnes, not to aunt Doe.

One afternoon, however, when Agnes was needed, it so happened that she was not there. She had gone in the trap on an errand to town and had taken Emma along for the ride. The other three were in the barn, hunting out old pieces of wood for the house they were building up in a tree, and during an argument between the two boys, a long shiny nail, sticking out of a plank, passed through one of Jamesy's fingers.

At first the boy felt nothing at all, but somehow the plank was stuck to him, and when he looked down to see why, there was the shiny point of the nail impaling the top joint of his finger and protruding two inches on the other side.

"Now look what you've done," he said to Chris, and his voice had the calmness of disbelief. "My finger's stuck on this duddy old nail."

49

Chris and Joanna were appalled at the sight. Neither of them knew what to do. Their father was miles away, up in the fields, and Agnes Mayle had gone into town.

"I'll have to fetch aunt Doe," said Chris. He dashed off quickly into the house.

Within a few seconds, aunt Doe was there. Jamesy, frowning, looked up at her, and his face, though calm, was deathly pale. No blood had come from the finger yet. Nor did he feel the slightest pain. The pain would come when the nail was removed.

"Look away," said aunt Doe, and her strong bony fingers closed over his. "Look away and take deep breaths. This won't take long, but you'll have to be brave."

Obediently Jamesy looked away. He fixed his gaze on the barn door and tried to think of other things as aunt Doe, without delay, eased the finger off the nail and wrapped a white handkerchief round his hand.

"There! It's done!" she said to him. "Now come indoors and we'll clean you up, and put a bandage on it, eh?"

Jamesy nodded, unable to speak. He went, under escort, into the house and through to the scullery, with its stone sink. The handkerchief was bloodstained now; his finger bore two bright red blobs; he saw them welling, and looked away. Aunt Doe turned on the tap and held his hand in the stream of cold water. Chris and Joanna stood and watched.

"It's a lucky thing the nail didn't go through the bone," said Chris.

"It's a lucky thing, too, that the nail was clean," said Joanna, "or he might have got lockjaw, mightn't he?"

"Fetch the first-aid box, will you, please?" Aunt Doe quelled them both with a frown.

Jamesy swallowed and said nothing. The injured finger was coming to life. He watched as the first-aid box was brought and a clean piece of lint was taken from it. Aunt Doe dried his hand, smeared the finger with antiseptic ointment, and bound it up with a gauze bandage, taken, new, from its paper wrapping. She snipped down the last ten inches of gauze, tied a knot between the two strips, and fastened them with elaborate care, round the finger, across the hand, and one last knot around the wrist.

"There, now, is that comfortable?"

"Yes, thanks," said Jamesy, in a husky voice.

But he was beginning to feel rather sick. The whole of his hand was full of pain. And aunt Doe, observing his pallor, sent the other two back to their games.

"Jamesy needs to rest a while. He can sit and watch me washing the eggs."

"Shall we go and tell dad?"

"Yes, go and tell him, certainly. But there's nothing for him to worry about. Jamesy'll be fine when he's had a rest."

The instant Chris and Joanna were gone, Jamesy, his face like candlegrease, turned and was sick in the scullery sink. He had always hated the sight of blood. Afterwards, when it was all over, aunt Doe gave him milk to drink and a lump of barley-sugar to suck. She took him into the living room and put him to sit in the big wing-chair, with his bandaged hand on a cushion to rest, and a favourite book for him to read.

"How do you feel now?" she asked. She leant over him, anxiously, and touched his forehead with her hand.

"All right, thanks," Jamesy said.

"It was a nasty thing to happen, and you were a very brave boy."

Jamesy's lip was tremulous.

"I don't call it brave, being s-sick!" he said, and, what with his shame and his self-disgust and the violent throbbing in his hand, he suddenly burst into childish tears and flung himself forward into her arms.

"Poor boy!" she said, holding him close, and his face was against her cool silk blouse. "I still think you were very brave."

In a little while, when he was more himself again, and all traces of tears had gone, he forced himself to meet her gaze.

"You won't tell the others I cried, will you?"

"Of course I won't! Whatever next?"

"You won't tell them that I was sick?"

"I won't tell them *anything*. Honour bright!"

And aunt Doe, as all four children were to discover, was a woman who always kept her word.

A little later that afternoon, Stephen came in with Chris and Joanna to see how Jamesy was getting on.

"I hear you've been in the wars, my son."

"Yes, but I'm all right now," Jamesy said. He showed his beautifully bandaged hand. "The puttee wallah bound it up."

"Puttee wallah?" Joanna said.

"That's what they say in India. A puttee's a bandage, did you know?"

Later still, after supper that evening, Chris and Joanna were out in the yard, helping their father to shut up the hens.

"Aunt Doe's all right, you know," Chris remarked, poking a chicken down from a tree.

"Of course she's all right! What did I tell you?" Stephen said.

In his heart he was much relieved.

*   *   *   *   *

So aunt Doe was accepted by them. When the house in the tree had been completed, she was their first visitor, and she brought with her an old salt-stained telescope that had once belonged to her uncle John, a seafaring man from Deal, in Kent. As she climbed the ladder up to the house, Chris watched anxiously from behind, one hand holding her by the skirts.

"I'm sorry about the missing rungs."

"It's better to have a few missing rungs, to baffle the enemy coming at night."

Exploring the inside of the house, she poked into corners here and there, and gave them unexpected advice.

"You want a few handy rocks, you know, for repelling invaders when they come. And you want some hard tack to store in that chest in case you need to withstand a siege. I'll let you have some biscuits and nuts."

On leaving she made them a present of the telescope.

Aunt Doe, they discovered, was always ready to take part in whatever scheme they had in hand: to bowl a few overs in a game of cricket; stand by with a watch to time their races; or hunt out a couple of old twill sheets for them to erect a tent on the lawn. Once she took part in a game of rounders and hit the ball right over the barn, into the yard on the other side, where it hit Reg Starling on the skull. And once when a sow got into the garden, she flung herself astride its back, caught hold of it by its flapping ears, and rode it through the open gateway, back to the stockyard where it belonged.

Whatever she did she did with verve and then, suddenly, recalled to a sense of domestic duty, she would give a cry and throw up her hands and hurry off, with her long mannish stride, back into the house again.

"I've got six beds to make before lunch," she would say, or: "The egg-man is coming at twelve o'clock."

She got through a great deal of work in a day, and she was a stickler for perfect detail. Her linen-cupboard was a model of tidiness and organization; beds were made most beautifully, with "hospital corners" and unwrinkled sheets; and all four corners of every pillow had to be insinuated meticulously into all four corners of the pillow-case, clean and white and stiff with starch.

"Aunt Doe's beds," Joanna said, "are a lot better dressed than aunt Doe herself."

She was also an excellent cook. They enjoyed the curries she made for them. Only Mrs Bessemer disapproved.

"I could never eat that. Oh dear me no. What'd my Bert have to say to me if I went home to him smelling of that?"

"What does he smell of," Agnes asked, "after his evenings at the pub?"

"She needn't eat it," aunt Doe said. "Chris and Jamesy will soon scoff that."

She enjoyed cooking meals for these young cousins of hers, with their hearty appetites, but one thing she could not abide and that was waste. If any food was left on a plate, she would point at it with a bony finger, and would fix the offender with a stern blue gaze. "The people in Calcutta would be glad of that!" she would say, and the phrase became a family joke, so that someone had only to leave a tiny morsel, such as a single green pea, to provoke the inevitable chorus.

One morning at breakfast, their father was the guilty one; he left some bacon-rind on his plate; but when the expected chorus came: "The people in Calcutta would be glad of that!", he looked around with a bland smile. "Oh no they wouldn't! – It's pig meat!" he said, and aunt Doe, clicking her tongue, snatched the plate away from him.

"I don't know who's the worst," she said, "you or these four scallywags here."

The household, under her influence, was gradually coming back to life. There was laughter in the house again; a sense of purpose, a meaning in things; a feeling that everything mattered again. It was not that aunt Doe had taken their mother's place with them: nobody could ever do that; but she was there, and they leant on her. She gave herself willingly to their needs, and allowed them to draw on her woman's strength.

Stephen, finding that this household of his went on the same though his wife was dead, was sometimes filled with hurt for her. Hearing laughter about the place, or aunt Doe's voice as she called to the hens; seeing the baskets of new-laid eggs, and remembering Gwen's pride in them; watching Joanna in the dairy, skimming the cream off the pans of milk in exactly the way Gwen had taught her: he would sometimes stand, arrested by pain, overcome by the sense of his loss.

But he was moved to wonder, too, and gave thanks for such as aunt Doe, another like Agnes, a giver of life.

By the time term began, aunt Doe had been at the farm almost a month. She was accepted. She was part of their lives.

* * * * *

Aunt Doe had been born in Sussex, but she was happy in Worcestershire, and one of the happiest things she did was to buy a second-hand bicycle. All through the tropical autumn that year, she rode about on it everywhere, eager for every sight and sound, and speaking to everyone she met. She was soon well-known all around Huntlip, riding her old ramshackle machine, and sometimes, in the fields at Holland Farm, the men while working would see her go by, rattling down the steep snakey lane, and would joke about it among themselves.

"There goes Miss Skeine on that warhorse of hers. Better keep off the roads today, if you value your lives, all of you."

It was certainly true that aunt Doe on her bicycle constituted a danger to the public at large, for her lamp battery was always flat, and her brake-blocks were worn to "no more than a cheese-rind" as Bob Tupper once said. One evening at dusk, careering at speed down Holland Bank, she passed so close to the elderly retired schoolmaster, Mr Quelsh, as he stepped from his gateway into the lane, that she knocked his Panama off his head.

"Dammit, woman, where are your lights?" the old man shouted after her.

"Next to my liver!" aunt Doe called back, and rode on merrily down the lane, tinkling her bell now and then lest anyone else should be fool enough to get in her way. As always, on a Sunday evening, she was late for evensong.

Aunt Doe's bicycle, with its sit-up-and-beg handlebars and its broken mudguards tied up with string, was a great embarrassment to Chris and Jamesy and Joanna. They knew how people laughed at her whenever she rattled through the village, and they heard the remarks of the men on the farm, and, since aunt Doe herself had no sense of the fitness of things, they decided to take the matter into their own hands.

One Saturday afternoon, when she was busy making jam, they wheeled the bicycle into the barn, lugged it up the ladder into the hayloft, and hurled it out of the hayloft door, down into the stackyard below. There, with relatively little noise, the wheels parted company from the frame, bounced a few times on the straw-littered ground, and at last lay still, buckled and broken beyond repair.

"Well!" said Chris, brushing his hands. "She'll never ride *that* old thing again!"

They were not present when Aunt Doe discovered the mangled remains. They were up in the fields with Tupper and Rye. But when they went to the stackyard again, the bits and pieces had all gone, and they found them later on the farm's golgotha, the rubbish heap behind the cartshed, among the old bits of harrows and ploughs.

"She may not know it, but we've done the old girl a good turn," Chris said as they walked away. "Sooner or later she'd have killed herself, riding that thing down Holland Bank."

"What do you think she'll say to us?"

"Oh, there'll be the deuce of a row, I daresay."

But in fact aunt Doe said nothing at all, and her sad silence in the days that followed somehow spoilt the splendid joke, bringing a feeling of anticlimax. The three children followed her example; they resolved to stay dumb as long as she; but after three days of this, poor Jamesy lost his nerve.

"Where's your old bike, then, aunt Doe?" he asked.

"I'm afraid something happened to it," aunt Doe said, looking at him sorrowfully.

"What sort of something?" Jamesy asked.

"As to that, I'm not quite sure, but I think it must have fallen from a very great height."

Jamesy gave a nervous snort. Chris and Joanna looked away. And little Emma, helping aunt Doe to make sausages, looked up at her sister and brothers accusingly.

"Aunt Doe's bike is all smashed in bits. There's nothing to laugh about in that."

"Who said there was?" Joanna asked.

Aunt Doe went everywhere on foot now. The children's father noticed it.

"Why no bicycle?" he asked.

"It needs a few repairs," she said.

The children met in the tree-house to discuss what they felt they ought to do.

"You know what I think?" Chris said. "I think we should buy her a new bike."

They were agreed. They fetched their money-boxes and tipped the contents onto the floor. Between them they had eleven-and-six. But before their discussion could go any further, a noise drew them to the window, and there was aunt Doe, riding triumphantly into the yard on another ramshackle bicycle, just as shabby as the first; bought, she announced when they gathered round, from a man with a junk-cart at Otchetts End.

"He wanted ten shillings but I got it for five. I haven't

shopped in the market-place at Ranjiloor all these years without learning a thing or two!"

Watched by the children, whose feelings were mixed, she rode round and round repeatedly, ringing her old rusty bell with such brio that Stephen came hurrying from the piggery.

"What do you think of my new bicycle?" she asked.

"New?" he said, incredulously.

"I think," she said, with a glance towards Chris and Joanna and Jamesy, "I shall have to keep this one chained up."

"Why?" said Stephen. "Does it bite?"

* * * * *

The long drought ended at last, and rain fell on the tired earth. Suddenly the weather was cold. The nights especially were sharp. But because of the heat stored in the soil, as soon as the rain soaked the ground, there was a quick growth of grass, so that brown parched meadows and brown leys were all a fresh bright green again before winter came to check their growth. The first sowings of wheat were up, green enough to cover the ground, and oats, sown as the first snow fell, were up in flag when the snow had gone.

By the end of November, water ran in the ditches again, and Copsey Pond was brim-full. Stephen went to the pond one day and stood at the edge, under the trees, watching a moorhen swimming across to vanish, darkly, among the reeds.

He had had the wire fence removed, so that cattle and sheep could drink there again, and had had the fletchers all cleaned out. But he himself had kept away. Now he had come, in secret, alone, to look at the place and test himself. But the pond, having filled with water again, was not a place of fear for him. He looked at it and was perfectly calm. It was the drought that had killed Gwen, and the word *drought*, with all it meant, would always strike terror into his heart and fill him with the sickness of hate. The pond itself was innocent. It was a place where moorhens lived; where the farm animals came to drink; where alders grew, and willows and oaks; and where, in the springtime every year, the martins collected mud for their nests.

Stephen turned and walked away. He was meeting his shepherd in Long Gains, to overlook the flock of ewes. The rams would be put in to run with them soon, so that the lambs would be born in May, and the flock be renewed. Rain fell on him as he walked. He drew his collar up to his ears.

Chapter 4

Early in the new year, the threshing tackle arrived. For days its smoke and smell filled the stackyard, and its noise could be heard all over the farm. John Challoner strolled over one afternoon. He was next on the list for the threshing team. He had come to see how long they would be.

"I can lend you a man or two if you like. Get done that much sooner, what do you say?"

"We can manage, thanks," Stephen said, pausing in his work of pitching the sheaves.

Challoner went to the grain-shute and took a handful of grain from the sack. He allowed it to run between his fingers.

"I hear you've got two horses sick. I can lend you a tractor if you like, to get this lot into town when you're done."

"We can manage, thanks," Stephen said.

"Suit yourself! Suit yourself!" Huffily, Challoner walked away, pausing only long enough to speak to the man in charge of the tackle. "You know your way up to my place by now? I'll expect you on Tuesday evening, then."

Stephen, on the stack, resumed his work, pitching sheaves down onto the drum. Tupper, beside him, gave a snort.

"He's in one of his lending moods. I wonder what he wants in exchange."

One morning at the end of the month, the hunt met at The Black Ram, up on the edge of Huntlip Common, and the chase led across Holland Farm. Billy Rye's son, a boy of thirteen, earned himself a shilling by opening the gate into Turner's Piece, and the hunt, trampling the soggy ground, ruined five acres of young tender rape.

The next day was market day. Challoner and Stephen met at the pens.

"I heard you were looking for two new tups. I think I can do you a favour there. A friend of mine from Porsham way —"

"There's just one favour you can do for me. You can damn well stop hunting across my land."

"Eh? What's that? Did we damage your rape? Hang it, man, you must send in a claim! We always pay for damage done."

"I don't want paying," Stephen said. "I only want you to keep off my land."

"You ought to join us," Challoner said, clapping Stephen on the shoulder. "Then you could get your own back a bit, hunting across the other chaps' land!" But, seeing that Stephen was not amused, he said: "I'll have a word with the M.F.H.. He's a reasonable chap. We *all* are. I'll tell him you lost that field of rape."

A few days later, half a dozen bottles of port were delivered at Holland Farm, with a message written on a card: "Apologies. The Crayle Hunt." Stephen was somewhat irked by the gift, but to send it back would be churlish indeed. He walked over to thank Challoner straight away.

"Think nothing of it," Challoner said. "I told you we always paid our debts."

"There is just one thing," Stephen said. "I still don't want hunting across my land. I've given orders to my men that no gates are to be opened for you."

Challoner went very red in the face.

"That's hardly sporting of you, man!"

"Then the port *was* intended to buy me off?"

"Dammit! Of course not! I never said that! We merely thought, the Master and I, that a show of goodwill on either side —"

"I made my feelings clear to you when I first came to Holland Farm."

"But it cramps our style no end, you know, to have your land out of bounds to us."

"The answer's still no," Stephen said.

"Well, Wayman, I'm disappointed, I must admit. I never thought you'd hold out like this. That port came from the Master's own cellar —"

"Maybe I'd better send it back?"

"No, no! Good God, that's absurd!" Challoner made a mighty effort and managed to laugh away his chagrin. "I'll come over and help you drink it if you like!"

"Yes, do," Stephen said.

Although he and Challoner got on quite well, Stephen could never really like the man, and later that year, in the middle of June, something happened that renewed his mistrust.

The sheep-shearing, shared as always between the two farms, took place at Outlands that year. Challoner's ewes were shorn first, and the fleeces were stacked at the end of the barn. Then Stephen's ewes were shorn, and the fleeces were loaded into his cart, drawn up in readiness out in the yard. When the first of his fleeces came, and Stephen went forward to pick them up, Eddie Templer, one of Challoner's men, spoke to him in an undertone.

"I'd count them fleeces if I was you."

Stephen stared. He was taken aback. The year before, and the year before that, his fleeces had gone uncounted to market and been sold there according to weight.

"Why should I need to count them?" he asked.

"It's the best way of making sure they're all there."

So Stephen, when he loaded the fleeces into the cart, kept a careful count, and at the end of the afternoon, instead of the ninety there should have been, there were only seventy-five.

"Seems I'm a few short," he said, as Challoner came up to him.

"Short? By how many?" Challoner asked.

"Short by fifteen," Stephen said.

"How the hell did that happen? Someone's been careless! I'll have his guts!" Challoner strode into the barn and called to his shepherd, Arthur Thorne, to bring fifteen fleeces from the heap. "Mr Wayman's fifteen short. Whose fault is that, I'd like to know? It's all this chatting and larking about! That's how these mistakes are made. If I'm not around to watch you men —"

The fifteen fleeces were brought out and thrown up into the cart. Challoner stood and counted them, in a loud voice, for all to hear. Eddie Templer was one of those who helped to bring the fleeces out. He took good care to avoid Stephen's eye.

"There! All correct?" Challoner asked.

"All correct," Stephen said. "I think I'll drive them down straight away."

"Before they can vanish again, eh?" Challoner gave a great hearty laugh. "I hope you don't think I'm to blame?"

"No, of course not," Stephen said.

Driving the load of fleeces home, he pondered over the incident. Although he had always mistrusted Challoner, he now found it difficult to believe that the man would stoop to such an act, merely for the sake of a few pounds' worth of wool. It could just as easily have been a trick, played out of spite by Eddie Templer, to cause his employer embarrassment. Challoner, as Stephen knew, was much disliked by the men he employed. Whatever the truth, it would probably never be known, for Challoner's manner gave little away and his greeting when Stephen met him again was as bluff and hearty as ever before.

But aunt Doe, it seemed, shared Stephen's mistrust.

"What was all that I heard about fifteen fleeces?"

"A misunderstanding," Stephen said. "They got in with Challoner's by mistake."

"By mistake? I wonder!" she said.

*　*　*　*　*

All through the spring and summer that year, when Stephen walked about the fields, it seemed to him there was always a wind. It whispered in the green corn and ran like the ghost of a grey-green hare through the long grass in the leys and meadows. Under the sunlight, under the wind, the green blades of grass and the green blades of corn bowed themselves down in humility, while the green stalks stood upright in their pride, flowering and coming to seed.

Every year, this miracle. A green excitement possessing the land; touching everything; sparing nothing. Stephen stood in the Home Field, and the green corn came surging up to his feet. He saw how the sheath at the top of each stalk was beginning to open, split by the ear, and he felt the excitement in spite of himself. He walked in the fields of mowing-grass, and the grassflowers touched him, blown by the wind. They left their coloured dust on him. He saw it, golden, on his hands.

By the middle of June the corn stood so high in the Home Field that Emma, creeping between the rows, could stand upright and not be seen. The cool green blades touched her bare arms, and the tall green stalks, with their green ears of grain, towered up above her head. She liked the cool greenness of the corn, and the whispering of the wind among the blades.

Once when she walked in the corn like this, she suddenly came on a hare in its form: a soft-furred doe, nursing her young, her ears drawn back and her eyes protruding as she crouched in her hollow in the ground. Emma stared at the crouching doe, and the doe stared through her with unblinking eyes; without so much as a twitch of a whisker. Child and hare were stillness itself, confronting each other in the green swaying corn. Then Emma turned and tiptoed away. Leaving the corn, she danced and ran. The hare was a secret that had to be shared.

But when she led Chris and Joanna and Jamesy there, creeping, small, between the rows, the hare and her young were not to be found.

"Are you sure this is the place?"

"I *think* it is," Emma said.

"You must have scared her away, then."

"No, I didn't. She stayed quite still."

"Well, she's not here now, is she?" said Chris.

"*If* she was ever here at all," Joanna said, walking away.

"She *was* there, I saw her," Emma said. "She had two babies suckling her."

"Well, I haven't got time to search the whole field. I've got better things to do. You can go on searching if you like."

The three older children went away. Emma was left alone in the corn. But although she searched up and down the rows, that day and on other days, she never saw the hare again, and the others often teased her about it.

"Seen your hare today, Emma?"

"Next time you see her, put salt on her tail."

"Or make a noise like a lettuce leaf. She'll follow you home if you do that."

Sometimes when Emma walked in the corn, she would hear aunt Doe calling to her from the garden, or her father calling across the fields. She would hear them saying to each other: "Where's Emma? Is she with you? Then she must have gone off with Chris and Joanna."

Hearing their voices speaking so close, Emma would laugh without sound to herself, knowing that she was hidden from them, although she walked upright in the corn. Gathering poppies and corncockles, or looking for larks' nests full of brown eggs, she would wander the corn-rows by the hour, while aunt Doe went searching everywhere, calling her name again and again.

* * * * *

"Where have you been?" Stephen asked, as Emma appeared in the cowshed doorway.

"I've been in the corn," Emma said.

"I hope you didn't trample it down."

"Of course I didn't. I walked in the rows."

"The others not back yet?" Stephen said. But he knew they were not. It was a Saturday afternoon; the two boys were playing in a school cricket match; Joanna was camping with the Girl Guides at Springs. "What about helping me wean this calf?"

The calf in question was six days old. Stephen had a pail of its mother's milk and was trying to persuade the calf to drink. He held his hand under the milk, his upturned fingers breaking the surface, but the calf ignored this enticement and nibbled the edge of the pail instead. Emma came close and watched, dark-eyed.

"Supposing you try," Stephen said. "Put your hand in under the milk and let him lick it off your fingers."

"No, I don't want to," Emma said. She put her hands behind her back.

"You're not afraid of a little calf?"

"Yes, I am. They always nip."

64

"That's not the reason," Stephen said.

"What is the reason?" Emma asked.

"You don't want to get your hands in a mess, that's your reason," Stephen said.

"How do you know it is?" she asked.

"I know my Emma!" Stephen said.

The calf was beginning to suck at last, curling its tongue round Stephen's finger. Gradually, he withdrew his hand, and the calf supped the milk till the pail was empty. Raising its head, it shook itself. Emma stepped back to avoid being splashed. She watched the calf as it licked its lips.

Nearby, in the straw, the farm cat, Maisie, also watched, waiting to lick up any milk that might be spilled over the cobbles. Emma went and picked the cat up, but it struggled free and leapt away, leaving a scratch on the palm of her hand. She licked away a drop of blood.

"Did she hurt you?" Stephen asked.

"Yes," Emma said. She showed him her hand. "But I forgive her. She's only a cat."

Stephen let the calf out into the paddock, to join the other, older calves. It lowed a little, wanting its mother, and the cow answered from the pasture behind the barn. Stephen turned back and looked at Emma, who was tying a handkerchief round her hand.

"I've got to go up to Blagg," he said. "Would you like to come with me and see Mr Maule?"

"No, thank you," Emma said.

"What are you going to do with yourself, then?"

"I'm making a sweetshop," Emma said.

"Well, aunt Doe's around if you want her," he said. "She's in the garden, hoeing the beans."

Sometimes it worried him that Emma, being so much younger than the other children, was often left to play by herself. Yet she never complained of loneliness. She would watch the others getting ready to go out: the boys assembling their cricket gear, Joanna dressing up in her Guides uniform and packing her rucksack to go to camp; and, waving to them as they set out, she looked a sad little figure indeed. "Can't I go to the cricket match? Can't I go camping?" she would ask.

But she never moped, once they were gone. She would play by herself for hours on end, heaping up empty flower-pots in the old garden shed, or painting the slatted garden-seat with a pot of white paint and a tiny brush, or scraping the moss from the farmyard walls. And when, at the end of these self-chosen tasks, she found that her smock had somehow become stained and grubby, she would run indoors to find aunt Doe.

"Can I have a clean pinny? This one's not nice!" she would say.

Today, when Stephen left her, she was already dragging a box across the yard to set up her "sweetshop" in the shade. She scarcely bothered to wave him goodbye. So long as he was about the farm, she would come to him many times in the day, to show him some prize or watch him at work, and it was the same with her sister and brothers. But once they were gone and she was alone, she became self-absorbed, in a world of her own, occupied until they returned.

The sweetshop was set up close to the door where the boys, coming home from their cricket match, were bound to see it. In little glass dishes, set out on the counter, were coloured pebbles, coloured beads, and small chips of stone wrapped in coloured papers. In front of each dish stood a carefully printed price-ticket.

"What's this? said Chris, easing his cricket-bag from one hand to the other; and Jamesy, his cap on the back of his head, his blazer slung over one shoulder, said: "Our little Emma is after our money."

"I'm selling sweets," Emma said. "The shop is still open, if you want anything."

"Have you got a licence for running a shop?" Chris enquired, with a solemn frown. "You'll get into trouble with the police if you haven't got a licence, you know."

"It's only pretending," Emma said.

Chris, with a nudge, drew his brother's attention to one of Emma's price-tickets: "Penny each or two for twopence." The two boys rocked on their heels at this. Emma surveyed them uneasily.

"Have I got the spelling wrong?"

"No, not the spelling," Jamesy said.

"Why are you laughing, then?" she asked.

"Because you're a cough-drop," Jamesy said. "Got any cough-drops by the way?"

"I'm afraid not," Emma said. "I'm expecting them in any day."

"What about bull's eyes?" Jamesy asked, and took a round pebble from a dish. He put it into his mouth, sucked it noisily for a while and then, apparently, swallowed it. "Went down like a stone!" he said to Chris.

Emma looked at him in dismay.

"It *was* a stone! You know it was!"

"I thought you said it was a sweet?"

"Only pretending," Emma said.

"Oh, cripes, I shall die!" Jamesy said. He clutched at his throat and gave a cough, turning despairingly to Chris. "Do something, quick, or it's all up with me! I've swallowed a stone! I shall die! I shall die!" His eyes were bulging hideously. He gave a horrible choking gasp. "Too late! I'm sinking!" he said with a moan.

Suddenly Emma burst into tears. The boys were all contrition at once. Jamesy stopped acting and spat the pebble into his hand. He held it out for her to see.

"I didn't really swallow it!" he said. "Laws, what a goose you are, to be sure! There, there, I'm not going to die. No need for weeping or gnashing of teeth."

"Tell you what, Emma!" Chris exclaimed. "We won our match like billy-oh! Two hundred and eight to their ninety-six. What do you think of that, eh?"

"Chris made forty," Jamesy said.

"Jamesy made twenty-three. Aren't you proud of your brothers, eh?"

Emma nodded. Her tears were gone. She straightened the bowl on her "weighing-machine" and flicked a beetle from her counter.

"I knew he hadn't really swallowed it."

"Of course you did. So did I."

"Jolly good sweetshop you've got here. I must come and buy your bulls' eyes again."

"Penny each or two for twopence!"

Spluttering with laughter, the boys went in. The joke

would last them a good many days. Emma, left alone, dismantled her shop. She returned the glass dishes to the kitchen cupboard, and threw the price-tickets into the stove.

"Where's your shop?" demanded aunt Doe. "I was coming to buy some sweets."

"It's closed for today," Emma said.

* * * * *

One day the children came home from school and found the hay in the Long Meadow cut, lying in its curving swaths, wave upon wave of dark seagreen rippling over the light bright green of the aftermath. They knew at once that the hay had been cut, for the smell of it came to them on the warm wind as they toiled homeward up the track. They ran to the meadow, drawn by the scent, and were just in time to see the machine, driven by Trennam in his haymaking hat, cut through the last long strip of grass and lay it sideways on the ground, completing the last long rainbow curve.

"You started without us!" Chris exclaimed. "What a dirty rotten trick!"

Chris was fourteen in July that year. He was tall, square-shouldered, sturdily built: "every inch the young farmer," as aunt Doe said; and Chris had no fault to find with that. The farm was his passion, first and last. School had become irksome to him. If only his father would let him leave!

"At fourteen years old?" Stephen said. He would not hear of such a thing. "There are all sorts of careers open to you. You could take your pick, the headmaster says."

"Farming's the only career I want."

"You're too young to decide that yet. You may change your mind in a year or two."

"I shan't," Chris said. "I know I shan't."

"Yes, well, we'll wait and see."

Haymaking days were the longest days. The sun seemed reluctant to leave the sky. Field after field of mowing-grass fell to the blades of the mowing-machine; grass became hay in the wind and the sun; and was carted home, swaying and creaking, to be built into stacks or stored in the barn.

All through the busy haymaking days, in the fields around the green corn grew tall, rustling dryly in the wind, the wheat striving upwards, spearlike, erect; the barley bowing its feathered heads; the oatsprays dangling, never still. The greenness faded, under the sun, and a luminous pallor took its place. The pallor went and colour came, deepening to a dusty gold.

But where was the wisdom, Stephen thought, in growing so many acres of corn? At market now, as he well knew, prices were falling all the time. His harvest that year was going to be good, but afterwards, when he threshed his grain, what price would it fetch in the market-place, competing against imported corn? He knew that cuts would have to be made. The men's wages, reduced once, would have to be reduced again, and one of the women, Agnes or Mrs Bessemer, would have to go. It would not be easy, even then, to pay his mortgage, tithes, and costs.

It was aunt Doe's idea that one of the two women should go, and Stephen gratefully agreed.

"Which one will you keep? Agnes, I suppose?"

"No, Mrs Bessemer," aunt Doe said. "It seems her Bert is losing his job when harvest is over at Outlands this year. Agnes's menfolk are all in work."

So Agnes Mayle left and Mrs Bessemer remained. There was more work than ever for aunt Doe, and Stephen, talking things over with his children, won a solemn pledge from them that they would help her whenever they could: in the house; the dairy; the poultry yard. He talked to them on equal terms and explained the need for economy.

"You could say I made a hash of things, taking up farming when I did. It's not going to be easy in the next few years, and I thought I ought to let you know. There won't be much money for luxuries. On the other hand, if I were to give up the farm and go back to practising the law –"

"But you can't do that! You simply can't!"

They were appalled. They cried out against it with all their heart. They would sooner go hungry all their days than think of leaving Holland Farm.

"It won't come to that, I hope," he said, turning the

matter off with a smile. "There's always plenty to eat on a farm."

"If I could leave school –" Chris said.

"Next year, perhaps, but not before."

"Think of the money you'd save on my fees."

"Why, would you work for nothing, then?"

"Anything to keep the farm!"

So Stephen knew that, whatever his folly in buying Holland Farm, his children at least would never reproach him. They would sooner remain on the farm, poor, than live in riches anywhere else.

"You have your answer," aunt Doe said.

"So it seems," Stephen said.

It was puzzling for them, even so, with the wealth of the growing corn around them, to understand the difficulties. At harvest time, when they helped in the fields, Joanna took up a sheaf of wheat and examined the fat, round, plumped-up grain. She took it to Tupper, building the stooks.

"Is it good, the corn we grow?"

"Best in the world," Tupper said.

"Then why doesn't it fetch a good price?"

"There's corn coming in from abroad, that's why, selling cheaper than what we grow. Canada, America, places like that."

"Why is it cheaper?" Joanna asked.

"On account of the way it's grown out there. Thousands and thousands of acres of it, and great big machines to harvest it. Don't ask me how or why, Miss Jo. I dunno. It's a mystery to me."

"There's something wrong somewhere," Joanna said.

"I reckon there is," Tupper said.

"What is it, exactly, do you think?"

"If I knew that —" Tupper said.

"Yes?" said Joanna. "What would you do?"

"I'd write a letter to *The Times!*"

"I'll tell you what's wrong!" Chris said, having listened impatiently while his sister displayed her ignorance. "It's this blasted government! That's what's wrong!"

"Ah," said Tupper, shaking his head. "You may be right,

Master Chris. Though speaking as one man to another –"

"Yes?" said Chris suspiciously.

"– there ent much to choose between none of them!"

* * * * *

"Mrs Bessemer pulling her weight, is she?" Stephen asked.

"Oh, we get done, eventually!" And aunt Doe added, with her keen blue glance: "You can see to read a book in the brasswork when Mrs Bessemer's finished with it!"

Aunt Doe herself was tireless. She kept on the move from morn to night. But she always made light of the housework and the gardenwork, and never wasted a moment of time. If she had to go from one part of the big roomy house to another, she would take a feather duster with her, to flick at the cobwebs on the way; and whenever she had to cross the garden, she would pull up a handful of weeds on the way or nip the dead heads from the daffodils.

No job dismayed her, however unpleasant. When Mrs Bessemer refused to clean out the kitchen drain, aunt Doe did it herself, plunging her arm in up to the elbow until it was coated with black greasy sludge.

"Oh! The smell!" Mrs Bessemer said, but aunt Doe retorted, with a curl of her lip: "I've smelt worse than that in Ranjiloor!"

One day, alone in the house, she fired Stephen's shotgun up the chimney, to bring down the soot. She then went, with a blackened face, to answer a knock at the back door. A red-faced farmer stood there. Behind him, in the yard, stood a sweating black mare.

"I hear you've got an entire," he said.

"An entire what?" aunt Doe enquired.

"An entire horse!" the farmer said. His face grew more red than it had been before.

"Oh, you mean the stallion?" aunt Doe said. "Certainly. Follow me."

She led the way to the stable yard and the farmer followed, bringing his mare. Aunt Doe was quite without fear or prudishness. She led the stallion out of his stall. The farmer, however, kept hanging back, although pulled about by his eager mare.

"Ent there a man about the place?"

"Oh, yes, there are plenty of those!"

She perceived the farmer's embarrassment, and tethered Lucifer to the fence. She went off in search of Bob Tupper. But over her shoulder she gave vent to her scorn.

"I've seen worse than that in Ranjiloor!"

* * * * *

One day towards the end of September, Stephen called the men together and warned them that their wages would have to be cut, from forty shillings to thirty-five.

"We knew that was coming!" said Morton George. "It's one damned reduction after another, ent it, now that the Wages Board is gone?"

"You see the papers," Stephen said. "I've got no choice as you well know."

"Seems to me we've done pretty well," Tupper said, in his quiet voice. "Wages been down a month or more on some of the other farms around. What can't be altered has got to be borne."

Stephen nodded and walked away. Morton George rounded on Tupper.

"Sucking up as usual? The old battalion? Toeing the line?"

"Shut your mouth," Tupper said. "If you was at Outlands instead of here, you'd have a lot more to skike about. There's men been turned off up there, you know, and it's much the same on other farms."

"The farmers need to be shown what's what. At the union meeting the other night –"

"What can the union do to them?"

"Sweet bloody nothing! I know that. There's not enough membership, that's why! Take all you lot here for a start –"

"Here we go!" Hopson said. "The music goes round and round, ooh-ooh-ooh-oh, and it comes out here! For God's sake let's get back to work!"

"Ah! Sweating our guts out!" George exclaimed. "And all for thirty-five bob a week!"

"Sweating?" said Tupper. "What, you? That's against the union rules, ent it?"

As harvest that year came to an end, and the first teams were out, ploughing the stubbles, Stephen discussed with Bob Tupper what sowings they would make that year. Less corn than hitherto, more grass and clover leys, more grey peas, more beans, more rape; and twenty acres of sugar beet, a crop much promoted by the government. Stephen also talked to his shepherd, walking with him in Long Gains. Sheep were a safer investment at times like this, and Stephen planned to increase his flock.

"It's always the way," Goodshaw said. "When farming is high, it's nothing but corn wherever you look. But when things is low, as they are now, grass comes back into fashion again and the shepherd is Somebody all of a sudden. Still, I ent complaining. Oh, no, not me!"

"Can you manage another hundred ewes?" Stephen asked in a tentative way.

"Is that all you're getting?" Goodshaw asked.

The other men were inclined to resent the growth in the number of sheep on the farm. When the first batch arrived, driven up the track by Goodshaw and his two collie dogs, the men stood watching over the fence. Hopson, in a voice loud enough for Goodshaw to hear, spoke to Reg Starling, at his side.

"Which do you dislike the most, Reg, sheep or shepherds?"

"Which is which?" Starling asked.

One day Challoner came over for his customary chat. He walked with Stephen about the fields, and noted the changes everywhere.

"What about this sugar beet they're telling us to grow now?"

"I mean to try it, in the spring. Twenty acres. That field up there. And you?"

"I'm not so sure. I had enough of that in the war, the government telling me what to do. But if you're going to try it up here –"

"Don't go by me, for God's sake. You've been farming all your life. I've been at it for three years."

"You made a mistake, giving up the law to try farming, eh?"

"No, I don't think so," Stephen said.

"What, all the money solicitors make, and you mean to say you've no regrets?"

"No, no regrets," Stephen said.

They walked in silence for a while, picking their way through a field of swedes.

"You know, Wayman," Challoner said, "it's time you thought of marrying again."

Stephen said nothing. He looked away. Gwen had been dead less than eighteen months.

"You're a young man," Challoner said. "Thirty-six is no age at all. It's no good trying to live in the past. You take my advice and look for a wife. I'd do the same, given the chance, but it's not so easy at my age. The market gets tricky when you're pushing on."

Stephen came to a sudden halt and turned to look Challoner in the eye. The man's coarseness offended him. The big handsome face, with its ready smile, was quite suddenly loathsome to him. He felt he could strike it with his fist.

"Am I speaking out of turn?"

"Yes," Stephen said, "I think you are."

"I know exactly how you feel. When my wife died, six years ago, I said I'd never marry again. I had my two boys John and Gerald, and for their sake I carried on. John's in a farm of his own now. Gerald will take over Outlands one day. They're good boys, both of them, and Gerald is company for me. But a man gets lonely all the same. Once you've been married, it's just no good. The loneliness gets into your bones."

Stephen felt guilty. His rage had gone. Challoner, whatever his faults, was just an ordinary feeling man.

"Supposing we talk of other things?" He resumed his walk down the edge of the field, to the pasture where Goodshaw was marking his ewes. "You can tell me what you think of my new flock."

* * * * *

One Saturday morning, during the winter, the children turned out in their oldest clothes to whitewash the inner walls and roofs of the farm buildings. Tupper showed them how to mix the lime into a wash, with a lump of fat floating in it to give it an extra stickiness, and, armed with big brushes, they transformed cowstalls, stables, piggeries, sheds, into dazzling white palaces, sweet-smelling and pure. They took pride in their work and Chris especially was a perfectionist. The lime must be scrubbed very thoroughly into every grain in the wood, into every crevice and pore of the ancient brickwork.

"The whitewash is meant to cleanse," he said. "It's no good leaving little cracks for the dirt and vermin to collect in."

Emma, wearing a clean white smock, stood watching Chris at work in the byre.

"Why can't I do the whitewashing too?"

"Don't be silly. You're too small."

"I want to try it," Emma said.

"Well, you can't, and that's flat!" Chris said. "You'll splash the lime into your eyes and that'll burn you and make you cry."

Emma, driven out of the byre, took refuge in the stables instead. Joanna and Jamesy were working there. Their stiff-bristled brushes went splish-splash, splish-splash, and Emma took care to sit out of reach, perched on the ladder leading up to the loft. Sitting there, she plaited her straws. She was making a workbasket for aunt Doe. And all the time, as her fingers worked, she sang to herself, in a monotone, the hymn she had learnt from Mrs Bessemer.

> "Jesus loves me, this I know,
> For the bible tells me so –"

Splish-splosh, splish-splosh, went the whitewash brushes on the wall, and Emma, above, plaiting her straws, returned for the umpteenth time that day to the chorus of her favourite hymn.

> "Yes! Jesus loves me!
> Yes! Jesus loves me!
> Yes! Jesus loves me!
> The bible tells me so!"

Jamesy, with a scowl, looked up at her, whitewash brush poised in his hand. He was sensitive to sound.

"Jesus doesn't love you!" he said. "Nobody loves you when you make that noise!"

After the whitewashing of the sheds, there were the farm implements to be painted. The boys set to work with loving zeal; a pot of blue paint, a pot of vermilion; and hay-turner, horse-rake, reapers, ploughs, were made to look as good as new. But Chris was not content merely to smarten the implements up: he wanted to know how everything worked; every tool and every machine must yield its secrets up to him, and he must learn to master them all.

And so it was with the tasks of the farm. He would talk to Tupper, Goodshaw, Rye, and pick their brains without shame. But he also read a great deal and kept up with new developments. The farm was his life. He wanted no career but that. He was determined to prove to his father in every way that this was not a boyish craze, but a man's decision, made for good.

Jamesy, on the other hand, though he loved the farm, had set his sights on a different future. He wanted to be an architect. Already, although only twelve, drawing was not just a hobby with him, but a thing that possessed him heart and soul. He saw everything in terms of design. Whatever he was talking about, he was sure to reach for a pencil and paper. "Here, I'll show you," he would say, and the mystery, whatever it was, would be resolved in a diagram.

"Even a cow chewing the cud!" Chris said to Joanna once. "Ask Jamesy how it works, and he'll do you a drawing, exactly to scale!"

Jamesy made drawings of all the great buildings in Chepsworth: the cathedral, the guildhall, the market cross; exteriors and interiors; exact in detail and true to scale. He made drawings of every building on Holland Farm: the house, the barns, the cottages; and when Hopson's cottage was renovated, and a lean-to extension was built on, Jamesy drew up the plans for it, and Mr Hake, the Huntlip builder, used them with only one or two minor alterations.

"So you want to be an architect, building houses and such, eh?"

"What I'd really like to do is to build a cathedral," Jamesy said.

Mr Hake stared. He gave a laugh.

"Well, if I hear of anyone wanting a cathedral putting up, I shall be sure to mention your name."

"Oh, I shan't build cathedrals until I'm old!"

"How old is old, if I might ask?"

"When I'm forty," Jamesy said.

The two boys, then, had already settled where their futures lay. But what of Joanna, now thirteen? Joanna varied with the wind. Doctor; dancer; courtesan; the model in a painting by Augustus John: Joanna yearned to spread her wings.

Early in 1923 a gipsy woman called at the farm and sold aunt Doe a dozen pegs.

"There are children in this house, I know, and one of them has a gift for music."

"Is that a fact?" said aunt Doe.

"A great gift for music. You mark my words."

She had no doubt looked in at the parlour window and seen the piano against the wall. Aunt Doe told the tale to the family as a joke, but Joanna, on hearing of the gipsy's words, felt sure that they referred to her. She resumed her piano lessons at school and practised assiduously at home. Everything else was quite forgotten. Music was the only thing. She saw herself, in her mind's eye, on the concert platforms of the world. She would always wear crimson, she told herself, for her school-friend, Elaine, said it suited her.

Often during the dark winter evenings aunt Doe would get out her violin, and, riffling through her music, brown with age, would find some piece that she and Joanna could play together. The family enjoyed these times. Stephen was very proud of his daughter, and the two boys, although they teased, were impressed by the progress their sister had made.

But one Sunday evening in late March, when she and aunt Doe were playing together, Joanna suddenly heard herself as though for the first time. It was the Bach Minuet, a piece they had played as a duo before, but she heard with sudden clarity that aunt Doe, on the violin, was carrying her and bearing her up. There was nothing there, in her own performance. She played the right notes and that was all. The music was coming from aunt Doe.

"It's no good, is it?" she said at the end, swinging round on the music-stool, and, although there were tears in her eyes, she was laughing at the same time. "I shall never really be any good! That gipsy was talking through her hat!"

"Come, now, Joanna," Stephen said, "Rome wasn't built in a day, you know."

Joanna still looked towards aunt Doe.

"Tell me what you honestly think."

"It all depends what you want to do. Your music will always give you a lot of pleasure –"

"But as a career! Have I got what it takes?"

"What does your teacher say at school?"

"My teacher says the same as you."

"Well, you're surely not going to give it up?"

"Oh, I shall play just the same, of course. But I know I shall never do great things." Joanna was perfectly matter-of-fact. She folded her music and rose from the stool. "Whoever it is in the family who has a great gift for music," she said, "it certainly isn't going to be me."

"Well, don't look at me," Chris said.

"No, nor me," Jamesy said.

There was a silence in the room.

"Perhaps it's me," Emma said.

Such a shout of laughter came from Joanna and the boys that Emma stared in frowning surprise. She had been sitting crocheting. The piece of work was in her hands, and the bright green wool was round the hook. Now she bent over it again and counted the stitches along the edge.

"Emma – musical!" Chris exclaimed.

"Now I've heard everything!" Jamesy declared.

"Poor little Emma," Stephen said. He drew her close to him, on the settee. "How do we know she's not musical? She may be. We shall have to see."

Emma resisted him, drawing away. She was trying to rescue a slipping stitch.

"I don't care if I am or not! Silly old music!" she said to him.

"Emma singing!" Jamesy said.

"Emma playing the snake-charmer's pipe!" Joanna said, with a grimace.

"That's enough!" said aunt Doe, putting away her violin. "Emma is very fond of music. She may surprise you all yet."

One afternoon, when aunt Doe went into the parlour, Emma sat at the old piano, frowning at the music on its stand. The keyboard was open, as it always was – the ivories would turn yellow otherwise – and Emma's hands hovered over the keys. But she snatched them away when aunt Doe came in and folded them in her lap instead.

"You could have piano lessons if you like, you know, and learn to play as Joanna does."

"No, I don't want to," Emma said.

"I could start you off at home."

"No," Emma said. She shook her head.

"What about the fiddle, then? Would you prefer to learn that?"

Emma was fond of the violin. The sound of it, when aunt Doe played, would always bring her into the room. And now, as aunt Doe took it out of its case and played a few bars of "Annie Laurie", there was a gleam in the child's dark eyes.

"Here," said aunt Doe. "You have a try. I'll help you to hold it while you start."

"Shall I be able to play a tune?"

"Not straight away. That takes time. But you'll soon learn, if I show you how."

"No, I don't want to," Emma said.

"Why won't you try it?" aunt Doe asked. "There's no one around to hear you try. The others are all out in the fields."

"I don't care if they are or not. I just don't want to, that's all."

"Very well," aunt Doe said.

She laid the instrument back in its case, but left the lid open, invitingly. She went out of the room and closed the door. Emma slid from the music stool and went to look at the violin. She put out a hand and touched the strings, and a little tremor broke the air, causing a shiver in her skin. She drew her finger, delicately, over the warm red varnished wood; she touched the bow where it lay in its clips; she felt the satin that lined the case. Then, suddenly, reaching up, she brought down the lid with a sharp little click.

Out in the dairy, scouring pans, aunt Doe saw Emma leaving the house; running across the stable yard, skipping and dancing in the wind.

"Where are you off to?" she called from the door.

But Emma pretended not to hear.

Chapter 5

Emma was very small for her age. Chris could carry her for miles; it was nothing to him, being so strong. He would run with her at high speed, pretending that he was a galloping horse, and Emma would bob up and down on his shoulders, shrieking with laughter when he neighed.

"You're just like a little doll," he would say. "I forget you're up there until you yell."

Emma at seven was so small she could scarcely reach the snecks of the doors. She had to stretch herself, up on her toes, and this was a joke to the other three.

"Poor Little Tich!" Jamesy would say. "Let me open the door for you."

They would reach things down for her from high shelves and would unscrew difficult jars for her. They would lift her when crossing a ditch on the farm.

"No! I can jump it! Leave me alone!"

"All right, let's see you," Jamesy said.

"She's bound to fall in," Joanna warned.

"Oh no I shan't!" Emma said.

"Very well. Go ahead and jump. But don't blame us, you silly thing, when you get yourself all black with mud."

Emma retreated a few yards and prepared to make a little run. But the ditch seemed wider, suddenly, and somehow the spring went out of her feet.

"There! You can't do it!" Jamesy said.

"Yes, I can. I've done it before."

"Then why don't you do it and not so much fuss?"

"Because you're watching," Emma said.

"Oh, all right, we'll look away."

But it made no difference whether they looked away or not. So long as they stood there, close by the ditch, Emma knew she would surely fall in, and the knowledge paralysed

81

her legs.

"Come along, little un!" Chris said to her. "You may as well let me give you a hand."

And Emma, yielding herself to him, was swung across to the other side.

She *could* jump the ditch, when she was alone, but they would never believe that.

Sometimes aunt Doe was cross with them, because of the things they did for Emma. When Jamesy fastened her shoes for her, or Joanna offered to cut up her meat, or Chris completed her jig-saw puzzle, aunt Doe reproved them, severely displeased.

"Emma is not a baby now. It's time you allowed her to grow up."

They only laughed at the idea. To think of Emma growing up! The sight of this tiny sister of theirs, coming behind the herd of cows, tapping her little stick on the ground and calling out, "Get over, old cow!" made them feel protective to her. She was so tiny; such a doll. They felt very big and strong beside her, and Chris especially, hoisting her up to sit on his shoulders, felt himself a man of great power.

"Emma's our mascot," he said once.

"That she is not!" declared aunt Doe. "Emma's a person, the same as you."

"Are you a person?" Chris teased the child.

"Yes," Emma said, "you know I am."

"First person singular, I suppose?"

The older children enjoyed the joke, but Emma herself was unsure, glancing at each of them in turn, and saying nothing.

"Take no notice of them," said aunt Doe. "They're not so smart as they think they are."

"Who's not so smart?" Stephen asked, coming into the room just then.

"These three children of yours," she said.

"I thought I had four," Stephen said.

He, according to aunt Doe, was just as bad as the rest of them. Emma was still a baby to him. He spoilt her and made a pet of her, for she was the one who was most like Gwen.

"There's plenty of time for growing up," he said, with his hand on Emma's hair.

At Easter, during the holidays, Chris spoke to his father again on the subject of his leaving school.

"If I'm to leave at the end of next term, we need to tell the headmaster soon."

"Are you sure it's what you want?"

"Absolutely. A hundred-per-cent."

"You're still very young," Stephen said, "to decide the course your life will take."

"Hang it all. I'll be fifteen by then. Gerald's been farming for nearly a year. So have Jeff Twill and David Mapp."

Stephen was not much impressed by this. He did not care for Challoner's son, nor for the other two sprigs thus named, and just lately, as he knew, Chris had been much in their company.

"I don't need to tell you that farming is in a bad way. There's not much scope for ambitious men."

"It'll get better in time. It must."

"I don't see much hope in the next few years. You'll get little joy but the work itself."

"It's still what I want. Honestly."

"Very well," Stephen said. "I'll write to Mr Priestman immediately."

"Thanks, dad!" Chris exclaimed. Jubilant, he shook Stephen's hand. "You won't regret it, I give you my word."

"I hope *you* won't. That's the main thing."

"I shan't," said Chris. "I know I shan't!"

The decision was taken; the headmaster informed. Chris would leave school at the end of July. Stephen still worried, all the same. He talked about it to aunt Doe.

"I hope I'm doing the right thing."

"Chris knows his own mind. His heart is in farming, there's no doubt of that."

"I hope his heart won't be broken by it. Older men's have been, these past two years."

"Why not look on the bright side? Four lots of school fees are a drain. Be thankful you'll soon be saving one."

"It *will* be a saving, certainly."

A few days later he heard that Miss Protheroe's Little

School, which Emma attended, was to close down at the end of the summer term. Emma would have to go elsewhere.

"Why not send her to the village school? You'd be saving two lots of school fees then."

"Is Emma's education to suffer, merely to save me a few paltry pounds?"

"I don't see why it should suffer at all. What does she learn at Miss Protheroe's that she wouldn't learn at the village school?"

"What would she learn at the village school that was better not learnt?" Stephen said.

"I've always heard it's a particularly good school."

"Yes. It is. Or so I believe."

"You ought to know. You *are* on the board of managers."

"It has a high standard, certainly. In fact it has the reputation of being one of the five best village schools in the three counties."

"In that case, I don't see what you've got against it."

"I've got nothing against it," Stephen said.

But the idea was new, and new ideas were hard to digest. His little Emma at Huntlip school, in the rough-and-tumble of that noisy playground, with labourers' boisterous daughters and sons? Cold-shouldered, perhaps, because she was different from themselves. If she had gone there from the first. . . .

"She'll soon get used to it," aunt Doe said.

"But will she be happy?" Stephen asked.

"She's made no friends at Miss Protheroe's. Perhaps she'll do better, nearer home."

"Labourers' children?" Stephen said.

"She talks to the labourers on the farm. Why not to their children, for goodness' sake?"

"I'm not being snobbish, you understand."

"No, of course not," aunt Doe said. There was a dryness in her tone,

"I only want what's best for Emma."

"You're afraid she'll be roughened, perhaps, down there, hobbing and nobbing with the villagers?"

"Isn't it possible?" Stephen said.

"That Miss Izzard, the mistress-in-charge. . . I was talking to her at the jumble sale the other day. She doesn't strike me as being rough."

"Of course she's not," Stephen said.

"She's a reasonably well-educated woman, isn't she?"

"I can see where you're leading me, you know."

"An intelligent woman, would you say?"

"Intelligent, yes, certainly."

"Yet she is a product of that village school, I understand."

"Very well. You've made your point. I shall think about it, I promise you."

So in time yet another decision was taken. Stephen went down to the village school and arranged that Emma should begin to attend there in September. As to the wisdom of the decision, only time would tell on that, but Emma herself was well pleased. She thought of the village school as her father's school, because it stood below the farm, and because the children who went there were allowed to play their summer games in her father's meadow, just behind.

"When am I going to daddy's school? Will they ring the bell for me? Shall I go down across the fields?"

As far as Emma was concerned, September could not come soon enough.

* * * * *

The flocks on the two farms were too big now to be shorn together on the same day. The two lots of shearers banded together as usual, but on different days, first at Outlands and then Holland Farm. And that, as Billy Rye remarked, meant two shearing-feasts instead of one.

"Shearing-feasts!" said Morton George. "They starve us all through the bloody year and give us a feast at shearing time! Are we supposed to be grateful for that?"

Wages were cut again that year. They were down to thirty shillings now. This was in accordance with the recommendations of the local "Conciliation Committee", set up to deal with such matters, but there was resentment all the same, and it showed in the faces of the men when, on a Saturday in July, they came to the office to be paid.

"Is that all I'm worth to you, Mr Wayman? Thirty

shillings?" Nate Hopson said.

"The slump hits all of us," Stephen said. "We've all got to make economies."

"God! I could spit!" said Morton George. He snatched up his money and walked out. His loud voice could be heard in the yard as he talked to Starling and Billy Rye. "Economies! Sweet Jesus Christ! What economies does *he* make, I'd like to know?"

The rest of the men said nothing at all. They took their money and slouched away, each one avoiding Stephen's glance. Their sullenness irked him; it got on his mind; and yet they had his sympathy. They were the ones who suffered most. It was their children who would go hungry when harvest was over and winter came.

All through the summer and autumn that year, there was a constant stream of men, most of them strangers to the district, calling at the farm in search of work. Aunt Doe would give them something to eat and perhaps put a shilling into their hands. But there was no work for them on the farm.

"Surely there must be something?" they would say. "Especially now, at haymaking time? Surely you need an extra man?"

But Stephen refused them, one and all.

"Any extra work I have goes to the local men," he said.

He made it a rule, and kept to it. He hardened his heart to these ragged strangers and watched them trudge towards Outlands and Blagg. Challoner, he knew, sometimes employed these casual men. He paid them less than their work was worth and, as he said to Stephen once, it kept his own men on their toes.

"They know, if they monkey with me, that I've got two or three chaps at my gate, ready to step straight into their shoes. That gives them something to think about, and keeps them from too much idling around!"

One man who called at Holland Farm was Eddie Templer from Outlands, the man who, at shearing time the summer before, had urged Stephen to count the fleeces.

"Challoner's given me the sack. I'm a union man and he hates our guts. It's been in the wind for a year or more. I've come to ask you for a job."

"I've got all the labour I can use."

"I done you a favour once, remember, when Challoner was trying to cheat you."

"Is that why you did it?" Stephen asked. "Against the day when you might want a favour in return?"

"What if I did? What's wrong with that?"

"Did Mr Challoner really try to cheat me that time? Or was it just a trick of yours?"

"Seems you've got a suspicious mind."

"You haven't answered, yes or no."

"Are you going to give me a job or not?"

"I've already told you, there's nothing here. I'm sorry, Templer, but I can't *make* work."

"Never mind the apologies! I can't keep my wife and kids on *them*! Seems I backed the wrong bloody horse!"

Less than half an hour after Templer had gone, aunt Doe came running up to the hayfield to say that the cattle were in the corn, in the twelve acre piece above Long Gains. Chris, coming home from school just then, was quick to believe that Eddie Templer was to blame. He had passed the man coming up the track.

"He's a bolshevik, one of the worst. Mr Challoner's well shot of him. Thank goodness you didn't take him on."

"We don't know for sure that he let the cattle into the corn."

"They're all the same, these unemployed. *Good* working men don't get the sack. They're either shirkers or bolshies or both and they ought to be put to mend the roads."

"Is that what Gerald Challoner says?"

"I do have opinions of my own."

"And no doubt they coincide with his."

"Yes, on the whole, I think they do."

"I think that's a pity," Stephen said.

"Dammit, dad! Gerald's my friend!"

"Yes, I know," Stephen said.

And that was a pity, too, he thought.

* * * * *

It was not only corn prices that had fallen so low. It was the same with cattle and pigs: the prices they fetched at market now hardly covered the cost of rearing them; and Stephen, going over his accounts, read the sad story on the page. Only the sale of fat lambs showed a worthwhile profit there. Sheep were keeping the farm alive. Sheep and aunt Doe's poultry yard.

Aunt Doe had savings in the bank, which brought her in fifty pounds a year. She wanted to remove her capital and give it to Stephen to pay off the mortgage on the farm. He would not hear of such a thing.

"Why not?" she asked. "I spend hardly anything on myself."

"Then it's high time you did," Stephen said, and he looked critically at her shoes, the laces of which were bits of string.

"You can talk! Just look at you! Ragged old jacket and that awful cap!"

"You'll want that money for your old age. I'm paying the mortgage gradually. Another two years should see it through. There's nothing for you to worry about. We're keeping our heads above water – just!"

"And *you* are wearing yourself to a shade."

Stephen's angular, loose-knit face, with its high cheek-bones and long lean jaw, had a tired look in it these days. She wished there was something she could do to smooth away the deepening lines and ease the burden of anxiety. But he would not take the money she offered, and she knew he would never change his mind. All she could do, she told herself, was to try and save him in every way.

Nothing was wasted in the house. Meatbones were boiled to make stock for soups; potatoes were always cooked in their skins; all manner of fruit was bottled and jammed. Used tealeaves were kept for cleaning the carpets, and soft soap was made at home. Cough-cure was made by baking onions with brown sugar, and all sorts of garden herbs were kept, for whatever ailments might come to the family. No one dared be ill in that house, for fear of aunt Doe's remedies, but her home-made wines were popular, especially the plum and the walnut-leaf.

Stephen would sometimes smile to himself, seeing her carefully hoarding the scraps that would go to make a curry for lunch the next day. Food, as he often reminded her, was the one thing that was plentiful on the farm.

"I like to think I'm helping you, even if you don't think my efforts are worthwhile."

"Of course you're helping me," he said.

* * * * *

One afternoon at the end of July, Chris left school for good. He celebrated in true Chepsworth style by hurling his "boater" from King Richard's Bridge, into the swirling river below, and watching it float away downstream.

"Poor old Wayman! He's a farmer now!" A school-friend stuck a straw in his mouth. "Don't forget to set your alarm."

"Or wind up the cockerel," another boy said.

"We'll think of you Wayman, milking the cows at four o'clock!"

"I'll think of *you* next term," Chris said, "sweating blood over Shenstone's impots!"

He and Jamesy ran for their bus.

A week later harvest began, and when the first field was cut, Chris was there in the first dim light, taking his place among the men, working beside them with his scythe. To his surprise nothing was said. There was no banter of any kind. The men worked in silence, in a row, cutting a way round the edge of the field so that the reaping-machine could get in.

The sun was not yet visible, and the men were shadowy, featureless shapes, mowing their way through the milk-white mist. Then the sun began to rise, burning over the earth's edge, touching the oats with its molten redness. The men's faces were crimson-flushed. Their scythe-blades, at every returning stroke, appeared for an instant to drip red fire. Only then did the mowers speak.

"Who's this new chap here with us, Billy?"

"That's the young master," Billy said.

"What, him what was only last week at school?"

"The very same," Billy said.

89

"Well, I'll say this for him, at any rate – he's no slug-abed, that's for sure. Nor he don't yap too much, neither, first thing. Seems to me we'll keep him on."

Chris, though he smiled to himself at this, said nothing in reply. He needed every ounce of breath if he was to keep pace with the other mowers.

The day came at last when Emma was to start at the village school. Stephen, as it happened, was attending a sale. He had to leave home at six o'clock.

"You'll take her down?" he asked aunt Doe.

"*I'll* take her down," Chris volunteered.

But when, at a quarter past eight, Chris came in to eat his breakfast, Emma was nowhere to be found. Her shoe-bag had gone from its place on the dresser. So had her luncheon, packed by aunt Doe. Emma had slipped off to school alone, and nobody had seen her go.

* * * * *

On ordinary mornings, Betony Izzard walked the mile from her home to the school, but today, the first morning of the new term, she asked her brother for a lift and rode with him in the workshop cart, sitting beside him on the box, with her big canvas hold-all on her lap. It was not yet eight o'clock. She liked to be early on the first day of term. And behind her, in the cart, among the timber and the carpenter's tools, stood two big baskets full of apples. The apples were her reason for wanting a lift.

When they arrived at the school, Dicky carried the baskets in and set them down as she directed, one in each of the two classrooms.

"I dunno what great-grumpa will say when he finds you've been at his precious apples. Nor dad and mother, come to that. They won't be best pleased if you ask me."

"They needn't know if you don't tell them."

"They'll notice the apples is in short supply."

"I shall say the mice have been eating them."

"Ah, two-legged mice!" Dicky said, glancing round at the empty desks. "You spoil them kids. You do, that's a fact."

Betony hung up her coat, closed the cupboard, and went

90

to her desk.

"One apple a day for each child! Do you call that spoiling, Dicky?" she asked. "For some of them – those whose fathers are out of work – that apple will be all they have to eat between coming to school in the morning and going home in the afternoon."

"And what they thieve in the fields on the way!"

"Do you grudge them a slice of raw turnip?"

"*You* can't feed all the poor of the parish and it's no use your trying," Dicky said. "But I ent got time to stop chatting here. I'm meeting dad at Mr Twill's. We're building him a summer-house to go with his brand-new tennis-court."

"And farmers complain that they have no money!"

"Seems to me I'd better be off, before you get on your hobby-horse."

The door closed and Dicky was gone. She heard him turning the cart in the playground. Stillness and quietness stole on her. She liked the hour between eight and nine, when she had the building to herself, and on the first morning of term, especially, there was always much to be done.

Out of her big brown canvas bag she took a roll of coloured posters, bought on a recent visit to London. She began pinning them up on the walls. They depicted people in history and were painted in bold lines and colours. Alexander taming his horse. Stephenson watching the boiling kettle. Captain Scott at the South Pole. Nurse Cavell, facing her captors. And others not so instantly recognizable, such as Ptolemy and Caractacus, William Willett and John Brown, to stir her pupils' curiosity. In the course of the term the children would come to know them all as intimately as they knew one another.

Next she took out a spray of hops and hung it above the classroom door. The scent of the flowers, and their stickiness, remained on her fingers and her palms. She wiped them clean on a piece of rag. She took out sprays of hips and haws, oakleaves and acorns, ashleaves and keys, and put them into a stoneware vase, up on one of the window-sills. The morning sunlight shone on them: scarlet rose-hips and crimson haws; acorns beginning to turn yellow; ashkeys already parchment-brown. She fetched a jug of water and filled the vase.

The school was really one large room. It was divided into two by a sliding partition of wood and glass. When Betony had first been made headmistress, there had been a hundred and nineteen pupils, but now, when the children reached the age of eleven, they went to the school at Middle Cross. There was more room at Huntlip now. When attendance was at its peak, there were sixty-seven children in all.

* * * * *

At half past eight Sue Vernon arrived. She was Betony's sole assistant. Small, neat, dark-haired and dark-eyed, she walked in with a sharp briskness as though impatient to start the day's work. She enquired after Betony's holidays and answered a query about her own, but her glance kept straying to the basket of apples standing beside Betony's desk.

"I brought them from home," Betony said. "There's another one in your room. The children can have one apple each when they stop for the morning break."

"How generous you are. I hope they appreciate it, that's all."

"The apples won't last long, I'm afraid. Not unless attendance is low."

"No doubt it will be, seeing the harvest is still going on. I saw some children in the fields as I cycled past Moat Farm just now. I nearly stopped and spoke to them, but I know your feelings on the subject, and I thought I'd better leave it to you. I can give you the names of three of them."

"No, there's no need," Betony said. She set up her easel and put in the pegs. "I shall know about it soon enough."

Sue Vernon's gaze was critical.

"Mr Pugh says it's a downright disgrace, these absences at harvest time. He says we teachers are to blame. We delay in reporting them to him."

Mr Pugh was the school attendance officer, a personal friend of Sue's family. He lived in the house next door to

92

theirs, in one of the better parts of Chepsworth.

Betony reached for the blackboard and lifted it up onto the easel. The argument was an old one between them. It varied little from year to year.

"The parents need the extra money. This year, perhaps, more than ever before."

"Well, I think it's very wrong indeed, that the children's schooling should be neglected just for the sake of a few coppers."

"What's the use of filling their heads if their bellies are empty?" Betony said. She took chalk and duster from the cupboard and placed them in the tray pegged to the easel. "A few coppers are not to be sneezed at, to a labourer with a family."

Sue Vernon walked away, into her own classroom next door, and laid her small suitcase on her desk. Miss Izzard's use of the word "bellies" was really rather typical. Sometimes she seemed to set out to offend. Or was the coarseness ingrained in her? Something that could not be overcome?

Miss Vernon, not for the first time, took herself severely to task. For she was the daughter of a church organist, a man of standing and refinement, and she had enjoyed advantages denied to such as Betony Izzard, whose father was a village carpenter. A good enough man in his way, no doubt – even well-to-do, in fact, for the family business was a flourishing one – but a countryman of no education: slow, simple, unlettered, uncouth, and almost laughably broad in his speech.

"Really," Miss Vernon told herself, "one must make allowances, after all."

Acting on her good resolution, she took a piece of paper from her case and carried it in to Betony.

"I've drawn up a list of hymns for the term. I thought you'd like to see it first."

One of Miss Izzard's disadvantages was that she could not play the piano. As mistress-in-charge she must feel it keenly. Miss Vernon therefore deferred to her whenever it seemed reasonable to do so. Betony took the neatly written list.

"Not three-three-one. At least not today. It's not very

cheerful, is it?" she said. "Let's have 'To be a pilgrim' instead. The children like it. So do I."

Miss Vernon drew a deep breath. Her good intentions were draining away.

"I haven't practised it, I'm afraid."

"I'm sure you can play it, even so."

"Oh, I can play it, certainly. But it won't be up to a high standard."

"The children won't mind. Neither shall I. We'll do our best to drown you out."

"Oh, how true!" Miss Vernon said, with more than a touch of bitterness. But when she met Betony's glance, she was gradually obliged to smile. "Oh, how true!" she said again, and the truth of it made them laugh together, with real amusement on both sides. "As for that dreadful piano in there – !" She returned once more to her own room.

Betony Izzard went to her desk. She took out pen-tray, inkwell, register. She opened the register out on her desk and wrote the date at the top of the page: Tuesday, September the 4th., 1923.

Her watch, which was pinned to the front of her dress, told her that it was five-and-twenty to nine. She stepped up onto a wooden form and looked out of the high window. The playground below was still deserted. No children had come to stir the dust. Only a movement in the "back-house" showed where the cleaner, Mr Miles, was filling a bucket at the tap.

Betony was proud of that tap. Not many country schools had a piped water supply indoors. It had taken three years to get it installed. But she was not so proud of the school privies, housed in a hut among the trees. How many years would pass, she wondered, before the managers would admit that four latrines were inadequate for sixty-seven children, girls and boys?

She was about to step down from the form when she saw a child in the playground. It was Emma Wayman from Holland Farm. For her first day at the village school Emma evidently meant to be in good time, but, finding herself alone in the playground, she stood uncertainly at the gate, swinging her shoe-bag on its string. A tiny thing, very small for her age, she wore a plain blue cotton frock and a clean white pinafore, crisply starched. Except that she carried a change of shoes, there was nothing to set her apart from the rest of the village children; nothing to show that hitherto she had gone to a private school in the town and mixed with the daughters of professional men. She was dressed like any Huntlip schoolchild. Plainly her aunt, Miss Skeine, had sense. Betony went to fetch her in.

* * * * *

"Didn't anyone bring you, on your first day?"

"No," Emma said, "I came by myself."

"Are they busy up at the farm?"

"Yes, they're harvesting," Emma said.

Betony took the child's hand and led her into the school porch. She showed her where to hang her bag, and watched while she changed into indoor shoes. Emma's movements were slow and precise. She looked about her curiously.

"I expect it seems strange to you after Miss Protheroe's," Betony said. "But you'll soon get used to it, you'll see. I'll take you into your classroom now, and you'll meet your teacher, Miss Vernon."

But Miss Vernon, in the smaller room, had removed the lower panel from the piano and was on her knees in front of it, tightening the pedals with a screwdriver. She looked fraught, and her hair was dishevelled. Betony tactfully withdrew.

"You'd better wait with me for a while, at least till the other children arrive. You can give me a hand with my morning chores."

Betony sat the child at a desk and gave her a box full of broken pencils. She gave her a sharpener shaped like an egg, and an empty carton to catch the shavings. And while Emma sharpened the pencils, Betony went to and fro, taking exercise books from the cupboard and sorting them into separate piles.

"Did you come down across the fields?"

"Yes," Emma said, "it's the quickest way."

"Are there still mushrooms in Cowpark Meadow? There

95

used to be when I was a little girl like you."

"I didn't see them," Emma said.

"Perhaps it's too early in the year."

Betony climbed onto the form and looked out of the window again. There were children in the playground now: six of them chasing an old rubber wheel; their booted feet kicked up the dust, and their voices shrilled with merriment. Betony got down again.

It made Emma smile to her see her headmistress bob up and down from the wooden form. Miss Protheroe would never have done such a thing. Miss Izzard was younger; she was light on her feet. She was fairer, prettier, more full of life.

"The children have begun to arrive now. Would you like to go out and play with them?"

"I haven't finished the pencils yet."

"That doesn't matter. You've done a lot."

"I'd sooner finish them," Emma said.

She liked this little task of hers, sitting at a desk in the sunny classroom, while her new headmistress passed to and fro. The pile of sharpened pencils grew, each one pointed beautifully, and the curly shavings filled the carton, tinged with yellow, red, and green. When she had finished, she sat quite still. She looked at the hops above the door; the hips and haws and the autumn leaves, catching the light on the window-sill; the coloured posters on the wall. She watched Miss Izzard, secretly, as she wrote on the blackboard with a chalk.

Outside, in the playground, the noise of playing children grew. From the classroom next door came a heavy thud as Miss Vernon replaced the front of the piano. She came and opened the connecting door.

"I'm going out to the playground now. There's a bit of a rumpus going on. The Tillotson boys, as usual. Goodbye to peace for the next three months!"

A few minutes later she was back, entering by the main door and ushering in, very formally, a young woman and a small boy.

"Miss Mercybright to see you," she said.

The young woman had auburn hair. It showed like

copper, gleaming bright, under her rather shabby hat. The little boy, on the other hand, was dark-skinned and had black hair. Yet there was enough likeness between them to show that they were mother and son. Miss Vernon's glance was shrewd and sharp.

"You did say *Miss* Mercybright, I believe? I'm sorry if I made a mistake –"

"Thank you, Miss Vernon," Betony said.

Miss Vernon withdrew, flushing slightly, and closed the door. Betony put her chalk away and wiped her hands on a clean duster. She moved between the rows of desks. Smiling, she stooped to the little boy, and lifted him up to stand on a form.

"Well, Robert, and how are you? I haven't seen you since ever so long. Not since we went to the Whitsun fair. Have you still got the fairing you won at the stalls?"

The little boy's hand went into his pocket. He held up the fairing for her to see. It was a tiny tumbler bell and he jingled it on the end of its string. Then he put it away again. Betony, laughing, looked at him.

"You look very smart in your corduroys. Are you glad to be starting school?"

Robert gave a little nod. A slight smile touched his lips. His mother reached up and removed his cap. She tried to smooth his straight black hair.

"He's very young to be starting school. He isn't even four yet. But I've got this job at Tinkerdine, doing the cleaning for old Mrs Frail, and dad said Robert should come to school."

"Robert will soon settle down with us. There are others here just as young, you know. It'll do him good to have company."

"He's always had company," Linn Mercybright said. "He's never been left alone in his life."

"But he's had no other children to play with. It's lonely out there in Stoney Lane."

"I suppose you think I've been too protective. But he *is* my son. Remember that." Linn, avoiding Betony's glance, pulled a thread from Robert's sleeve. "You and your family have been very kind. You've helped us for his father's sake –"

"We've *tried* to help," Betony said. "Tom was brought up with my family – is it so strange that we should want to help his son?"

"Robert is all I've got left of Tom. If Tom had lived, we'd have shared him together, but I'm not going to share him with anyone else."

"Why should you indeed?" Betony said. "Except in those ways that are best for him?"

"I'm the one to decide what's best."

"Well, at least you've allowed him to come to school."

"As to that, I have no choice, if I'm to work for Mrs Frail. We need every penny we can get."

Linn's tone had an edge to it. There was a coldness in her face. If it had been any other school she would have found it easier, but Betony, being the little boy's godmother, had a special claim on him, and Linn would have given anything rather than yield him up to her. Betony apprehended this. She sought to set Linn's mind at rest.

"Robert will be in Miss Vernon's class. He won't come to me until he's eight. There's nothing much to worry you."

"Oh, I'm not worried!" Linn said. She turned it off with a little shrug, pretending not to understand. "He'll soon settle down, I'm sure of that."

All the time, while the two women talked, the little boy stood on the form, watching them with a deep dark gaze. Once he turned his head and looked at Emma, sitting primly at her desk, but otherwise he scarcely moved.

"I hope there won't be any trouble from the other children."

Linn spoke carefully, with some hesitation, but Betony knew what she meant to say. Robert was illegitimate. In a village like Huntlip, this would be known to everyone.

"He's not the only love-child here. There may be remarks from time to time, but that's something that's got to be faced, isn't it?"

"So long as it isn't worse than that."

"I shall watch over him, never fear."

"Yes," said Linn, "I'm sure you will."

Suddenly she coloured up. The tartness this time had

been unintended. Confused, she turned to her son again, straightening his collar and tightening his tie. She forced herself to meet Betony's gaze.

"Do you see Tom in him?"

"Yes, in his stillness," Betony said. "And because he's so dark, of course. But he's got a look of your father, too, especially about the eyes."

She gave the little boy her hand and encouraged him to jump from the form. She walked with him and Linn to the door.

"How is your father nowadays?"

"His leg is giving him trouble," Linn said, "though he'll never admit it, needless to say."

It was time for her to go. She found it hard to leave her son. She forced herself not to touch him again, but looked at him with severity.

"Be a good boy on your first day at school. I'll call for you at three o'clock. And do remember what I said! – You mustn't say 'aunty Betony' – you must say 'Miss Izzard' like everyone else." And, turning to Betony, she said: "I hope it doesn't slip out, that's all. I've told him about it often enough."

"It won't be the end of the world if it does. He is my godson, after all."

At the outer door, Linn turned to wave. Robert answered by waving his cap. Then suddenly she was gone, and a shadow flickered across his face. Betony gave his hand a squeeze.

"Come along, Robert. I'll find you a friend."

She took him to Emma, who sat with folded hands in her lap.

"This is Robert, my godson," she said. "He's never been to school before. Will you be his special friend?"

Emma nodded. She and Robert exchanged a stare. When she stood up, small though she was, she felt herself tall compared with him. Shyly, she took his other hand.

"It's not worth your going out to play now," Betony said. "They're all coming in in a minute or two. I'll take you into your own room."

"Can't we stay in here with you?"

"No, Emma, I'm afraid you can't."

Emma was in Standard I; Robert was in the Infants' Class; they had to go into the smaller room, and Miss Vernon was the teacher there.

Betony went to ring the bell. Half a dozen peals, and then a hush. But within a short space of time, the school resounded to the trampling of feet, the slamming of desk-lids, the shifting of forms. Fifty-eight children, girls and boys, stood in their places in the sunlit room; the panelled partition was slid back half way; and Miss Vernon sat at the ancient piano. Gradually the noise subsided. Betony said the morning prayer.

"Give to thy children gathered here a day of peace, Oh Lord, and strength to be dutiful in thy sight."

When the opening bars of the hymn were played, she spared a thought for Sue Vernon. The piano was indeed old. Two strings were broken and many were loose. But fifty-eight pilgrims, undismayed, lifted their voices to the roof and sang with all their might and main.

> "He who would valiant be
> Gainst all disaster –"

* * * * *

Emma sat at the back of the room; Robert with the "babies" in the front.

"Silence, everyone!" Miss Vernon said. She tapped with a ruler on her desk.

The first day of term was always like this. The children were slow to settle down. The basket of apples drew all eyes.

"Miss Izzard has kindly brought them for you. One apple a day for everyone but *not* until eleven o'clock."

Through the glass-panelled partition, now closed, Emma could see Miss Izzard in the room next door, the sunlight on her smooth fair hair as she stood talking in front of her class. Emma sat very straight and still. *She* would wear a little watch pinned to the bosom of her dress, when she grew up, she told herself.

"Pay attention," Miss Vernon said.

Out in the playground, during the break, Robert was surrounded by older children, who wheeled him about in the gardener's barrow. Emma sat under the chestnut tree, on one of the knobbly outcropping roots. Florrie Ricks came and sat by her.

"Ent you going to eat your apple?"

"No, I'm keeping it," Emma said.

"You can't be very hungry, then."

"No. I never said I was. I've just had my elevenses."

"Lucky thing," Florrie said. "I ate all mine on the way to school."

"What did you have?" Emma asked.

"Bread and scrape," Florrie said.

The two were silent for a while. Emma waved away a wasp. Florrie picked at a hole in her sleeve.

"Where's your father? Is he dead?"

"No," Emma said. She looked away. "He's gone to Wales."

"Your mother's dead, though, isn't she? Hilda Bowers said she was. You've got an aunt looking after you."

Emma made no reply. She breathed on her apple yet again and polished it on her pinafore. Florrie gave a little sniff.

"You won't have no apple left if you keep on rubbing it like that."

"Oh yes I shall."

"If you don't want it, you should ought to put it back."

"Back where? Back on the tree?"

"Back in the basket, clever dick."

"Well, I'm not going to, so there."

"I knew you wouldn't," Florrie sniffed.

"I'm going to keep it," Emma said.

But the apple, placed on her desk during the rest of the morning's lessons, had somehow vanished by dinner-time.

"What have you lost?" Miss Vernon asked.

"I've lost my apple," Emma said. "Somebody must have taken it while I was giving out the books."

"That's not a very nice thing to say."

"*Somebody* took it. They must have done."

"Perhaps when you have your apple tomorrow it will

teach you to eat it up at once instead of hiding it away just to tease the other children. Now run along home, child, or you'll be late for lunch."

When Emma reached the Brooky Field, Chris was waiting at the stile. He put her to sit astride his shoulders and jogged home with her up the steep track.

"Somebody slipped off to school by herself and never said nothing to nobody!"

Because it was Tuesday, there was curry for lunch. Aunt Doe was filling a bowl with rice. Joanna and Jamesy were both there because school had not started for them as yet.

"How's our little Emma, then, and what did she think of the village school?"

"Put her to sit in dad's chair. She likes that when he's away."

"What are the children like down there?"

"Were the teachers nice to you?"

"What sort of lessons did you have?"

"Ordinary lessons," Emma said. "We did our arithmetic on a slate."

"Do you like it? asked aunt Doe.

"Yes, it's all right," Emma said.

When she returned to school after lunch, one of the children, sniffing her breath, made a face of great disgust.

"What've you been eating, for goodness' sake?"

"Curry, of course," Emma said.

Emma shared a desk with Jenny Quinton, a child with wire-rimmed spectacles and a bulging forehead that shone like wax. When Jenny broke the point of her pencil she took Emma's from its slot in the desk and put the broken one in its place. She raised her hand to gain attention.

"Please, miss! Emma Wayman's broken her pencil."

Emma was allowed to sharpen it, while Miss Vernon waited impatiently.

"You mustn't be so careless next time."

"*I* wasn't careless," Emma said.

"Don't answer back, if you please."

Breaking your pencil was a grave sin in Miss Vernon's eyes. It was also a sin to allow your chalk to squeak when writing with it on your slate.

"Really, Emma! Must you make that dreadful noise?"

"It isn't me, it's the chalk," Emma said.

There was a titter from the other children, and Emma looked round at them in surprise. Miss Vernon's irritation grew.

"Were you allowed to make that noise when you were at Miss Protheroe's?"

"We didn't have slates there."

"Emma, my child," Miss Vernon said, "I'm aware that you've been to a *better* school, but we do our poor best here in Huntlip, you know, and you will have to get used to us."

Emma did not understand what she meant. The village school had a bell on the roof, a playground with a chestnut tree, and stained glass windows in the porch. It was a much better school than Miss Protheroe's.

Stephen came home from the sale in Brecon, bringing gifts for all of them. A sleepy Emma sat on his lap, nursing a doll in Welsh national costume.

"How did you get on at your new school?"

"All right, thank you."

"She won't tell you much," Chris remarked. "We know. We've already tried."

Emma removed the doll's tall black hat and then put it on again.

"Winnie Aston's got a loose tooth."

"Has she, now? Fancy that."

"She's got a hammer toe as well."

"The things one hears at a village school!" Joanna said disdainfully.

Jamesy leant forward and tweaked Emma's hair.

"You're a cough-drop. That's what you are."

"Oh no I'm not!" Emma said. She nestled against her father's chest. "I'm not a cough-drop, am I, dad?"

"You're a little girl who should be in bed and I'm going to take you there," Stephen said. "Come along, sleepy head! Up the Wooden Hill to Blanket Street!"

Later that night, sitting alone with aunt Doe, he spoke to her about the child.

"Is she going to be happy there?"

"Give her a chance. It's only one day."

Certainly Emma seemed happy enough. She was ready for school betimes in the morning and glanced repeatedly at the clock.

"What would you like for elevenses?" aunt Doe asked.

"Bread and scrape," Emma said.

* * * * *

Emma and the boy, Robert Mercybright, stood in a warm patch of sun, leaning against the toolshed wall. He was eating the last of his apple. When he had finished, she offered him hers. He refused it, shaking his head.

"Don't you want it?" Emma asked.

"I mustn't take things from anyone."

"Did your mother tell you that?"

"Yes, and I promised her," Robert said.

"Go on, have it. She won't know."

But Robert again shook his head. He could not be persuaded, small though he was. Emma ate the apple herself.

"Can I see your little bell?"

He held up the bell for her to see, and jingled it on the end of its string. He put it into his pocket again. Emma took a bite out of her apple.

"Tell me about when you went to the fair with your auntie Betony," she said.

While they stood by the toolshed wall, a group of children, forming a ring, danced up to Robert, surrounding him, and began to draw him into their game. Emma hung on to him, by the sleeve. She tried to push the others away.

"No!" she said. "You leave him alone!"

"He can play if he wants to, bossy thing!"

"He doesn't want to. He's talking to me."

"Bossy old thing!" said Evie Wilkes. "You ent his sister or anything!"

"I'm his *friend*."

But the children had hold of Robert's arms, and he was pulled from Emma's grasp. In another moment he was part of their ring, dancing with them across the playground.

Emma sat on the toolshed step. Winnie Aston joined her there.

"I dreamt my tooth came out last night and when I woke up it really had." She drew back her lip and revealed the gap. "I planted it in the garden," she said. "It'll grow to be twopence in a day or two."

"How will it?" Emma asked.

"Mum will put the money there." Winnie sucked at the space in her mouth. "Do you ever dream much, Emma?" she asked.

"Sometimes I do," Emma said.

"What sort of things do you dream about?"

"All sorts of things, the same as you."

"Yes, but what? Can't you remember?"

"Once I dreamt about aunt Doe's violin."

"Yes? What happened?" Winnie asked.

"I dreamt I could play it, that's all."

"You can't really, I don't suppose."

"No," Emma said, "it was only a dream."

Her apple was just a core now. She threw it into the nettles nearby.

"Can *you* play the violin?" she asked.

Winnie Aston gave a shrug.

"I could if I wanted to," she said.

At home these days, when Emma talked, they noticed a change in her way of speech. Working out a sum aloud, "It's fivepence-three-fardens!" she announced, and, talking of the spaniel, Sam, who was sick, "He's off his fettles," she explained.

Chris and Jamesy were much amused.

"Our little Emma is getting quite broad."

"Broad your own-self!" Emma said.

The two boys were beside themselves, but Joanna fiercely disapproved.

"Don't encourage her!" she said. "She shouldn't be allowed to talk like that. 'Coal-skiddle' and 'cloe's-hoss'! That's what she's picking up at school!"

"If she picks up no worse than that," said aunt Doe, "I for one will not be too worried."

And Stephen, taking his cue from her, smiled at Emma

105

across the table.

"Emma's doing well at school. She got ten out of ten for Scripture today and nine out of ten for composition. She's quite a good scholar, aren't you, Emma?"

He worried about her, all the same, because he had thrust her into a school where the children were an unknown quantity. He would have to keep an eye on her, especially in these early days.

But this was September, and he was busy. The weather was open so far, and ploughing was going on apace. Often, with the other men, he ploughed from first light to mid-afternoon, and sometimes, with a fresh team, carried on until darkness fell. He was putting more and more land down to grass; growing more rape, more kale, more swedes; and planning to grow more sugar-beet. The open weather could not last for ever. There was much to be done before it broke.

"If we had a tractor," Chris said, "we could get done in no time at all."

"I can't afford one," Stephen said.

On Chepsworth Fair Day the weather broke and from then onwards there was endless rain. All landwork was at a halt and Stephen had time for other things. He had time to think of his little daughter, setting out for school every morning, dressed in her oilskins and rubber boots. Was she happy at the school? It was difficult to tell.

"Next year when I'm eight," she said to him, "I shall be in Miss Izzard's class."

Chapter 6

Joanna had a new ambition. She thought she would like to be an actress. Aunt Doe was inclined to approve; she had had some experience of amateur theatricals in her youth; and she suggested that the children should put on a play for Christmas, inviting all the men from the farm, with their wives and families. Joanna was taken with the idea, but what play could they perform with the limited cast that they could muster?

"When I was a girl," said aunt Doe, "we always used to write our own."

Once again she had sown a seed, and this was how Joanna and Jamesy, one Saturday morning in November, came to be sitting in the attic, biting their pens. It was a dark and dreary day. The little lamp had been lit on the table. Emma was trying to knit a scarf.

"Am I going to be in the play?"

"No, you're too small," Joanna said.

"Can I help to write it, then?"

"Don't be silly. You wouldn't know how."

"I would if you showed me," Emma said.

"Do be quiet! I'm trying to think."

Chris, who had a few minutes to spare, found his way up to the attic.

"What's it about, this play of yours?"

"Pirates, for one thing," Jamesy said.

"Oh no it isn't!" Joanna said.

"Well, the bit I've written is, so there!"

"What's it going to be called?" asked Chris.

"'Captain Terror'," Jamesy said. He had been to the cinema recently, and Douglas Fairbanks was his god.

"Really! I ask you!" Joanna said, spreading her hands to Chris in dismay. "How can I act in a play about pirates?"

"That's easy," Chris said. "You'll be the plucky heroine, held to ransom on the high seas. A proud, beautiful haughty girl –"

"Why don't you join us and write it down?"

But Chris was a man now; he worked on the farm; the writing of plays was kids' stuff. What little leisure time he had was spent upon more robust pursuits.

"I'm waiting for Gerald as a matter of fact. I only looked in for a moment or two. But you're quite welcome to use my ideas –"

"Rats to you!" Jamesy said.

He threw his bunjy at the closing door and went back to biting his pen. Joanna by now was making notes. Emma, on her knees under the table, was disentangling her ball of wool, which had rolled around the legs of her chair.

"Do stop jogging!" Joanna said. "Can't you see I'm trying to write?"

Emma put her wool on its needles, dropped her knitting into its bag, and slipped quietly out of the room. The other two hardly heard her go.

*　*　*　*　*

There was an old disused quarry between Holland Farm and Outlands. Thorn trees and rowans grew from its sides, with clumps of bramble and gorse and briar, and water collected in its bottom. Up on the rim, against the fence, a spindle tree grew, leaning over the edge.

Emma had to climb onto the fence and stand on the topmost rickety bar, leaning out over the quarry, before she could reach the spindleberries. The tree shook when she broke off the sprays, and a shower of raindrops fell on her. The fence creaked under her and one of its bars, breaking with a crack, let her down suddenly. Her arms and legs were badly scratched, but she had her sprays of spindleberries, and she was well pleased. She walked along the path skirting the quarry and down into Stoney Lane.

There was a cottage in the lane. A tiny place, in need of repair. One of its windows hung awry, and its roof was patched with a piece of tin. The little boy, Robert Mercybright, stood perched on a ledge inside the gate, leaning over it, dangling his arms. Emma stopped and stared at him.

"Is this where you live?" she asked, surprised.

Robert answered with a nod.

"Is your mother indoors?" she asked.

"No, she's gone to the shop," he said. "Granddad's at work. The thresher's come."

The noise of the threshing machine could be heard, throbbing away over at Outlands, and smoke could be seen among the trees. Emma looked at the little boy and showed him the sprays of spindleberries, coral-coloured, waxy, smooth, breaking from their rough pink husks, among the russet-coloured leaves.

"I'm going down to the village," she said. "You can come with me if you like."

"No, I mustn't," Robert said.

"Come just a little way, down the lane."

"No," he said, "I dussn't dare."

"Your mother won't mind. I'm sure she won't. I shall look after you, little boy."

"Mother always says to stay."

"I daresay we'll meet her, if we go down. We'll be able to help her to carry things. She's probably nearly home by now."

It took a long time to persuade Robert to open the gate and step out into the lane with her. He looked at her with anxious eyes. But Emma took him by the hand and he went with her down past the farm; then up the track to the wicket gate; and out onto the open hill.

He really was very small, and the way he put his hand into hers, tiny fingers finding their way, stealing in warmly and clinging to hers, made her feel very grown-up. She looked down at him from a greater height, and he looked up at her, dark-eyed and grave. She liked his dark eyes and straight black hair, and she liked his small features, so neatly made. Her only wish was to see him smile.

"They used to have Punch and Judy shows up here. That's why they call it Puppet Hill. A long time ago, my father says."

"I want to go back now," Robert said.

"Come just a little way further on."

"How much further on?" he asked.

"Down to those chestnut trees in that lane."

Kicking through the leaves in Cricketers Lane, Robert forgot about going back. He became absorbed in watching his feet, moving forward so rapidly, stirring up the damp dead leaves so that their colours were constantly changing, a red-brown flurry around his legs. Emma too kicked up the leaves, and they danced together along the lane, the wetness soaking the front of their clothes.

All the way across the village playing-field, they saw no sign of Robert's mother, nor was she coming along the road. They stood outside the gate for a while, but the road was empty in both directions. The village lay to the left of them. Emma turned towards the right.

"No!" Robert said. "I want to go home."

"You can't go home by yourself," Emma said. "Don't be silly. Come along."

"This ent the way to the shop," he said. "We should've gone the other way."

But Emma's strength was greater than his. She was able to pull him along. And soon they stood at two tall gates, peering through the bars into a yard, stacked up high with timber planking. To the right of the gate, above the hedge, stood a large wooden notice-board, painted boldly in black on white. Tewke and Izzard, carpenters, est. 1850; and beyond the great square stacks of timber, stood the old carpenter's workshop, backed by bushes and nut-trees.

This was Saturday, nearly lunch-time. There was not much activity in the workshop; only the sound of a man sawing wood and the jaunty whistling of a tune. Emma and Robert moved on, turned left down a narrow lane, and stood at yet another gate. Beyond stood a big old timbered house. It had enormous twisted chimneys. Smoke rose from one of them.

"Do you know this place?" Emma asked.

Robert nodded. He looked at her.

"Whose house is it?" Emma asked.

"Auntie Betony's house," he said.

"Does anybody else live there?"

"Uncle Jesse. Auntie Beth."

"Anyone else besides them?"

"Uncle Dicky. Granna Kate." Robert thought for a moment or two. "Great-grumpa Tewke, he lives there too."

Emma stood and frowned at the house. A great many people lived in it. Were they all at home today? Its windows, shadowed, gave no clue.

"Why don't you go and knock on the door?"

"No," Robert said. He resisted her shove.

"Are you frightened?" Emma asked.

Robert's gaze was deep and still.

"I ent frightened. No, no not me."

"Why won't you go and knock, then?"

"I don't want to. I want to go home."

"Don't you want to see your auntie Betony?"

"I seen her yesterday, in school."

Emma, reluctantly, turned away. She took the little boy's hand again.

* * * * *

Betony had spent the morning in Chepsworth, selling poppies from door to door, raising money for Earl Haig's Fund founded to help ex-servicemen. For today was the eve of Armistice Day, when people everywhere would remember their dead, and some would spare a thought for the living.

At one house, in Albion Square, a well-dressed woman of middle age sighed as she searched her purse for a coin.

"Five years afterwards," she said, "and we're *still* paying for that dreadful war!"

Across the square, on the other side, two old soldiers stood in the gutter, one on crutches, the other blind. The blind man played an accordion, the man on crutches played a flute. A collection box stood on the ground and on it the one word "Passchendaele."

"*They* are the ones who are still paying," Betony thought as she crossed the square.

Just before lunch-time she was driving through Huntlip on her way home. She had passed over Millery Bridge when she saw the two children, Robert and Emma, coming towards her along the road. She stopped the trap and spoke to them.

"You're a long way from home," she said. "What are you doing right out here?"

"We've been for a walk," Emma said.

"Just by yourselves, the two of you?"

"Yes. We came over Puppet Hill."

Betony looked at the little boy and saw the anxiety in his eyes.

"Does your mother know where you are, Robert?"

"His mother wasn't there," Emma said. "She'd gone out and left him all by himself."

"So you decided to take him for a walk?"

Emma nodded. She looked away. Her small face was blank, abstracted, still.

"You shouldn't have brought him away like that," Betony said quietly. "His mother will worry when she gets home."

"His mother's gone to the shop," Emma said. "We thought we'd meet her on the way." She looked directly at Betony. "You said I was to be his special friend."

"Yes, that's right. So I did."

"I brought him to see you. We went to your house. But Robert was shy. He wouldn't knock."

"Why did you bring him to see me?"

"I don't know. I just thought I would."

"Well," said Betony, hiding a smile, "I think it's time you were both back home."

She took them up into the trap and turned back into the village. There was no sign of Linn on the way. The shop, when they passed it, was closed for lunch. She drove out to School Lane and turned off up Holland Bank. The two children sat close to her, Emma with her sprays of spindleberries cradled in the crook of her arm.

"What beautiful spindleberries – where did you find them?" Betony asked.

"Up by the edge of the old quarry."

"Isn't it dangerous up there?"

"Oh, no," Emma said.

When they reached the track leading off to the farm,

112

Betony stopped and let the child down.

"Wait, you've left your berries," she said.

She picked up the sprays from the seat of the trap and leant down to give them to the child. Emma refused them. She shook her head.

"I don't want them. I picked them for you."

She turned and went dancing up the track.

Betony, as she drove on, put her arm round the little boy and gave him a reassuring squeeze. His face was still puckered with anxiety and when, on nearing Lilac Cottage, he saw his mother out in the lane, his hand crept into Betony's.

"Where have you *been,* you naughty boy? How dare you disobey me like that?" Linn's angry gaze switched to Betony. She stood accusingly by the trap. "What do you mean by coming here, waiting until my back is turned, and taking my son away with you? I've been worried out of my mind. Coming home to an empty house! Nothing to tell me where he'd gone! If such a thing ever happens again –"

"I didn't take him," Betony said. "He went for a walk with Emma Wayman. It seems she passed here, earlier on, and persuaded Robert to go with her."

"Emma Wayman?" Linn said.

"One of the children from Holland Farm."

"She had no right to do such a thing!"

"They took the pathway over the hill. They thought they'd meet you on your way back from the shop."

"I didn't come across the hill. I had a lift in Ricks's cart."

Linn reached up to her small son and lifted him down with a show of roughness. She leant over him, straightening his clothes.

"You're a naughty boy, going off like that! I've always trusted you before and now you've gone and let me down! I'm disappointed in you. It seems I can't trust you after all."

Robert was silent. He hung his head.

"You'd better go in now and wash your hands." She sent him on his way with a gentle push. "I'll have more to say to you presently."

"Don't be too hard on him," Betony said.

"He really must be made to obey."

"I'm sure it'll never happen again."

"What about this Wayman child? Why should she come and entice him away?"

"I suppose she wanted company. She knows Robert at school, you see, and I asked her to be his special friend."

"What are her family thinking of, letting her wander about like that, right away from her own home?"

"Lots of children go out alone. It isn't so very far after all."

"She's only a little thing, isn't she? Supposing something had happened to her?"

"Nothing did happen," Betony said. "I've just delivered her at the farm."

"But things *do* happen. You know they do. Mr Wayman's wife, for a start. She was suffocated in the mud of a pond, in broad daylight, on a summer's day, and no one around to hear her call. There's a lot of carelessness, if you ask me, up there at Holland Farm."

"You may be right," Betony said. She thought of Emma, out alone, picking sprays of spindleberries from a tree that grew by the edge of the quarry. "Things do happen, as you say."

"Thank you for bringing Robert back. I'm sorry I snapped at you as I did."

"Don't be too severe on him."

Because of the difficulty of turning the trap in the narrow lane, Betony drove straight on and so went homeward by Outlands and Blagg.

* * * * *

On her way down Craisie Lane, she stopped to speak to Fred Cox. Fred worked at Outlands Farm. He was an honest, intelligent man and was secretary of the local branch of his union. Betony knew him and his wife, for they had three children at the school and the eldest boy, Billy John, would almost certainly, next year, win a free place at the Grammar School in Chepsworth. Fred was on his way home from work, his dinner-satchel over his shoulder, a can of milk in his hand. He walked with a heavy, slouching, tread.

"You look down-hearted," Betony said.

"How many people, nowadays, ever look anything else?" he asked.

"Not many, if they work on the land."

"We've had an Irishman's rise this week. That's the second time in six months." He meant that his wages had been reduced. "We're down to twenty-seven-and-six. I feel I could just about jump in the brook."

"What about the local Conciliation Committee? Surely they'd have something to say to that?"

"My master, Mr Challoner, he don't take no account of them. Nor don't Mr Twill of Dunnings neither. Wages there is even worse. They're down to twenty-five bob there."

"Oh, but that's infamous!" Betony said. "Can't your union do anything?"

"Not many chaps belong any more. They can't afford fourpence for the fee. There's only two of us left at Outlands and our days is numbered, I daresay." Fred's voice had tears in it. He was a man at the end of his tether. "What sort of winter's it going to be? No bloody Wages Board any more! No bloody union left to fight! We'll just about be starved off the land!"

Shrugging, he apologized. He made an effort to cast off his gloom. He spoke of the coming General Election.

"We've got a man putting up for Chepsworth. A union man, one of our own. He's worked on the land since he was a boy. Now if *he* could get in we'd be getting somewhere, cos he knows our problems inside out. I want him to hold a meeting here in Huntlip, but with no village hall nor nothing, he says it wouldn't be worth his while. Folk won't stand about out of doors, not in this weather, after dark. Nor they won't trouble theirselves with travelling into Chepsworth neither."

"What about holding it in the school?"

"Should we be able to, do you think?"

"I don't see why not."

"Your board of managers, that's why not! Tories, every one, I bet!"

"Leave it to me," Betony said. "I'll speak to the vicar as soon as I can. You'd better see your candidate and let me know what date you fix. You'll need some posters putting up –"

"I'll see to that! There's no problem there!" Fred's face was quite transformed. Hope had brought him back to life. "Christ, Miss Izzard, you're a brick! Just supposing our man got in?"

"That I can't promise," Betony said. "I haven't even got a vote." She would not be thirty for another two years.

"You would have, by God, if I had my way! If women had the vote at twenty-one, we'd soon see a change of government, and Labour once in would be in for good."

"You seem very confident, anyway."

"If you can get us the use of the school –"

"I shall certainly do my best," she said. "I'll be in touch when I've got some news."

She saluted him and drove away.

When she reached home and drove through the archway into the fold, her father and brother were at the pump, splashing their faces and hands in the trough. They had come from the workshop, covered in sawdust.

"You're late, my blossom," her father said. "Did you bring the paper like I asked?"

"Yes, I've brought it," Betony said.

"I hear there's some Labour chap putting up. He's got a nerve, putting up round here. Why, we've had a Liberal man for Chepsworth ever since never, practically. We've never voted for nobody else. Nobody else ent never stood."

Dicky, going to see the pony, gave his sister a broad grin.

"Dad's not the only one who's got it, you know. It's spreading like wildfire everywhere."

"What are you talking about?" she asked.

"Election fever!" Dicky said.

In the kitchen, when Betony went in, her mother was taking a pie from the oven and granna Kate was mashing the swedes.

"Did you bring my buttons?" Beth asked.

"And my lozenges?" granna asked.

"Yes, I brought them," Betony said. "And great-

116

grumpa's nasal drops."

"Did you sell all your poppies?" Beth asked.

"All except a handful, yes."

"That there Earl Haig!" granna said. "Strikes me he's doing a proper job. I reckon they ought to make him a Sir."

Beth and her daughter exchanged a smile. Granna's sayings were all of a piece. At seventy she was full of her years, and was always a little out of touch with what was going on around. Great-grumpa Tewke, on the other hand, although he was turned ninety-two, was just as astute as granna was vague. He might be stiff in his joints these days; short of breath when he climbed the stairs; but not much escaped his memory. He came into the kitchen now as Dicky came in at the other door.

"Did you finish them trestles for Edgar Mapp?"

"Yes, I finished them," Dicky said.

"Did you take them down to him?"

"I took them down at ten o'clock."

Dicky was rather pleased with himself. He did not always emerge so well from the old man's catechisms. Betony took the opportunity, now that great-grumpa Tewke was there, of mentioning a troublesome fault in the trap.

"That offside tyre is still loose. One of the rivets is nearly out. The tyre was rattling all the way home."

Great-grumpa's head came round at once.

"Ent you fixed that rivet yet? You get it done this afternoon! If need be, take it down to the forge, and get Will Pentland to deal with it."

Dicky, swearing under his breath, took his place at the table, next to Betony.

"There goes my afternoon off!" he said. "Did you have to mention that damned tyre?"

"I wanted it done," Betony said. "I'll be needing the trap in the next few days."

The tyre had been loose for a week or more; Dicky and her father would let things slide; any old day would do for them; it was great-grumpa Tewke who got things done. Although "retired" from the carpenter's business, he always knew what was going on, in the workshop and in the house, and a word from him would still be obeyed.

The family sat down to their meal. Beth began to cut the pie. Jesse was still immersed in his paper. He put it away reluctantly and took his place at the foot of the table.

"There's all sorts of chaps putting up this time. Liberal, Conservative, Labour, the lot. Poor Mr Crown will have to fight. I reckon that's hard on a man of his age, after being our Member all these years."

"He'll get in just the same, you mark my words," said great-grumpa Tewke.

"How do you know that?" Betony asked.

"The Liberals have always held Chepsworth, that's why, and that ent a town to change its coat."

Great-grumpa Tewke voted Liberal, as every right-minded person did, and the outcome to him was therefore unquestionable.

* * * * *

"I'm afraid not, Miss Izzard," Mr Netherton said, when Betony called at the vicarage. "The Labour candidate? Oh dear me no! Such a thing would never do."

"What about the other candidates? Will they be allowed to use the school?"

"The matter hasn't arisen," he said. "No one's approached me on that score."

"Supposing they do? How will you answer them?" Betony asked.

"The only promise I can make is to raise the matter with the managers and see how they react to it. But I'm quite certain they will refuse."

"If they disagree with Labour principles, they can always come to the meeting themselves, to voice any criticisms they have."

"Well, speaking for myself, as a Liberal –"

"You would naturally want to hear both sides. Will you come to the meeting if it is held?"

"No, I think not," Mr Netherton said. "As vicar of the parish, you know, I'm afraid my attendance at such a meeting might influence my parishioners."

Secretly Betony doubted it. Mr Netherton had been vicar

118

of Huntlip for two and a half years and the only effect he had had on his parishioners was to cause them intense irritation. In the pulpit he had great eloquence, but out in the parish he was weak. He tried too hard to please all men and was therefore destined to please almost none.

"If you were to forbid a Labour meeting in the school, however, you might be influencing them in the other direction."

"I neither forbid nor accede, Miss Izzard. The decision is not just mine alone."

"But you could influence the board."

"I'm not sure that I want to do that."

"Mr Netherton," Betony said. "When the General Election is held, the school will be used as a polling station. If people can go there to vote for the Labour candidate, surely they can go there to hear him speak beforehand?"

"I will raise the matter with the managers. That is as far as I will go."

Betony knew he was stalling her. He would leave the matter until it was too late. She therefore went to see Fred Cox and together they planned their course of action. Four days later the posters arrived. She had them put up throughout the village. The vicar met her after school.

"Really, Miss Izzard, I must protest! I did not consent to this meeting of yours –"

"Have you seen the managers?"

"No, not yet, I must admit."

"Would it be better if I saw them myself?"

"You've left it rather late, haven't you, seeing these posters are everywhere?"

"It would certainly be very awkward if the meeting had to be cancelled now. People would say – and there would be some truth in it – that a man had been denied freedom of speech."

Mr Netherton was annoyed.

"You've deliberately forced me into this position, Miss Izzard, and it's no good looking to me for support. It seems I'm obliged to yield to you, but let me say categorically, that I don't for one moment approve of it, and when the managers tackle me – as they surely will – I will make my

119

position clear to them. Furthermore, I hold you personally responsible for the conduct of the meeting in the school, and everything connected with it."

"Yes, of course," Betony said.

Within a few days, many more posters had appeared. The day of the meeting was announced on them as Friday November the twenty-fourth. Tea and refreshments would be served.

One of the posters was nailed to a tree in Rayner's Lane. Chris, who was taking two horses to be shod, stopped in the rain to read what it said, and Gerald Challoner, out shooting, came across the field to him.

"I suppose you'll be going?" he said with a grin.

"What, to hear some socialist spouting rot?"

"Might be fun in it," Gerald said.

"Are you thinking of going, then?"

"There's two or three of us going, my boy. We've got some ideas for making the meeting go with a swing. Coming with us or are you too young?"

"Just try and keep me out, that's all!"

When Chris had gone, leading the horses down the lane, Gerald reached for the rain-soaked poster and pulled it from its nail. He screwed it up into a ball and thrust it into the nearest ditch. It was the third he had dealt with that day.

Chapter 7

The night of the meeting was cold and wet. When Chris arrived at The Black Ram, up on the edge of Huntlip Common, Gerald was there waiting for him, with Jeff Twill of Dunnings, Jackie Franklin of Lucketts End, and David Mapp of Letts. They drank outside, keeping away from the lighted windows, for all of them were under age and their drinks were passed out to them by the maid. When their glasses were empty, Gerald took a look at his watch.

"Eight o' clock! Let's go!" he said, and the five of them set off down the hill, boots pounding the rough stony road.

Chris was among his equals tonight. The five of them, as they strode together, were united by a common bond. They were all farmers' sons, and each boy's father owned his farm. They were little lords of the land, and the knowledge gave them a fine swagger. Laughing and joking, they descended on the village school, where lights shone in the high windows, and where the doors stood fastened back, open to welcome all who came.

* * * * *

Inside the schoolroom, the panelled partition had been removed, and so had all the children's desks. Betony, helped by Fred Cox, had carried everything out to the playground and covered the pile with a canvas sheet. Wooden benches had been brought in, mostly from the workshop at Cobbs, and a table and chairs had been set in front for the speaker and his supporters. On the wall above hung a printed poster: Vote for Bob Treadwell: Vote for Action and Employment. Of the school furniture, only the cupboards and piano remained, and these had been pushed into a corner. Because the night was wet and cold,

Betony had kept the stoves alight, and beside each stove stood a scuttle of coals. None of Betony's family were there. Dicky had come, bringing the benches, and had helped to carry them into the school. After that he had gone away.

"Politics is nothing to me. You can have my vote for half-a-crown!"

By half-past-seven, when the candidate arrived, there were fifteen people gathered in the schoolroom, mostly labourers from the farms around. By eight o' clock, when the meeting was timed to begin, a few younger labourers were drifting in, having come, it was plain, from The Rose and Crown. Three of these were dressed in their best and wore Tory blue favours in their coats. Others wore the Liberal yellow and one or two the Labour red.

Betony, standing inside the door, surveyed the assembly. She knew all the people there by sight, and could put names to most of them, especially those who had children at school. There were three men from Holland Farm, two from Outlands, and two from Letts. Fred Cox had brought his wife, and there were three other women there.

"Not much of a turn-out," Fred remarked. "Not for a village the size of Huntlip. Most of these youngsters ent got a vote and as for the rest – Bob'll be preaching to the converted."

"Let's wait a few minutes," Betony said. "Perhaps there'll be some late-comers."

But the only late-comers were the five fresh-faced young farmers' sons, led by Gerald Challoner, who arrived just as the doors were closed and hammered loudly for admittance. They swaggered in, these corduroy lordlings so full of themselves, and stood for a moment glancing about, eyes narrowed against the light. Then they shouldered their way to the front and slumped together on the foremost bench. They were well aware of the pause in the hum of talk around, and the many eyes that were turned their way, and they glanced at each other, smirking and winking, pleased with the stir their arrival had caused.

"Any of your lot here, Chris?" Gerald asked in an undertone. "There's two of ours, needless to say, but I knew *they'd* be here, they're union mad."

Chris looked over his shoulder and counted three of his father's men. Only two of them sat together: Reg Starling and Billy Rye; the other man was Morton George and he sat with Tommy Long of Letts.

"There are three of ours," Chris said. "But only one is a union man. The other two are all right."

"They could still vote Labour, couldn't they?"

"Yes, well, I suppose they could."

At twenty-past-eight the meeting began. Fred Cox, in the chair, introduced the candidate, Bob Treadwell, who arose to the sound of ragged applause.

"Ladies and gentlemen!" he began, and a few young labourers booed at him. He bore it all with a friendly grin and when it was over he began again. "Comrades, I'll say, if you prefer it –"

"Get away!" said a voice from the back. "Get back to Moscow where you belong!"

"Friends, then!" the candidate said.

"We'll have to think about that!" said the voice. "We'll have to take a vote on it!"

But the candidate made his start at last and spoke for a while without interruption. He had a good voice and a sense of humour and he made his audience of farm-workers laugh by explaining the blue-black mark on his cheek.

"Not, as you might think, a heckler throwing a rotten egg, but a cow I was milking early this morning who was rather careless with her tail!"

Soon, however, he became serious, talking of conditions on the land and unemployment in particular. Something would have to be done, he said, and a Labour government, once elected, would soon show that they knew the answers to the problems.

"Don't we all!" Gerald said, in a tone of heavy sarcasm.

The candidate merely carried on.

"The disgraceful treatment by employers of men, and most especially on the land, where conditions are worsening all the time –"

"Who pays their wages?" Gerald asked.

"Wages?" the candidate replied. "Down to thirty shillings a week and in some cases even less! Does the young

123

gentleman call that a wage?"

"Where would the labourers be without it? You tell us that!" Gerald exclaimed.

"Wages in 1919 were forty-six shillings a week –"

"Prices were higher then," Gerald said. "Now where are they? Down the drain!"

"I know what problems the farmer has to face –"

"The labour problem for a start!"

"The flaming union!" shouted Jeff Twill. "That's one of his problems, to name but a few!"

"If the young gentlemen will hear me out –"

"Yes, let him speak!" said Billy Rye's wife. "He's the one we came to hear, not you half-grown bits of lads!"

"Aren't we allowed to air our views?"

"We know your views! We hear nothing else! The farmers get their say all the time. The papers is full of what they say! So you pipe down and let the man speak!"

"Yes, let the man speak!" Gerald said. "Let's hear what he's got to say about solving our problems for us. How he's going to stop foreign corn –"

"I will come to those things," the candidate said, "but first I want to deal with the labourer –"

"Let's deal with *him* by all means!" Jackie Franklin said with a sneer.

"No problems are going to be solved while conflict continues to exist between the farmer and his men."

"Who causes the conflict?" Chris demanded. He felt it was time he had his say. "The union causes it by sowing discontent! The average labourer would be happy enough if it weren't for the union stirring him up."

"Happy be blowed!" said one of the men from Lucketts End. "It's up to us to say whether we're happy or not!"

"You're still wet behind the ears, young fella," said an elderly man, just behind Chris. "You want to go back home to your dad and wait till you've growed up a bit before you start talking on our behalf."

After a while, order of some sort was restored, and the candidate began again. But he had not proceeded far when Gerald, turning to his friends, spoke out in a loud voice.

"Not much of an audience here, is it, in spite of all the

posters about? I expected a lot more folk than this. It's hardly worth the poor chap's trouble."

"If I could perhaps be allowed to proceed –"

"Just a minute!" Gerald said. "Two of my friends don't feel too well."

He nudged Jeff Twill and Jackie Franklin, and the two of them lumbered to their feet. Each held a handkerchief to his mouth, and, making a great deal of noise and fuss, left the schoolroom and slammed the door.

"Where have they gone?" whispered Chris.

"You'll see in a minute," Gerald said.

"My object in coming here tonight," the candidate went on in a ringing voice, "is to offer some hope, some ray of light, to those who are groping in the darkness and gloom enveloping our country at this time." Pausing, somewhat surprised at the silence, he took the chance of a deep breath. "My party *is* that ray of light. . . ."

* * * * *

Betony, at the back of the room, sitting with Billy Rye and his wife, listened with only half an ear. She was worried about the two young men who had just gone out.

"I don't think we've seen the last of them. I think I'll go out and lock the porch door."

Billy half rose to accompany her, but Betony motioned him to stay. She walked quietly to the door and passed through into the porch, which was lit by a single hurricane lamp hanging from a beam in the roof above. The outer doors were still fastened back, but before she had time to loosen the hooks, there was a sudden scurry outside and three wet sheep pattered into the porch. They were quickly followed by five or six more and coming behind them, urging them in, were the two young men, Twill and Franklin.

"Get these animals out at once!" Betony cried furiously. She stood in the way, trying to turn them. "Do you hear me? Get them out!"

But Jeff Twill, ignoring her, was already opening the inner door, and Jackie Franklin, wielding a stick, was driving the sheep into the schoolroom. They lolloped in, confused and frightened, blinded by the glare of light, their ears back and their eyes rolling. Seeing the people gathered there, they came to a halt, defensively, and one or two of the older ewes stamped with a fore-foot on the floor. Gerald Challoner and David Mapp now sprang up with a loud halloo. They darted forward with arms outstretched and sent the sheep lurching around the room.

"That's more like it! Here they come! Are they all good union members? Make way for them, it's only fair! They've got a right to have their say and bleat along with the rest of you!"

The frightened sheep went careering about, and most of the audience rose at once, trying to shove them towards the door. The benches, thus vacated, were sent toppling in all directions, and one of them, sliding along the floor, struck two young men behind the knees, bringing them down together in a tumbled heap. Angrily they scrambled up and lunged towards Chris and Gerald. Chris got a stinging blow on the mouth and Gerald was hurled against the stove. Bellowing because he was burnt, Gerald rushed towards his attackers, but was knocked down and winded by one of the ewes. David Mapp and Jackie Franklin were wrestling with two young labourers and were getting the worst of it by far. Chris mopped the blood from a cut on his lip and reluctantly went to their aid. The noise by now was terrible. The whole of the schoolroom was in an uproar.

The older men, such as Fred Cox and Billy Rye, were doing their best to catch the sheep and hurl them out through the open door, and their womenfolk were trying to help by driving the sheep in the right direction. But the younger men were out of hand. They had formed themselves into two camps, one at either end of the room, and were pelting each other with coal from the scuttles. One young man, Leslie Smith by name, having snatched up a chair that came flying his way, had seated himself at the school piano and, in the manner of a cinema pianist, was playing a spirited accompaniment to the mêlée around him.

The battle raged across the room, and there was a crash of splintering glass as a lump of coal went through a window. The music came to a sudden stop, and the young pianist looked down in surprise as blood dripped into his lap from a cut in his forehead, neatly opened by flying glass. Chris, during a lull in the battle, saw the pianist's bloodied face and watched as a woman led him away. The sight of the blood made him feel sick. He wished he had never come to the meeting. Gerald and Jeff Twill, he saw, had opened one of the school cupboards and were hurling inkwells across the room.

The sheep were driven out at last. Three men went with them across the playground to drive them down to the village pound. Billy Rye sent his son to fetch the constable from Slings, and the candidate, on hearing this, thought it was time he slipped away. His motor car was brought to the door.

The coal-slinging battle was at its height when someone shouted: "The constable's coming!" Hostilities ceased miraculously. The opposing factions skeltered away.

"Come on, let's go!" Gerald said, and his fellow lordlings, with blackened faces and hands and clothes, joined him in a rush for the door. Chris for a moment hesitated. Then he too followed the rest, taking to the fields in the wind and the rain.

By the time the constable arrived, only the older men remained, with Betony and three of the wives. The constable opened his little book and listened to the story he was told.

"There was five of the young sods altogether, but my young master from Outlands, like, he was the ringleader," Johnny Marsh said.

"It was the young chap from Dunnings, though, that went and brought in the bloody sheep. Him and that cross-eyed lout from Letts."

"They all came together, the five of them. You could see they meant mischief the moment they walked in at that there door."

"Ah, and my master's son was one of them, the cheeky young swine!" said Morton George.

"Names, if you please," the constable said.

He knew well enough who the culprits were, from these

remarks bandied about, but he had to observe the formalities and write in his notebook as informed. So the five names were given to him: Gerald Challoner; Jeffery Twill; Christopher Wayman; Jackie Franklin; David Mapp.

"All farmers' sons," the constable said. "And these are the ones you say are to blame?"

"They are the ones that started it, there's no doubt of that," said Fred Cox. "We was having a quiet meeting here and they was determined to break it up. They're the ones to blame all right. No two ways about none of that."

But Betony, when they had all gone and she stood alone in the empty schoolroom, surveying the wreckage and the dirt, knew that as far as the vicar was concerned she and she alone would be held to blame for what had happened there that night.

She put on her hat and coat and scarf, turned out the last of the lamps in the room, and quietly let herself out of the school. She locked the door on the chaos within and walked away towards the village. She went at once to the vicarage.

* * * * *

Mr Netherton heard her through with an angry tightening of his lips and a gathering of colour in his cheeks. He sat without moving in his chair.

"I was against it from the start. I don't have to remind you of that, I hope? And now you see the sad result of flying in the face of my opinion."

"You can't have foreseen what would happen tonight?"

"I lay no claim to such a thing, but a Labour meeting such as this –"

"It was those who support the opposite side who caused all the trouble," Betony said.

"The inescapable fact is that if you had regarded my views on the matter, none of this would ever have happened."

"I shall of course take full responsibility for all the necessary repairs."

"I'm afraid the matter will not end there."

"No. I didn't think it would."

"As soon as this regrettable affair is known to the school managers, they will come to me for an explanation, and I shall have no alternative but to tell them the truth: that you went against me in this matter and allowed the school to be used for this meeting without my approval or my consent. I have no doubt that the consequences for you will be very grave."

"How grave?" Betony asked.

"I'm very much afraid, Miss Izzard, that after what has happened tonight, the managers are bound to feel that you should be asked for your resignation."

"And what if I refuse to give it?"

"The chances are that you will be dismissed."

"Will that be the course you recommend when meeting the managers?" Betony asked.

"I certainly don't feel that I can speak up on your behalf, either to the managers or to the education secretary when I see him. How can you expect such a thing when you went against me so wilfully?"

Betony rose and drew on her gloves.

"I don't expect it, Mr Netherton, and I wouldn't dream of asking it."

She said goodnight and took her leave.

When she got home it was past ten o' clock, and the faces of her family, waiting up, told her that they had heard the news. The incident, apparently, was all over Huntlip. Dicky had heard of it at The Rose and Crown. Jesse, her father, was much disturbed.

"Whatever possessed you, my blossom," he said, "to let that Labour chap speak in the school?"

"Why shouldn't he speak?" Betony said. "He speaks for the hungry, the unemployed."

Jesse shifted in his chair.

"I know there's a lot of talk these days about poverty on the land and that, but I dunno that it's really so bad as some of these Labour chaps make out."

"Don't you, father?" Betony said. "Haven't you seen those half-starved men tramping the lanes hereabouts as they go from one workhouse to the next? Haven't you had them in the yard, offering to do a day's work for a bite of bread and a bowl of stew? Even those who *are* in jobs – have you any idea how much they earn? Have you seen their wives, as thin as laths, old and grey before their time? I've got children in my school whose only breakfast before they leave home is a slice of bread dipped in the water that has boiled an egg for their father's dinner!"

"All right, girl!" great-grumpa said. "No need to get in such a lather about it. There's always been poverty in the world. Hungry folks ent nothing new."

"You'd better tell my father that. He seems to think it's a fairy tale."

"About this meeting," Jesse said.

But Betony had had enough. She made her excuses and went to bed.

*   *   *   *   *

Chris, going home after leaving the school, loitered for a time in the cartshed, watching the windows of the house. He waited until they were all in darkness before he stole quietly in to his bed. The following morning, at five o' clock, he arose after a sleepless night and took himself off across the fields, lit only by a sprinkling of stars. He still had a lot to think about but when he returned, an hour later, his mind was not much clarified.

News of the incident at the school reached the farm just before six, when the men arrived at the milking-sheds. Morton George spoke to Stephen about it, and Stephen went in search of Chris. He found him in the kitchen, drinking a cup of hot sweet tea.

"Have you got something to tell me?" he asked.

"I daresay you've heard it from Morton George!"

"It would have been better if you'd told me yourself."

"I needed time to think things out."

"I hear you behaved disgracefully, you and young Challoner and the rest. A pack of hooligans, raising Cain! If it was only half as bad as Morton George says it was, you've got some explaining to do, my boy."

"It *was* pretty bad," Chris said. He stared miserably into the fire. "Everything somehow got out of hand."

"Was there much damage done to the school?"

"I don't know. I daresay there was. Somebody let the sheep in, you see, and after that there was hell to pay."

"Were you a party to all this?"

"I had nothing to do with the sheep, but I'm naming no names," Chris said.

"I know all the names. Be sure of that."

"We only intended it as a lark. We went to heckle, and what's wrong with that? You should have heard that Labour chap and all the rot he talked last night!"

"There's only one thing to be said for these piffling excuses of yours! – At least they show you have some sense of shame!"

Stephen was angry, a rare thing when dealing with his children, and he looked at Chris with hot, hard dislike.

"Had you been drinking at all?" he asked "Morton George seemed to think you had."

"One pint, that's all, outside The Black Ram."

"I won't have you drinking at *any* pub, inside or outside or anywhere else! You're only fifteen. It's against the law."

"It's a damn silly law, if you ask me."

"I am *not* asking you!" Stephen said. "I'm not interested in your views on *anything* till you show some signs of maturity. And as a first step towards that end, you can go in due course and call on Miss Izzard, and apologize for your behaviour last night."

"But I can't do that! I simply *can't!*"

"Oh yes you can. Indeed I insist."

"Well, I'm not going to!" Chris exclaimed.

"Then I must do it for you, that's all. I shall have to see her in any case, but it seems I shall also have to explain that my eldest son, although fifteen, is too much of a coward to make his own apologies."

Stephen returned to the milking-sheds and worked there until eight o' clock. He then went in to his breakfast; washed and shaved with extra care; and changed out of his working-clothes. Chris had taken himself off again. The younger children were eating their porridge. Aunt Doe saw Stephen as far as the door.

"What's all the atmosphere about?"

"I haven't got time to tell you now. I'll tell you later, when I come back. Or, if my eldest son comes in, you can ask *him* what it's all about!"

But aunt Doe did not have to wait for Chris. She heard the story from Mrs Bessemer.

* * * * *

Because it was Saturday, Stephen intended to walk out to Cobbs, expecting Miss Izzard to be at her home, right at the farthest end of the village. On nearing the school, however, he saw that the doors were wide open and that chairs and benches stood outside. So he crossed the playground and went in.

Inside the schoolroom, Betony, with a broom and shovel, was sweeping up the coal that littered the floor and putting it back into the scuttles. Most of the coal was dust by now, trodden into the wood-block floor, with the sheep-dung and the broken glass and the bits of broken inkwells. Stephen looked round, grim-faced. He saw the black marks on the white-painted walls, where the flying lumps of coal had exploded, and he saw that the coloured posters and maps and the pictures painted by the children had been taken down, torn and blackened, to lie in a pile on the teacher's desk. Betony stopped what she was doing and turned to face him. Her eyes in the light from a nearby window were a very clear bright shade of blue.

"I hardly know how to start," he said, "except that I've come to apologize."

"On behalf of your son?"

"I hope, when he's had time to think, he will come and apologize for himself. At the moment he's too ashamed. But I'd like to make it quite clear that, whatever the cost of the damage done, I expect to pay the bill."

"Your son wasn't the only hooligan involved, Mr Wayman. He was merely one of a group. As for the damage done here, my brother is coming in to paint the walls and replace the window-pane, but thank you for offering all the same."

"Isn't there anything I can do to ease my conscience in

132

this matter?"

"I'm more concerned with my own feelings at the moment, Mr Wayman, rather than giving relief to yours."

"I share your anger, I assure you, especially now that I see this mess."

"Your son is very young to be taking such an interest in politics."

"Much too young, I quite agree."

"He's against socialism and the union. It seems he's against free speech as well. Does he take his stand from you?"

"If he does," Stephen said, "he much mistakes my attitudes."

"You're not against the union yourself?"

"The one union man I've got on my farm is a poor advertisement for the rest. You must make allowances for my son if he takes a somewhat jaundiced view."

"On some of the farms in this district, men run the risk of losing their jobs if they join the union, so I'm told."

"There's bound to be prejudice, I suppose."

He knew there was truth in what she said, but he did not wish to be drawn into an argument concerning his neighbours' actions, and he therefore looked for another subject. He turned to the pile of children's paintings lying, tattered, on the desk.

"Will they be upset, seeing their pictures spoilt?" he asked.

"They will no doubt be puzzled," Betony said, "at the strange behaviour of their elders and betters."

"Is there anything of Emma's here?"

"No, there's nothing, I'm afraid. She did have a picture put up in class, but she took it down and threw it away."

"Why did she do that?"

"She told Miss Vernon that it wasn't good enough."

There was a pause. Betony looked at him absently. She leant her broom against the wall, and dropped her shovel into the scuttle. With her hands in the pockets of her pinafore, she turned again, considering him.

"You are interested in Emma's school work, then, Mr Wayman?"

"That's a strange question to ask, isn't it, seeing that I'm her father?" he said.

"You were not at our Parents' Day last Friday. That's why I ask."

"I didn't know it was Parents' Day."

"Every parent was sent a note. The children wrote them out themselves. They copied the words from the blackboard."

"I never had mine. I must ask the child what became of it."

"Would you have come, if you'd known in time?"

"I might have done, certainly. A lot would depend on the work of the farm –"

Stephen broke off, looking at her. He saw that her smile was sceptical.

"Miss Izzard," he said in a gentle tone, "are you taking me to task?"

Betony chose her words with care.

"Emma seems a lonely child. She doesn't seem to have any friends. It's all right while she's in school . . . She talks to the other children here . . . but out of school it's a different matter and she seems at a loss for something to do. Forgive me for saying so, Mr Wayman, but I don't think she ought to be allowed to wander about by herself so much."

Stephen's feelings were beginning to change. Amusement was yielding to irritation.

"I don't think I neglect my children, Miss Izzard, if that is what you are trying to say."

"Perhaps neglect is too strong a word –"

"Use whichever word you like so long as you say what you really mean!"

"Seeing that your eldest son is running wild, it shouldn't be too difficult to understand what I mean."

"Running wild?" Stephen said. "That is something of an exaggeration! Chris as a rule works very hard. He works a full day on the farm with me. Last night was the first occasion of its kind and if the Labour candidate who addressed your meeting had not been so provocative –"

"What he said was only the truth."

"Part of the truth, but not the whole."

"How do you know? You weren't there."

"I've heard Bob Treadwell speak in the town. He neglects the farmer's point of view. The prices we're getting for our produce now –"

"Do you know what wages are paid at Outlands these days?"

"My neighbour, Mr Challoner, –"

"Do you know what they are at Dunnings?"

"I know what they ought to be," Stephen said.

"They're down to twenty-five shillings."

"How do you know about these things?"

"I make it my business to know!" she said.

Once again there was a pause. They looked at each other, and each drew breath.

"I've always heard you were a firebrand, Miss Izzard, and now I begin to see it's true."

"Then it may satisfy you to know that because of what happened here last night I may well lose my job."

"What?" Stephen said. He was appalled. "What in heaven's name makes you think that?"

"The vicar made it plain to me when I went to see him last night. And now, if you will excuse me, I do have rather a lot to do."

"But this is unheard-of!" Stephen said. "I really must get the matter clear."

"I'm sorry, Mr Wayman, but I haven't got time. My brother is coming in at ten and I have to get this room clean enough for him to start work." She took up her shovel and her broom. "Thank you for coming on your son's behalf. It was kind of you to take the trouble."

As she began to sweep again, the coal-dust rose and hung on the air, the particles glistening in the pale sunlight. She was intent on what she was doing. Stephen felt himself dismissed. He stood for a moment, watching her, then swung away and left the school.

* * * * *

He went straight to the vicarage and was shown into the vicar's study.

"What's all this about Miss Izzard losing her job? You

135

surely can't be serious. Where's your good sense?"

Mr Netherton was taken aback. He drew up a chair for Stephen to sit.

"I feel that Miss Izzard acted irresponsibly in allowing the meeting at the school. She chose to ignore my considered advice. I knew the managers would be incensed when they heard about the disgraceful affair and I warned her last night what the probable outcome would be. I've already had Major Jeans here this morning, with Mrs Talbot of Crayle Court, and they both insisted that I should call a special meeting of the managers for Monday next at twelve o' clock. Miss Izzard will be required to give an account of herself and as she is quite unrepentant I'm afraid they will ask for her resignation."

"I am one of the managers," Stephen said, "and I shall ask for no such thing."

"The major made his feelings plain. So did Mrs Talbot, needless to say. And some of the other managers, I'm sure, will feel that Miss Izzard ought to go."

"Then it's up to us to change their minds!"

"Is it?" said the vicar, doubtfully.

"She's good at her job, isn't she?"

"Well, of course, there's never been any question about that."

"Then we should be foolish to let her go."

Stephen sat quiet for a while, watching the vicar as he polished his glasses. Then he spoke again with vehemence.

"If Miss Izzard is dismissed I shall resign from the school board and make known my reasons for doing so. I may tell you also, speaking from my knowledge of the law, that Miss Izzard might well have grounds for bringing an action against the managers for wrongful dismissal. The education secretary would probably support her in such a course. *I* certainly would!"

"Wrongful dismissal?" the vicar said.

"I shall go along and see Mrs Talbot straight away and do my best to talk some sense into her. I shall see Major Jeans and the other managers, too, if need be."

"It would appear that you feel very strongly about this matter, Mr Wayman."

136

"My son was one of the troublemakers. No doubt you've heard who the others were. Is Miss Izzard to lose her job because of the bad behaviour of a handful of boys? No, Mr Netherton, it will not do!"

"Yes, well, I begin to think you're right," Mr Netherton said. He rather liked Stephen Wayman because Stephen, alone of the farmers in the parish, never grumbled about paying his tithes. "I will certainly speak for her at Monday's meeting and that, together with your eloquent representations, should sway the rest of the board, I think."

"I should damn well hope it does indeed!"

"Nevertheless, there are still grounds for criticism, I think, in that Miss Izzard allowed the school to be used for a political meeting without obtaining the board's consent. I feel therefore that when she is called before us on Monday she should receive a reprimand."

Stephen got up and went to the door. He had a full morning in front of him.

"Reprimand her if you must but I will not be present at the meeting to witness such a piece of flummery."

Walking through the village, out towards Crayle, he smiled to himself in a wry way. His concern for her feelings at Monday's meeting was probably quite unnecessary. It would take more than the vicar's reprimand to put *that* young woman out of countenance, he thought.

* * * * *

In the attic at Holland Farm, Joanna and Jamesy were trying on costumes for their play. Chris, with his hands in his breeches pockets, sat on a corner of the table, watching them as they flounced to and fro.

"What's the good of choosing the clothes when you haven't even written the play?"

"We've written some of it," Jamesy said. "It's the Second Act we're stymied on."

"If you're so clever," Joanna said, sweeping Chris with a swirl of her cloak, "why don't you help with writing it?"

"I've got better things to do."

"Such as smashing up poor Emma's school?"

"Sssh!" said Jamesy, with a warning glance, but Emma, rummaging in aunt Doe's tin trunk, gave no sign of having heard.

Chris slid from the edge of the table and slouched about the room. He picked up Jamesy's cardboard cutlass, gruesomely stained with crimson paint, and tried on Jamesy's three-cornered hat. More than once he glanced at his watch. It was almost eleven o' clock. He went to one of the barred windows and stood looking down over the fields. His father was coming up the track.

"Where are you off to?" Jamesy asked.

"Never you mind," Chris said.

He left the playroom and hurried downstairs. He met his father in the yard.

"Well, I've had a busy morning of it, thanks to you," Stephen said. "I've seen the headmistress of the school. I've seen the vicar and three of the other managers, and I've seen the young man whose face was cut by glass last night. I've also called on the constable."

Stephen looked pointedly at his son. Deliberately he paused, waiting, and Chris at length muttered his thanks.

"You'll be relieved to know that the young man with the cut face is recovering from the shock and bears nobody any grudge," Stephen said. "You'll also be relieved to hear that no summons will be brought against you for the damage you did to the school. The constable will be calling on you to give you a piece of his mind, but otherwise there will be no action from the law, because no one intends to bring any charge."

"What about the headmistress? I bet she had plenty to say!"

"She said nothing that wasn't deserved. She called you a hooligan, and so you are. But you may be interested to know that she blames me as much as you. She thinks I neglect you and let you run wild."

"Oh, what rot!" Chris exclaimed.

Hands thrust into his pockets, he stood without speaking for a while, kicking a stone with the toe of his boot.

"I've been thinking over what you said, about making my apologies to her. There's no sense in putting it off. I'd better get it over with, hadn't I?"

"If you go straight away," Stephen said, "you'll probably find her still at the school."

Chris went swinging away down the track. Somehow his mood was lighter now. He felt he could do almost anything. Phrases were forming in his mind.

As Stephen turned towards the house, little Emma came running out.

"I've been talking to your headmistress," he said. "She says you had a note for me, about the Parents' Day last week. What happened to it, I wonder?"

Emma frowned. It seemed she had trouble in remembering.

"I must've lost it on the way home."

"That was careless, wasn't it? But why didn't you tell me about the note? You could easily have remembered what it said."

"It was only about the Parents' Day."

"Didn't you want me to come to it?"

"I didn't want aunt Doe to come."

"Why ever not?" Stephen asked.

But it was easy to guess why not. Aunt Doe was a figure of fun. Fond though the children were of her, she was a source of embarrassment to them. They would grow out of it in time.

"Very well. You run along. But mind you take care of any notes you have for me in future."

When he had gone, Emma went across the yard and let herself into the little orchard, where the rows of hen-coops stood and the chickens were pecking about in the grass. She opened the lid of a nesting-box and looked inside it in search of eggs.

* * * * *

Standing outside the school door, Chris could hear voices from within, and the sound of a scrubbing-brush in use. For an instant he thought of turning back; he hadn't bargained for an audience; but while he stood indecisively, watching the smoke from a pile of rubbish burning on the waste-ground by the sheds, Betony came out of the school with a bucket of water to throw down the drain. Seeing the boy, she came to a halt. She knew who he was. She left him to speak.

"I say!" he exclaimed, swallowing. "I'm terribly sorry about all this! Last night and everything, I mean, and all the mess!"

"So you should be sorry," she said.

"I'd no idea it would turn out like that. If I'd known beforehand about the sheep –"

"Would you have stopped it?" Betony asked.

"Yes! I would most certainly! It was a rotten thing to do!"

"I suppose your father sent you here?"

"I know I ought to have come before but I was in a bit of a state and I wanted to think out what to say."

"At least you have come. None of the other hooligans have. Not so far, anyway."

No, nor would they, Chris thought. Gerald, David, Jackie, Jeff: *they* would never apologize; and he suddenly felt himself better than they. Though younger in years, he was more mature. He had learnt a few things about himself during the course of his sleepless night. He knew that Gerald and the rest were not the friends he really wanted.

"I would like, if I may, to make an apology on their behalf." Words were coming more fluently now. He sensed that he had her sympathy. "I would also like to say that I think it's jolly decent of you to take it all so well as you have."

Betony inclined her head. A smile hovered about her lips. Chris sent a glance towards the school.

"I wondered if I could give you a hand with clearing up the mess in there."

"I've got plenty of helpers, thanks, mostly people who were here last night. The cleaning is very nearly done."

"I'll be getting along, then. I've got a few more calls to make and a lot more apologizing to do."

"You"ll find it easier," Betony said, "now that you've had a bit of practice."

Chris gave a grin and walked away. Then he stopped and retraced his steps.

"We're doing a play at Christmas time. My sister and

brother and I, that is. I suppose you wouldn't care to come?"

Betony hesitated, thinking of the angry words that had passed between his father and herself, earlier that morning. She thought, too, of the threat to her job. But clearly the boy knew nothing of that.

"Thank you," she said, "I will certainly come."

"That's really very decent of you. I'll let you know when we've fixed the date."

He walked away with a jaunty step. An unpleasant duty had been accomplished and had not been so difficult after all. Next on the list, he told himself, was a visit to the village constable.

Close upon lunch-time, when he got home, he sought out Jamesy and Joanna, who were still busy up in the attic, painting an old calico sheet as a backcloth, all sea and sky and black scudding clouds.

"I say, you two! We've got to get our skates on, you know, if we're to put on that play for Christmas. I've invited someone to come and see it."

"Who?" said his sister and brother together.

"Miss Izzard, that's who," Chris said.

"Cripes!" Jamesy said, making a face. He splashed white paint on his foaming green sea.

Joanna handed Chris her notes.

"It's up to you to write Act II."

* * * * *

The schoolroom was filled with the smell of wet paint. Dicky worked quickly and with skill, disguising the smudges and scars on the walls. Betony's other helpers had gone. The wood-block floor had been scrubbed clean, and she was on her hands and knees, with a brush, a cloth, and a tin of polish.

At one o'clock they stopped for lunch. There were sandwiches and cherry cake. The day was reasonably mild, and they thought they would eat their lunch outside, sitting on one of the benches there.

"Hello, what's this?" Dicky said. "Someone's been in and

141

we never heard."

On the table in the porch lay a tiny spray of winter jasmine, just beginning to come into flower, and beside it three brown chicken's eggs, lying in a nest of crumpled paper.

"One of your kids, who wishes to remain anonymous?"

"I know who it is, though, all the same."

"Teacher's perks, eh?" Dicky said. "You'd better make the most of them if you're going to get the push next week."

* * * * *

By Monday morning, the schoolroom was restored to order again, and a few new pictures hung on the walls. Miss Vernon, smelling the new paint, had to be given an explanation, and her pupils, who had heard all about the rumpus at the meeting on Friday night, were able to fill in the details for her, which they did with some embellishments.

Betony approached Emma in the playground to thank her for the eggs and the spray of jasmine.

"How did you know it was me?" Emma asked.

"Ah, now, I wonder!" Betony said.

At twelve o' clock, in the course of her luncheon break, she presented herself at the vicarage and stood before a meeting of the school board, specially convened for the purpose and chaired by Mr Netherton. The managers had plenty to say and Betony heard them through in silence. To her surprise, the vicar spoke in her defence, and nobody asked for her resignation. When she emerged at a quarter past twelve, she was still headmistress of Huntlip School.

"How did it go?" Miss Vernon asked, coming to meet her in the playground.

"I was given a reprimand," Betony said.

Chapter 8

It was Saturday, the First of December, a day of keen winds and sharp stinging showers. From the steps of the Corn Exchange the Member of Parliament for Chepsworth, Mr James Crown, was addressing a gathering of some three score of his constituents, reminding them that in five days' time they would be asked to cast their votes. Mr Crown had been Member for Chepsworth for seventeen years. His election campaigns had been smooth and painless. He had never had to fight for his seat, and he was unused to the cut-and-thrust, the pertinent question, the jeers and abuse and derisive laughter that were coming his way from the crowd this morning.

And the one person who had started it all was a young woman, apparently alone, dressed in a bottle-green coat with a high collar and a pillbox hat trimmed with fur. Being only of medium height and surrounded mostly by men, she had climbed onto the edge of a horse-trough, and was thus head and shoulders above the crowd, looking stright across at the Member for Chepsworth. Her questions rang out across the town square and Mr Crown had the greatest difficulty in following the speech he had prepared. It was pretty much the same speech he had made in previous election campaigns. His simple beliefs were embodied in it. It had always been heard with respect until now.

"Would the fair-haired young lady in dark green – who is wearing a very entertaining hat – be good enough to repeat her question?"

And the young lady, quite unmoved by the compliment, was only too willing to oblige. The questions came, thick and fast, and Mr Crown was kept busy. Would he say that the coalition government, during its term of office, had done well by the unemployed? Was he reasonably well satisfied with the sight of ex-servicemen begging their bread in the town's gutters? And could he promise, if returned to his seat again, that these atrocious conditions would be maintained and that perhaps a new and even worse record might be achieved?

Stephen stood at the back of the crowd, having come from some business in Millichip Street. James Crown was known to him: he owned an estate at Newton Childe and farmed six hundred acres of it himself; Stephen had sometimes bought sheep from him. Crown was a good enough man in his way; he scarcely deserved his fate here today; and Stephen, smiling to himself, braced his back against the wind and settled down to watch and listen. Betony Izzard was now asking questions about conditions on the land.

"Why is there no national insurance for farm workers?"

"Because they don't need it," the Member said. "There is plenty of work on the land."

"Take us to it!" a man shouted, and a few others took up the cry.

"You are a landowner, Mr Crown," Betony said in her clear-ringing voice. "Will you give these men a job?"

"I already employ more than twenty men."

"How much do you pay them?" Betony asked.

"They don't complain!" the Member said.

"It seems to me you're evading the question. What are the wages on your farm?"

"I think we're getting away from the point —"

"Why don't you answer?" Betony asked. "Is it because the wages you pay your men would not satisfy the Conciliation Committee?"

There was a ripple in the crowd, and a dozen voices began to chant, "Answer her! Answer her! Answer, answer, answer her!" The Member suddenly became aware of the cold; he hunched his shoulders and buttoned up his coat; and at that moment the rain came down, cold and white and saturating, dispersing the crowd to the shelter of doorways, here and there about the square.

Stephen, as the crowd thinned, ran across to the Corn Exchange and sheltered under its portico, with James

Crown and his canvassers.

"Take courage, man!" he said. "The elements are on your side!"

Betony Izzard, he could see, was sharing an elderly man's umbrella, between two buttresses of St Winifred's church.

"That young woman!" Crown exclaimed. "I wish the rain would drive her off home!"

"Has she got you rattled?" Stephen asked.

"It's all very well for you to jeer. I've never had much of this before. It's always been a clean, straightforward affair, and I've always been allowed to say my piece."

"I can see she's been giving you a rough ride."

"Young woman like that! You'd think she had something better to do. If I had a daughter as troublesome as that, I'd keep her at home under lock and key!"

"I happen to be acquainted with her. I'll see if I can take her off your hands."

"Do that," Crown said, "and I'll send you a couple of brace of pheasants."

"Right, it's a bargain," Stephen agreed.

As the shower eased, and people emerged again into the square, Stephen went across to St Winifred's and met Betony coming away.

"Miss Izzard!" he said, raising his cap. "This is a very pleasant surprise."

"Is it?" she said, sceptically.

"For me it is, anyway. Will you come and have coffee with me?"

"I'm sorry, Mr Wayman, I don't think I can. There are certain things I want to do."

"Perhaps you're still out of charity with me. We exchanged some sharp words the last time we met. But our argument was cut short and I'll be glad of the chance to pick up the threads."

He could see the reluctance in her face. She was glancing across the town square to where James Crown, on the Corn Exchange steps, had a crowd in front of him again.

"I would also be glad of the chance to talk about Emma."

"What about her?" Betony asked.

"Come and have coffee," he said again, and this time she

agreed.

* * * * *

"The thing about places like this," he said, looking around the tiny teashop, "is that they are citadels of femininity and men are only allowed in on sufferance."

"Women will not be satisfied, however, until they have stormed and taken a few of the citadels guarded so jealously by men."

"You are a socialist, Miss Izzard?"

"I don't have a vote yet, Mr Wayman, so it hardly matters what I am. But in fact I haven't made up my mind."

"You held a socialist meeting in your school."

"It was a meeting of *people*," she said. "Anyone was welcome – even farmers."

Stephen smiled.

"It's a great pity I didn't come. But I take little interest in politics."

"You vote, however, I daresay."

"Surely you don't grudge me that?"

"You grudge it to *me*," Betony said.

"*I* do?" he said, much astonished. "It's hardly my doing that women can't vote till the age of thirty."

But the truth was, as he had to admit, that his thoughts on the subject had never been clarified, even to himself. It amused him to think of women having the vote; he couldn't understand why they wanted it, since men took care of things like that; but in fact he had more respect for women than many men did who were loud in support of equality. His own attitude to women was such that he didn't see why they should want more freedom than he already extended to them. He tried to explain this to Betony.

"My household is ruled by women," he said. "By my cousin, Miss Skeine, on the one hand, and by Mrs Bessemer on the other. But I don't storm *their* citadels. I merely take refuge in the barn."

Betony smiled. She was used to this kind of chaffing patronage. But she would not make the mistake, as some women did, of pursuing the subject in seriousness merely that men might be amused.

"Most women don't want to rule their menfolk, Mr Wayman. They ask only to rule themselves."

"I'm glad you agreed to have coffee with me. It shows you bear me no grudge, after all, for my son's behaviour at the meeting last week."

"I have no reason to bear you or your son a grudge. I am not to lose my post after all. But, as one of the managers, you must already know that."

"As one of the managers, and the father of a child at the school, I am extremely glad to hear it."

He did not mention his own part in influencing the rest of the board. In fact it hardly crossed his mind. He was watching her as she poured the coffee.

"I've been thinking over what you said about Emma being neglected," he said. "I've got three other children, as you know, and Emma is very much their pet. She gets her fair share of spoiling, I assure you, but she's a lot younger than the others and she does get left out of their games, I'm afraid."

"That's why she wanders off alone."

"I asked her about the note you mentioned and she said she lost it on the way home." He helped himself to sugar and stirred it round in his coffee. "I don't think she wanted any of her family to come to the Parents' Day. I get the feeling that she wants to keep her new school all to herself. Don't ask me why. It's a mystery to me. You probably understand her better than I do."

"Emma is not yet in my class, but I keep an eye on her, of course, and Miss Vernon talks to me about her. Emma, like all children, wants attention, but sometimes, when she's got it, she retires into herself."

Betony drank the last of her coffee and set down her cup.

"I feel I should withdraw that charge of neglect, Mr Wayman. It was made somewhat hastily and I apologize."

"You spoke as you found," Stephen said. "I hope you will always do that."

There was a pause, and he drank his coffee. Betony refilled his cup and when he took it from her she noticed for the first time that the fingers and thumb of his right hand were twisted and scarred.

"I was hit by shrapnel," he explained. "But the hand still works reasonably well. There aren't many jobs I can't do on the farm. It's a bit stiff in winter, unfortunately, and then the cows don't like me milking them. The milk comes out crooked, my cowman says."

"Where were you, in the war?"

"Flanders, first, and then the Somme. Sezerincourt and Mametz Wood. I was gassed a bit at St Hélène. It left me with a husky voice."

Betony nodded. She had heard that huskiness in men's voices before; had seen many scars like those that puckered Stephen's hand; and had seen that tiredness which even now, six years afterwards, was like a shadow at the back of his eyes. And suddenly she remembered, with a cold sense of shock, that this was the man whose wife had died in a tragic accident, less than half a mile from home.

"How long were you out at the front?"

"Only ten months in all. But – I was glad not to have to go back again."

Across the small table, with its coffee cups and its plate of biscuits, they looked at each other and were silent a while. He rather liked her straight, calm gaze, but something was nagging at the back of his mind.

* * * * *

There was a story he had heard, of her jilting her fiancé on the wedding day. How could a woman do such a thing? There must be some hardness in her, he thought, although it was not to be seen in her face. And, looking at her, he wondered about her, wishing he could read her mind.

Outside the teashop, when they left, they met the Member, James Crown, who, with a group of laughing attendants, was just coming in in quest of lunch. He raised his hat with exaggerated politeness to Betony and gave Stephen a broad wink.

"Much obliged to you, Wayman, I'm sure. I'll do the same for you some day. Though half an hour in such pleasant company was no great sacrifice, I don't suppose?"

"Quite the reverse," Stephen agreed.

The rain had died out altogether now. A pale, unwarm sun was struggling forth. He walked with Betony to The Plough, where she had left the pony and trap.

"What did Mr Crown mean?"

"He was thanking me," Stephen said, "for having taken you off his hands while he said his piece to the crowd in the square."

Betony faced him.

"Was that your object in asking me?"

"Not exactly. It was a joke."

"You are easily amused, Mr Wayman."

"Come, now, Miss Izzard! You're surely not hipped?"

"Nobody likes having their time wasted."

"It wasn't wasted as far as I am concerned. As Crown just said, half an hour in such pleasant company –"

"No gallantry, please, Mr Wayman. I've had enough masculine patronage for one morning. Thank you for the coffee. I'll bid you good-day."

She nodded coolly and turned into the livery yard. Stephen made his way to The Revellers in Lock Street. Had his "gallantry" been patronizing? Well, yes, perhaps it had. It was certainly not his usual style. But did the young woman have to take herself so seriously? He decided to put it out of his mind.

On the way home, however, he caught up with Betony on the road and drove behind her for about a mile. When she looked back and saw who it was, she pulled over onto the grass verge and stopped, signalling to him that he was to pass. Instead he drew up close beside her and they looked at each other, glimmeringly, while the two ponies, the black and the grey, leant together, nose to nose.

"Really, Miss Izzard, don't you think this is absurd? I asked you to have coffee with me because I wanted to talk to you. That I did Crown a favour at the same time was just a joke and nothing more. I certainly wouldn't have asked you merely on his account alone."

"And yet you will vote for him, probably."

"In the absence of someone better, yes, I daresay I shall."

His answer, somehow, was unexpected. It brought a

smile to her lips. In another moment they were laughing together and all her frostiness was gone. He spoke again.

"My son would never have forgiven me if I had seriously offended you. Neither would Emma, come to that. I hope there'll be peace between us from now on."

"I don't see why there shouldn't be."

The two traps kept shifting a little. The ponies, having become bored with each other, were growing restive between the shafts. Betony drew in the slackened reins.

"Will you go ahead, Mr Wayman?"

"No, I'm waiting for you," he said.

So Betony pulled out into the road again and touched the pony to a trot. Stephen followed close behind, rather enjoying the advantage it gave him, of watching her and the way she drove. You could learn quite a lot, he told himself, from the way a person handled a horse, and as far as her driving was concerned, he had no fault to find in her. But there was something else as well; something he admired even more; and that was her easy naturalness. Plainly the girl was conscious of him: she would not have been human otherwise; but there was no affectation in her; she felt no need to act a part merely because he was watching her. She had a clear view of the world. Whatever happened, she would be herself.

At Rider's Cross, knowing that he would be turning right, she looked round and nodded to him, raising her whip in a little salute. He responded by raising his cap. And all the way home along Rayner's Lane he carried in his mind an image of her, sitting erect in the pony trap, her fair hair, in the old-fashioned style, twisted in a knot at the nape of her neck, under the fur-trimmed pillbox hat.

When he got home, aunt Doe was in the garden, cutting broccoli for lunch. He leapt from the trap and went over to her.

"What was that tale about Miss Izzard, jilting her fiancé on the day of the wedding? – Do you remember it?" he asked.

"Yes, I remember it," aunt Doe said. She stood erect and turned to him. "It was something to do with her foster-brother, a boy brought up with her family. I believe he was

150

blinded in the war. The day Miss Izzard was due to be married, he was in trouble with the police. She put off her wedding to go to him. Her fiancé couldn't forgive her for it, so the wedding never took place at all."

"And her foster-brother? What happened to him?"

"It seems the poor boy was desperately ill. That's why Miss Izzard was so concerned. I believe he died that very day." Aunt Doe looked at Stephen's face. "I don't remember the ins and outs. But Mrs Bessemer's sure to know. If you want the details, you'd better ask her."

But Stephen, although he was interested, had no intention of gossiping with Mrs Bessemer. It was enough for him to know that, whatever the details of the story, Betony Izzard had not jilted her finacé out of caprice or out of wilful cruelty. He said something of this to aunt Doe, and she gave a little impatient shrug.

"You could tell she wasn't *that* sort of girl, just by looking at her, I would have thought."

"Perhaps you're right," Stephen said.

* * * * *

There had never been a general election like this one. Huntlip was full of fluttering posters, and slogans were chalked up everywhere. On polling day, at eleven o'clock, Mr and Mrs Talbot of Crayle Court drove up to the school to cast their votes, and behind them, in a huge brake drawn by four horses, came their employees from the estate. Mr Talbot wore the Tory colours in his lapel, and Mrs Talbot, who was very young, wore a hot-house carnation, dyed blue, pinned to the bosom of her coat. When they emerged from the school and drove away, the estate employees stood and cheered. They then went in to cast their own votes, and five of them at least voted for the opposite party.

Betony was busy throughout the day, driving about in the pony trap, fetching voters from outlying places. She wore no colours about her person; sported no posters on the trap; she was no more than a ferryman and observed a strict neutrality. She did not stop for lunch, but ate her sandwiches as she travelled about, and at three o'clock, when darkness fell, she lit the two lamps and carried on.

At six o'clock, as arranged, she returned home to Cobbs. Her father and mother and great-grumpa Tewke, dressed in their best as befitted the occasion, stood waiting in the fold, and Betony, jumping to the ground, relinquished the trap in her father's favour. Granna Tewke was not going to vote, but she had come out to see them off.

"I'm too old for that caper, driving out in the cold," she said. "And so is some others that I could name." She gave great-grumpa a prod in the back. "Gadding about at your age and you so comical these past few days!"

The old man had not been too well. The doctor had warned him against exertion. But he was determined to cast his vote, and, helped up by willing hands, he heaved himself into the trap.

"Where's Dicky?" Betony asked.

"There's no room for him in the trap. He says he'll go later when he's finished work."

Betony followed granna indoors, and granna gave her a cup of tea.

"You ent going out again, I hope? Not on a nasty night like this?"

"Yes, I am, when the trap comes back. But there aren't many more calls now."

"I pity that pony," granna said.

At half-past-six the trap returned, and Betony went off again. It was cold and wet, but she wore a mackintosh cape and hood, and had goloshes on her feet.

Beth Izzard went indoors, but Jesse and the old man went to the workshop, where, beneath the hanging lamps, the carpenters were still at work. There were eight men there, besides Dicky, and eight faces now looked up, wearing a bright expectancy. Great-grumpa Tewke spoke to them.

"I suppose you're hoping I'll say you can leave early, on account of the polling, eh?"

"It'd be a great kindness, gaffer," said Albert Tunniman.

"All right. You can go. But mind you all vote for the right man!"

The eight carpenters reached for their coats. In three minutes they were gone. Great-grumpa Tewke went into

152

the house. Dicky remained at the bench, working.

"Ent you going to vote?" Jesse asked.

"I'll go when I'm finished," Dicky said.

"The polling shuts down at eight o'clock. Do you think you'll have finished that job by then?"

"It don't take *me* a month of Sundays to put a new floor in a damned tumbril!"

Dicky, it seemed, was in a bad mood. He did not often sneer at his father. But Jesse, aware that he was slow, and a poor craftsman compared with his son, took it all in good part.

"I reckon I'll leave you to it, then. It ent worthwhile my starting again, seeing I've got my best suit on and all. I reckon I'll follow your great-grumpa in."

But before he reached the door of the house, Beth came hurrying out to him, to say that great-grumpa had collapsed.

"All right, wife, keep calm!" Jesse said. He himself was far from calm. "Is it bad, do you suppose?"

"Yes," Beth said, "he's slumped in his chair."

"Laws!" Jesse said. "Oh, glory be!"

He returned to the workshop and shouted for Dicky to go for the doctor. Dicky set off, white-faced, at a run.

When Jesse entered the kitchen, Beth was loosening great-grumpa's clothes. His collar and stock were very tight and she had trouble removing them. His face was a dark and terrible colour and there was a wetness on the skin. He was making a noise as he fought for breath. Granna stood weeping on the hearth. She had her pinafore up to her face.

"Silly old obstinate man!" she said. "I knew he shouldn't have gone to the poll. He's done for hisself, he has, that's a fact. He won't never recover now."

Beth and Jesse exchanged a glance.

* * * * *

News always travelled fast in Huntlip. Betony heard of the old man's collapse from a group of voters outside the school. She drove home immediately. By the time she arrived, great-grumpa Tewke was conscious again, and he

153

had been got upstairs to his bed; and he had enough of his old spirit left in him to have ordered the doctor out of the room.

"You're not taking me to no hospital and that's all-about-it, young fella-me-lad! If I'm going to die – and I surely am – I'd sooner do it in my own home!"

Dr Day was with the family in the kitchen when Betony arrived.

"It's probably better for him to be at home. Rest and care, that's what he needs, and he'll have them here."

"He ent going to die, is he, doctor?" Jesse asked anxiously.

Dr Day spread his hands.

"Anno domini, Mr Izzard. He's a wonderful age, you must admit. I'll call in again tomorrow morning."

"There!" said granna, when the doctor had gone. "As good as done for! What did I say?"

The others were silent, lost in their thoughts. The old man was ninety-two; he had had a good innings certainly; yet the thought of his death was hard to accept. House and workshop would seem very strange without William Tewke to order the comings and goings there. Jesse Izzard looked at his wife. Dicky looked at Betony. Dicky felt the need to be occupied.

"I'll go and see to the pony," he said, "and there's lamps to be douted in the workshop too."

Betony went upstairs and quietly entered the old man's room. She sat in a chair beside the bed and after a while he opened his eyes. His face was now as pallid as yeast, and his voice when he spoke was just a whisper.

"I know you're there, child, watching me."

"Is there anything I can do?"

"You can tell me how the voting went."

"From what people say, it looks as though Mr Crown will win, but we shan't really know until tomorrow, of course."

The old man closed his eyes. His breathing, though heavy, was regular. Betony sat in her upright chair and kept watch over him while he slept, and at ten o'clock, quietly, her mother came and took her place.

The next morning he was better. When Betony left for

school, he was eating a breakfast of porridge and milk. Janie, her married sister, had come and was sitting with him, pouring his tea. At eleven o'clock the doctor came and pronounced himself pleased with the old man's condition. He advised him, however, to stay in bed.

Jesse gave orders that no noisy work should be done in the workshop that day. There was plenty of painting the men could do. But the old man missed the hammering; the noise of the saw at work in the sawpit; the voices shouting in the yard.

"What's the matter with them all down there? Why ent they working?" he said to Beth.

Only with the customary sounds coming from the workshop and the yard could he lie peacefully in his bed.

After lunch the vicar called.

"Are you in a hurry to bury me?" the old man demanded with a scowl. "I see you've brought the books along."

"I thought perhaps a short prayer. . . ."

"Can't do much harm, anyway. But don't expect me to join in. I've got things to think about."

The vicar read the eighty-fourth psalm, followed by a prayer for the sick. The old man sat propped against his pillows and listened patiently to the end. Abruptly he spoke.

"What worries me is them gates!" he said.

"Gates?" said Mr Netherton. His mind being full of piety, he thought of St Peter and the gates of heaven. "What precisely do you mean?"

"The churchyard gates, of course, what else? You've been needing new ones these two years past. Have a word with Jesse while you're here. Better still with his boy Dicky. He'll let you know what that'll cost."

*   *   *   *   *

He would not have granna in the room. "Her long face makes me sick," he said. Only Beth was allowed to sit with him, and Betony when she came home; and by then he was weak again; he was beginning to talk to himself.

"Better to bring the old tree down, once the rot's got in at

155

the roots. Put a couple of wedges in . . . and bring it down, clean and straight . . . out of the way of them bits of saplings."

Betony looked at her mother's face. Was the old man wandering? – Talking of the oak in the workshop yard, felled in the autumn of 1913? No, he wasn't wandering. After a lifetime working with timber, he saw himself as an old tree. He had stood like a stubborn oak for years. No one had ever seen him yield. And now, when he knew his time was come, the woodman had no fears for him.

At three o'clock, Dicky came into the house with a newspaper, fetched hot-foot from Jeremy Rye's. It contained the latest election news. In Chepsworth, as Betony had said, the Liberal member had kept his seat, but in the country as a whole, there had been a swing to the left. The next government would be a Labour one.

"Laws!" Jesse said. He was much upset. "A Labour government! I dunno! I'd have thought the country had more sense!" He dropped the paper in disgust. "Your great-grumpa Tewke won't care for that. He won't care for it at all."

And then Betony came in to them, to say that great-grumpa Tewke was dead.

* * * * *

On the day of the old man's burial, the carpenter's shop was closed all day. The carpenters attended the funeral and six of them, with Jesse and Dicky, bore the coffin to the grave. The vicar prefaced his address with words from Ecclesiasticus: "Let us now praise famous men, and our fathers that begat us." For William Henry Tewke, carpenter, had been a famous man in his way, as the many mourners gathered in the church testified. He had lived to a great age, and before he died there had been five generations of his family living in the parish. Now he was gone and the four generations remaining sat in the church to honour him. . . .

As Dicky said afterwards, the vicar might not be much of a mucher outside his church, but in the pulpit there was no one to beat him.

Later that day, at Cobbs, when the last of the mourners had left the house, Dicky went to the workshop yard and walked about, his hands in his pockets, among the criss-crossed stacks of timber, good oak and elm, ash and beechwood, and the softwood planks of foreign deal. He was gazing into the sawpit when his father came looking for him.

"At least we can get rid of this lot now." Dicky kicked at a baulk of timber, so that it toppled into the pit. "We can get all our stuff from the sawmill now, instead of sawing it all by hand as though we was Noah building his ark."

Jesse looked at his son in horror.

"That ent no way to talk, boy, with your great-grumpa Tewke hardly cold in his grave."

"He wouldn't care," Dicky said. "He was no humbug, I will say that. The living came first with him all along. He wasted no time on 'em once they was dead."

"You should show some respect all the same. Your great-grumpa Tewke, he started this place. He was its founder, as they say."

"The business has got to carry on."

"Ah. But you was talking of making changes."

"Shall we be keeping the sawpit, then, just cos great-grumpa started it, way back in 1850? Shall we still be sawing by hand in another ten or twenty years?"

"I never said that," Jesse said.

"There's got to be changes, you know, dad."

"H'mm, and it seems you've decided how, where, and when!"

But Jesse, in fact, was quite content to allow Dicky to take the reins, and Dicky knew it. Jesse rarely asserted himself. His wife, his daughter, and his son, could impose on him just as they pleased. His wife knew best in everything, and he trusted her. His first-born child, Betony, was always the apple of his eye. And Dicky, shedding his youthful feck-lessness, was already showing signs of the drive that would keep the business flourishing.

In the days following the funeral, the changes were already showing themselves. When Joe Kyte called, to discuss the repairs at his granary, Jesse at once summoned

Dicky.

"My son is the chap you need to see. He'll come along with you to the farm and give you an estimate of the cost. You'll find there's a lot of old Mr Tewke in him. He's got a better business head than I'll ever have in a hundred years."

* * * * *

But there was one small business matter, not connected with the workshop, which Jesse always dealt with himself. He owned a cottage known as the Pikehouse, which stood three miles out, on the old Norton road. It had been left to him by his mother; he was its owner, and he alone; and the ownership gave him a certain importance. He let the Pikehouse, for a weekly rent of one-and-sixpence, to a stonemason named Horace Nash, and every Friday on his way home from work Nash called at Cobbs to pay his rent.

Jesse always looked out for him and made a fuss if he was late. The money went into a small cashbox, which was carefully locked afterwards, and the rent-book was signed with immense pains: always in ink, never in pencil; always carefully blotted dry, and breathed upon for good measure. It was a family joke at Cobbs and Beth said once to Betony: "Your father can sign a rent-book more slowly than anyone else in the world."

It happened one night that Nash came early, in Jesse's absence. Beth took the money and signed the rent-book. And Jesse, coming in, was almost angry. He looked at the money as though it were defiled.

"That's *my* job to sign for the Pikehouse rent. It ent no one else's, I'll be bound."

"How could you sign it when you wasn't here?"

"Nash could've waited, couldn't he? You knew I'd be in by seven o'clock."

"It doesn't matter who signs the book. It's just a sort of formality, that's all, to show that the rent has been paid."

But Jesse was not to be persuaded. He returned to the matter again and again. His Friday evening had been quite spoilt.

"It's *my* job to sign for the Pikehouse rent. If Nash comes early another time, you make him wait."

Every two or three months or so, Jesse took the money out of the box and paid it into the post office. This was another great day in his life, and for some time beforehand, whenever he went to the cashbox, he would give it a little shake and say, "That's beginning to get fuller again. I'll soon have to go to the Huntlip bank." Once he said to Betony, "That's twenty-one shillings in there. It's amazing how quickly it all mounts up."

"Seeing that you're so rich," she said, "why not give it to the Fund?"

There was a scheme afoot in the village to raise money for a parish hall, and Betony was on the committee.

"Oh, no!" Jesse said. "That's Pikehouse money, and it goes in the bank, cos I never know when that might be needed to pay for repairs. But I daresay I'll find something for your Fund."

He gave her ten shillings the very next day, but the rent-money must never be touched. It was sacred, Dicky said.

On December the fourteenth, there was a concert in the school, to raise funds for the parish hall. Jesse was rather shocked that Betony should join in the entertainment, less than a week after great-grumpa's funeral, but all the rest of the family went, even granna, and Jesse as always was over-ruled.

"It'll be a good thing if Huntlip gets a parish hall," Dicky said when he got home. "I spoke to the vicar about it tonight and he promised that we should have the job of building it."

"Laws!" Jesse said. "Did you ask him outright?"

"I don't believe in passing things by."

Dicky, as foretold, was treading the path great-grumpa had trod. Doing business was in his blood.

Chapter 9

On December the twenty-first, when the village school broke up for Christmas, the children were given those pieces of work which they had done during the term and were allowed to take them home. Emma had a small raffia basket, a peg-doll dressed in blue paper, and a knitted kettle-holder. But out in the playground, before going home, she gave these things to Winnie Aston, who gave her a pear-drop in exchange.

"Surely you want your little doll? I think she's nice, all dressed in blue."

"No, you can have it," Emma said.

"I shan't give them back, once I've took them home."

"Nobody's going to ask you to."

Emma, twirling her shoe-bag on its string, walked backwards to the gate. Miss Izzard and Miss Vernon stood outside the school porch, wishing their pupils a happy Christmas. Miss Izzard wore a dark blue suit, and had a black band of silk sewn to one sleeve. She had worn the black band for a fortnight now and Emma knew, having asked Florrie Ricks, that it was because Miss Izzard was in mourning for her great-grandfather, William Tewke.

"Happy Christmas, Emma!" Winnie said.

"Happy Christmas, Winnie!" Emma replied.

Emma walked up Holland Lane. It was too wet to go by the fields. The weather just lately had been very bad. When she was half way up the lane she stopped and took something from her pocket. It was her end-of-term report. She took it from its envelope and read her marks. She then read the sentences at the bottom, written by Miss Vernon in a large clear hand. "Emma must try and concentrate. She is too much given to day-dreaming." Emma tore the report to bits and scattered them in the dark puddles. Swinging her shoe-bag, she went on her way, sucking the pear-drop Winnie had given her.

* * * * *

All over Christmas the weather was cold, with sleet and snow showers coming by turns. This was the hated time of year, when the farm became a sea of mud, and the men as they squelched about the yards were inclined to be surly and quarrelsome.

"I hope it's cheerful, this play of yours," Stephen said to his older children. "We could do with cheering up a bit, especially the men."

"D'you think they'll come?" Chris asked.

"I don't see why not. They've received their invitations, I understand. I heard Tupper and Rye talking about it this morning."

"What were they saying?" Joanna asked.

"Tupper was wondering," Stephen said, "whether he ought to wear white tie and tails!"

Up in the attic with Jamesy and Joanna, Chris gave a reading of Act II, which he had completed on Boxing Day.

"The curtain rises on the posh drawing-room of a house in Kent –"

"Posh?" shrieked Joanna, outraged. "You can't say *posh*, for heaven's sake!"

"I don't see why not. The audience won't see the stage-directions."

"If we are going to do this wretched play, at least let us do it properly." Joanna spoke with a touch of hauteur. She was already feeling her way into the part of her heroine, the Lady Rosina Cavendish.

"Oh, very well," Chris agreed. He altered the word in his exercise book. "The curtain rises on the *elegant* drawing-room –"

"That's better," Joanna said. "But whereabouts in Kent exactly?"

"Cripes!" said Jamesy impatiently. "When are we going to start rehearsing?"

Rehearsals brought new difficulties. Joanna, as the

haughty heroine, having been abducted by the wicked pirate, Captain Terror, and thrown into the hold of his ship, *The Scourge,* was there to find the hero, Chris, lying unconscious on the floor, bleeding from a wound in his right temple.

"A goodly looking youth but *reeks* of garlic!" Joanna cried tragically. "How am I to bandage his wounds?"

"*Bind* his wounds, not bandage them!" Chris reminded for the seventh time. "They didn't have bandages in those days."

"You're supposed to be unconscious."

"I can still hear you making a muff of your lines."

"Order! Order!" Jamesy said, bringing his cutlass down, smack, on the side of his gumboot. "Or I'll have you marooned, you mutinous dogs!"

Downstairs, in the bedroom she shared with Joanna, Emma stood in front of the wardrobe, looking at herself in the long mirror. She wore a black silk band on her arm and a tiny tin watch, taken from a Christmas cracker, pinned to the bosom of her frock. She folded her hands in front of her and bowed her head.

"Lighten our darkness, we beseech thee, O Lord, and by thy great mercy defend us from all perils and dangers of this night. . . ."

Below, in the hall, a door closed and aunt Doe's voice called up the stairs. Emma pulled the black band from her arm and threw it into an open drawer. She unpinned the watch and set it aside.

"Emma, where are you?" aunt Doe called. "I've got a little job for you."

"All right, I'm coming!" Emma replied.

* * * * *

New Year's Eve was cold and wet. All day at the farm, fires burnt in the sitting-room and dining-room, and the children were busy with their preparations. With the connecting doors removed, the two rooms became one, and when all the inessential furniture had been removed, there was space enough for six rows of chairs. The "stage," at one end, consisted of two shearing-platforms, and drawstring curtains hung in front from a wire fixed to a beam in the ceiling. At the back of the room, behind the rows of seats, a trestle table had been set up, covered with a clean white sheet, and by seven o'clock in the evening aunt Doe, with Mrs Bessemer's help, had filled the table with all sorts of food.

At seven o'clock, the farm-hands arrived with their wives and children, all dressed in their best clothes. Only Morton George stayed away and, as Chris remarked, who cared about him? The vicar was there with his wife and daughter; Agnes Mayle was there with three of her younger brothers and sisters; so were some friends of aunt Doe's from the Women's Institute; and a few of the neighbouring farmers came, including John Challoner and his son Gerald.

Aunt Doe, in a brown woollen dress, ran to and fro without pause, showing people to their seats and going "backstage" now and then to help the actors with their costumes, their lines, and their last-minute nerves.

"My gosh!" said Jamesy, having peeped through the curtains at the audience. "There's no end of a crowd! Where the deuce is my three-cornered hat?"

Chris had no nerves. Although in a state of some excitement, he was in command of himself. He was even brave enough to walk out into the hall, wearing his costume, to welcome Betony when she arrived.

"I'm so glad you could come, Miss Izzard, and after my behaviour at the meeting that time, I think it is more than I deserve."

His welcoming speech was well-rehearsed. He had spent some days perfecting it. And, dressed as he was in his best fawn breeches and the "cutaway" coat aunt Doe had made him, with white lace ruffles at throat and wrists, he delivered his lines with a certain panache. But his smile and his look were genuine enough and Betony responded to them.

"I wouldn't have missed it for the world."

"It's only a bit of a lark, you know. It's something Joanna and Jamesy dreamt up and I got roped in to give them a hand."

He took her coat and hat and hung them up. He ushered her in to a seat at the front, specially reserved with her name on it. He treated her as the guest of honour.

"I'm afraid I shall have to leave you now, but you will excuse me, won't you?" he said.

He walked away down the side of the room and there was a little round of applause from the Holland Farm men and their families before he vanished behind the curtains. Betony, turning in her seat, looked round at the rest of the audience. They were all known to her, especially the children, and she exchanged greetings with them. When she turned back again, she found Emma sitting beside her.

"Aren't you going to be in the play?"

Emma said nothing, but shook her head.

"Oh, well, never mind. I expect you'd sooner watch, like me."

A voice called out and the lights were dimmed. The audience stopped talking and applauded instead. The curtains parted to reveal the stage, lit by a single hurricane lamp, carried by Jamesy as the villainous pirate, clad in striped pyjama trousers, a shirt painted with the skull and crossbones, and a scarlet bandana round his head.

"Easy does it, you lubberly rogues!" he snarled to an imaginary crew behind. "Belay there and hold your noise! Easy on the tiller, you fool! Now! – Fire a shot across her bows!"

Stephen, outside the sitting-room window, set off a charge of gunpowder in an old iron stovepipe to simulate the cannon's roar. He was then able to go indoors and take his place at the back of the audience, glad of the room's enveloping warmth after the wind and rain outside. He could see Betony, six rows in front, sitting next to his youngest daughter.

* * * * *

All through rehearsals, Chris had taken the play very seriously, and had often been vexed by Joanna's carelessness with her lines. But now, tonight, there was a change. Aware of the audience watching him, he suddenly

164

saw the play for what it was, and an imp of mischief got into him.

"A goodly looking youth – " Joanna cried, remembering to project her voice; and Chris, who should have lain still, being unconscious, gave a little modest cough and put up a hand to straighten his cravat; " – but reeks of garlic!" Joanna said, reproving him with a sharp kick.

Chris however was unrepentant and when, later on in the same act, his part required that he should lift Joanna into his arms, he deliberately allowed his knees to buckle and staggered with her across the stage.

"Fear not, my love! You are but a sylph!" he gasped. "I could carry you to the end of the world!"

The audience responded with a cheer. The play was giving them a good many laughs. And when Chris, setting Joanna down at last, knocked over the "ship's table" and it was seen to be a box stencilled with the words "Hardy and Hawker's Binder Twine", there was another loud cheer. Joanna by now was furiously angry. She set the box upright again, with the treacherous words hidden from sight.

Exits and entrances were through a door to the right of the stage. In the last act, due to a shortage of actors, aunt Doe made a brief appearance as one of the pirate crew. Wearing a scarf tied over her head and a black patch over one eye, she opened the door with such force that Jamesy's cutlass was knocked from his hand. She fixed him with her one ferocious staring eye and delivered her only line in the play.

"What orders, Captain?"

Her voice was immense. It took the principals by surprise. Chris and Jamesy got the giggles and Jamesy for a while was quite unable to answer her.

"What orders, I say?" aunt Doe bellowed.

"H-hoist the mains'l!" Jamesy said.

"Splice the main-brace and batten the hatches!" Chris shouted, carried away. "Weigh anchor and man the oars!"

These lines were not in the written play. Nor were many of the others that flew across the stage in the next few minutes. But the story moved to its appointed end and the wicked pirate met his desserts.

"See where he hangs from yonder yard-arm!" And Chris pointed to where poor Jamesy, hooked to a rope hanging from the rafters, was brandishing a puny fist. "England is safe from one black-hearted villain at least!"

"Let me down!" Jamesy piped, forgetting to pitch his voice to a growl. "Let me down, you mutinous swabs, or I'll have you keel-hauled, every man jack of you!"

"*I* am the captain now!" Chris declared. He danced a hornpipe, whistling the tune. He at least was enjoying himself, but Joanna, crimson in the face, looked as though she could murder him. "The skull and crossbones fly no more from yonder masthead! Instead I have hoisted the flag of St George! We sail for England – and Holland Farm – where this fair maid shall be my bride!"

"Stop it, you're spoiling everything!" Joanna hissed.

Chris merely took her into his arms. Reverently he kissed her cheek.

"Are you happy, my Lady Rosina?"

Joanna's answer was inaudible. Secretly she was pinching him, twisting the flesh at the back of his neck. He bore it bravely and kissed her again.

"What did you say, my shyest one?"

This time her answer was audible, but only to him, and he, with the greatest aplomb in the world, turned to face his audience.

"She's blissfully happy and I'm standing on her foot!"

There was loud applause from the audience, and a great deal of stamping of feet. The stage curtains began to close but became stuck half way across. Aunt Doe, still in her eye-patch and bandana, tugged at the drawstrings and broke them off. She went and closed the curtains by hand, swearing at them in Hindustani.

* * * * *

"I suppose," said Bob Tupper, enjoying a plateful of cold ham and pickles, "our young master here will be going on the films next."

"Tomorrow morning," Chris said, "I shall be out with you in the Bratch, making a start on that sugar-beet."

166

"What, in them clothes?" said Billy Rye.

Chris was still wearing his stage costume. He grinned at the men and moved away. Joanna and Jamesy, with their father, were standing talking to the vicar.

"I'd no idea your children had such a comic talent, Wayman."

"Neither had I," Stephen said.

"As for the beautiful heroine –"

"When I've got time," Joanna said, "I intend to write a *proper* play."

Emma had a plate of hot mince-pies and was offering them to Betony. But Betony's plate was already filled with sausage-rolls and sandwiches. She was talking to Mrs Billy Rye. She smiled at Emma, and the child went away. Chris, too, was hovering. Mrs Rye gave way to him. He carried a bottle of ginger wine and he refilled Betony's glass.

"At least the food and drink are all right, Miss Izzard, even if the play was not up to much."

"The play went down very well," she said, "and now the food is doing the same."

She rather liked this boy of fifteen. Tonight he was gay and debonair; the occasion had filled him with ebullience; but underneath this evening's mood, she thought, there was seriousness of purpose and great resolution. He would not be slow in growing to manhood.

"The idea was to cheer everyone up a bit. Things are rather gloomy on the land just now."

"And elsewhere."

"Do you think the new government will mend matters, Miss Izzard?"

"I'm not a crystal-gazer, I'm afraid. All I can do is hope for the best."

Chris was called away by John Challoner. He excused himself with great politeness. Betony, still with her plate in her hand, went to speak to a group of children, gathered where the table was most full of food. She saw that two of the Starling boys were cramming their pockets with apples and nuts. She spoke to them and they put the things back. She returned to where she had left her glass.

From across the room Stephen watched her, although he was talking to Arnold Twill. A little while later he came to her. The hubbub around them was very loud. He had to speak up to make himself heard.

"It was kind of you to come, especially on such a bitter night. Can I get you another drink?"

"Thank you, no, I've got plenty."

"I was sorry to hear of your great-grandfather's death. I only met him once or twice, but I knew his reputation as a craftsman, and as a man of forceful character."

Betony smiled.

"You will hear people say that he was a hard, unyielding man, and there is truth in what they say, but a piece of old Huntlip has died with him, I think, and perhaps a piece of old Worcestershire."

"Do you regret its passing?" he asked.

"Most things take on a special colour, once they are in the past," she said.

"Will the present bad times do the same, do you think, when we look back on them in years to come?"

"It depends how long the bad times last."

"Let's drink to the future, anyway," he said, and raised his glass. "I wish you good health, Miss Izzard, and a happy new year."

"A happy new year!" Betony said.

When she left Holland Farm it was close upon midnight, and by the time she got home to Cobbs the hour had struck. It was 1924.

* * * * *

The following morning, Chris started work on the sugar-beet, in the fifteen acres known as the Bratch. He worked with Starling and Morton George, Harry Ratchet and Billy Rye, and cold wet dirty work it was too. The sugar-beet, loosened in the ground by the plough, had to be pulled up by hand and knocked together to shed the soil. The green tops were then cut off and the beets were thrown into the waggon. But the beets were too wet to shed the soil. Icy cold and covered with slime, they stung the men's hands until

168

they ached. And the language heard in the field that day sometimes reddened Chris's ears.

Once Stephen came into the field and took a turn at lifting and topping. But with his badly twisted fingers he was less deft than the other men, and after an hour his hand was useless, the fingers seized up in a painful cramp. He threw down his bill-hook and walked away, and as soon as he was out of earshot, Morton George gave a grunt.

"That's a great help, I must say, his doing that! How many beets did he throw in? We should get on famously if we all done as much as the master done!"

Chris, though angry on his father's behalf, went on with his work and said nothing. Morton George was beneath his contempt. Chris never spoke to him if he could help it.

At Outlands, when they lifted their beet, it was left in great mounds beside the road, to await collection by motor lorry. Chris thought this a grand idea. He wanted his father to do the same. But Stephen wouldn't hear of it. Each load must go to the factory as soon as lifted.

"Hang it all!" Chris protested. "Think of the time we should save."

"No," Stephen said, "I want that beet taken in straight away."

Three days later the hard frosts came. Chris was at Outlands on an errand one day and Gerald showed him their sugar-beet crop, heaped by the roadside, ready to be taken to the factory. Gerald kicked at it savagely. The rotten pulp was all over his boots and the sweetish carroty smell of it was very strong on the frosty air.

"So much for the Ministry's precious beet! I'm damned if we'll grow that stuff again!"

"You should've carted it straight away, the same as we did," Chris said.

He did not often get a chance to score off Gerald. He went home whistling up the hill.

There was a friendly rivalry between the two boys as they went about their work on the two farms. If they met at the boundary, they would stop for a chat. But Chris was much less in Gerald's company these days, and much less inclined to repeat his opinions. Stephen noted it and was glad.

* * * * *

In the middle of January there was a heavy fall of snow. Then the rain came again and washed it away. It was bitterly cold on high ground, and in the valleys there were floods.

At the village school, children who came from outlying places arrived soaked and shivering. Their faces were pinched, their hands and feet numb. At such times as these, Betony set routine aside. Coats and shoes were put to dry; forms were drawn up around the stoves; and the children sat as close as they could, steaming dry in the heat of the fires and drinking the cocoa that Betony had heated for them on the hob.

The first lessons of the day were taken round the stove, but instead of following the timetable, the children were encouraged to talk about the terrible weather and the things they had seen on their way to school. In the smaller room, Miss Vernon did the same with her younger ones, who soon lost their shyness as the game went on.

"I seen one of Mr Franklin's turkeys swimming for his life when I came by. The brook was up as far as his barn."

"I seen a dog with a fish in his mouth, running along Withy Lane."

"Old Mrs Tarpin at Collow Ford, she'd got a great mattress in front of her door, to stop the water getting in. But it *got* in all right. She was upstairs hollering at the window and the blacksmith was reaching her up her milk."

All the children had something to tell, even the "babies" of three and four. Only Emma Wayman remained silent.

"Well, Emma, and what about you?" Miss Vernon said cheerfully. "What did you see on the way to school?"

"I didn't see anything," Emma said.

Rain continued all day, and Betony decided to cut the afternoon short, but already, at two o'clock, word was coming in that the Derrent brook had burst its banks and had flooded the road at Slings Dip. Eighteen children used that road and Betony went down with them to see for herself how matters stood. Sure enough, the road was impassable for two hundred yards or more, the water being

170

a good two feet deep. She was herding the children back to the school when a cart came down from Holland Lane and drew up beside her. Stephen Wayman leapt to the ground.

"Tupper told me the road was flooded. I thought maybe you might need help."

"Indeed we do!" Betony said. "These children would have a three mile walk if they had to go round by Lippy Hill."

Stephen wasted no time. He began lifting the children into the cart, and Betony helped him. The bigger ones clambered in by themselves. There was a lot of laughter among them as the cart, creaking, began to move. Their journey through the swirling waters became a mighty joke indeed. The mare, Phoebe, splashed her way through and, reaching the unflooded ground beyond, gave vent to a thankful whinny. The children, once they had been set down in safety, stood watching as Stephen, with some difficulty, turned the horse and cart in the road. They watched it make its return journey, then they scampered off towards home, some to Steadworth and some to Bounds.

Betony stood outside the school gate. Stephen stopped to speak to her.

"Is that the lot living out that way?"

"Yes. And I can't tell you how grateful I am."

The rain had stopped for a little while, but the gale still blew ferociously, whipping the words from Betony's lips. She had to lean forward into the wind to keep her balance against its buffets. She had to hold on to the skirts of her coat to keep them wrapped close about her legs.

"What weather!" she said, looking up at him, and she laughed because of the rollicking wind that threatened to knock her off her feet.

"Would you care to be driven home?"

"No, thank you, I've got things to do."

"Then I'll bid you good-day," Stephen said.

She returned to the school. He drove up the lane. The afternoon sky was very dark, the black clouds rearing up thick and fast, blown by the wild north westerly wind.

After the floods, there were frosts again. One morning when Betony arrived at school, she found the stoves still unlit, and the caretaker, Miles, waiting to see her.

"Seems we're out of coal," he said. "A skiddle of slack, that's all there is."

"But we had half a ton not long ago! The heap was up to the back-house window."

"That's just the trouble," Miles said. "Anyone can get at that coal. They've only got to climb the fence. It ent the first time we've had thieves in here in the cold weather."

"It's the first time they've left us without any coal whatsoever! Do they want the children to freeze to death?"

Betony went to the post office and sent a wire to the coal merchant, ordering half a ton of coal to be delivered at once, that very day. She returned to the school and, with Miles and Miss Vernon to help, moved the desks to the back of the room. When the children arrived, they were told to keep their coats on, and Betony, standing in front of them, led them in a game of "O'Grady Says." After an hour of this, Miss Vernon played the piano and the children sang songs of their own choosing, for singing too helped to keep them warm. At eleven o'clock, however, a telegram arrived from the coal merchant to say that the coal could not be delivered till the following Monday. The maximum temperature in the school was thirty-eight degrees. Betony had to admit defeat. She sent the children home and closed the school.

As she and Miss Vernon were leaving, Stephen and two of his men arrived, with twelve sacks of coal in the back of the cart, brought from his own stock at the farm.

"Emma tells me you're out of coal. She's very upset at being sent home. Will this see you through till your order comes?"

Certainly it would see them through. Betony unlocked the gate again to let the horse and cart drive in. She watched the three men unload the coal.

"If you have trouble with your order, let me know," Stephen said, "and I'll send in to town to fetch it for you."

By twelve o'clock the stoves were lit. By half-past one the rooms were warm. The desks were all back in place again, and Betony rang the school bell, to tell her pupils throughout the village that the school was open after all. Miss Vernon came and stood by her.

"Mr Wayman is very kind. That's the second time he's come to our rescue. He never used to take such an interest in the school. Not such a *personal* interest anyway. But now he can't do enough for us."

Betony pulled on the bell-rope and the bell rang out in its turret on the roof.

"Not so surprising as all that, now that he has a child here with us."

* * * * *

There were outbreaks of foot-and-mouth disease in the area that spring. A farmer at Stamley lost his pedigree herd. Everywhere, throughout the district, precautions were taken against the infection, so mysterious in its ways, and the movement of cattle was controlled.

At Holland Farm, as on other farms, there were buckets of antiseptic fluid at every entrance, and anyone who had been beyond its boundaries had to dip his booted feet in this and sluice the wheels of vehicles. Stephen was in the cartshed one day when Morton George drove straight through the gateway without stopping, although he had come from Steadworth Mill.

"It's all a waste of flaming time!" he said when Stephen challenged him. "How do we know it does any good?"

"How do we know it doesn't?" Stephen said.

He made the man dip his boots in the bucket and sluice the axles and wheels of the cart.

"If you disobey me again over this, you'll get your cards without delay!"

The outbreaks died away at last. Stephen and his neighbours breathed again. The weather improved in April, although not much, and the ploughs were able to get out on the land.

"If we had a tractor," Chris said, "we should soon catch up on all this lost time." He was bitterly jealous of the two tractors so busy at Outlands, crawling about the green and brown fields. "Surely now that you're saving on my school

173

fees –"

"But I shouldn't be saving them," Stephen said, "if I spent the money on a tractor instead."

"It would pay for itself in no time at all if you were to sack one of the men."

"I prefer to keep men in work."

"Even Morton George?" said Chris.

"Look," Stephen said, somewhat curtly, "I said you could come and work on the farm, but I didn't say you could take over!"

But he smiled to soften his words a little, and passed *The Farmer and Stockbreeder* across to the boy, open at a page on beet-growing.

Chris tried to enlist Bob Tupper's support, but Bob was a horse-man through and through.

"Don't speak to me about tractors," he said. "A tractor ent human, like a horse. And it don't seem natural to me, neither, to hafta look back on your work all the time instead of forrards, the proper way."

"At least a tractor doesn't eat its head off when it's not working."

"No, nor it don't manure the land, neither."

"Hah! Manure!" Chris said in disgust. "We're up to our ears in it on this farm!"

"You speak for yourself, young master," said Bob.

Chris was very keen to plough. He wanted to do every job on the farm. Once he and Bob were in the same field; Bob was ploughing with Beau and Bonnie; Chris with the geldings, Spick and Span; while over on the other side of the hedge, in an Outlands field, Gerald on his tractor lurched to and fro, completing four furrows in less time than Chris could do one. Once he came to the hedge and shouted.

"How're you peasants doing up there? Have you ever heard of a thing called progress?"

Chris took no notice but ploughed on, his young face tight-set under his cap.

"Peasants!" he said, later, to Bob. "That just about hits the nail on the head! Why not use oxen and be done with it?"

But, as Bob remarked to Stephen one day, in spite of the

boy's bitterness, his work in the field was always good, whether ploughing or drilling, and he was improving all the time. He might look down on the use of horses but his team was always well turned out and he worked them with as much patience as Bob did himself.

Sometimes Stephen had worried about Chris, coming so young to the work of the farm, without having seen the outside world. He feared that the boy would become cloddish. But Chris had a busy, adventurous mind. He read a great deal; kept abreast of new things; he was outward-looking, ambitious and keen. He was the sort of young man who would build the future of agriculture – if only he were given the chance. Stephen wished he could give in to him and bring modern methods to Holland Farm, but he felt that the bad times had come to stay and his instinct counselled cautiousness.

"Take John Challoner," he said. "He spent big while the going was good. Now he needs to pull in his horns and he's finding it difficult to do."

"At least he's got tractors," Chris said. "At least he's got electricity." Then, after a moment, he said: "At least he keeps hunters and rides to hounds."

"Do you want to ride to hounds?" Stephen asked.

"I'd like to be able to afford it, that's all."

"That's just it, Challoner *can't* afford it," Stephen said.

* * * * *

The weather turned wet again. Very little ploughing was done. The two war veterans, Tupper and Hopson, were heard singing the hymn-tune, "Holy! Holy! Holy!" as they went about the farm. But the words they sang were those they had so often sung in Flanders: "Raining! Raining! Raining! Always bloody well raining!" And Tupper said to Morton George, "I don't think it's stopped since this ruddy government of yours got in!"

The lambing season was bad that year. Stephen was out at all hours, helping his shepherd, Henry Goodshaw, but their losses were heavy all the same, and he grew quite hardened to the task of burying dead lambs.

175

One day in the pasture at Wood End, he found three dead lambs in an old disused well. Morton George had thrown them there.

"I didn't think it'd hurt," George said, "what with the weather being so cold."

"Have you smelt them?" Stephen asked.

"It ent my job, anyway. It's the shepherd's job to bury his lambs."

"Then leave them where he can see them, man, and don't go flinging them into holes."

This was a trying time for Stephen. He was suffering from lack of sleep. He knew he must keep a check on his temper whenever he dealt with Morton George, for the man was growing more slovenly and every day brought cause for complaint. Pig-swill inadequately boiled; barn-doors left swinging in the wind; coils of barbed wire thrown down and left where cattle could entwine their legs.

"If that was me I should sack him as soon as look at him," said Chris. "He's more trouble than he's worth."

"I've never had to sack a man yet and I hope I never shall," Stephen said.

Round about the middle of April, however, something happened that changed his mind. The mare, Tivvy, was in foal. It was a month or so to her time, and she was therefore excused from work. Yet Morton George, with a heavy load of manure to cart, put Tivvy into the shafts and drove her uphill to the Eighteen Acre. It happened that Tupper was in the field. He unyoked the mare and led her home. But the harm was already done by then. Tivvy miscarried and the foal was born dead. Bob Tupper was beside himself. He threatened to take Morton George apart.

"Bloody lazy pigging sod! He took the mare because she was nearest! It saved him fetching Beau from the meadow. You'd better keep him away from me, Mr Wayman, cos I'm in the mood to break his neck!"

But Stephen himself had had enough of Morton George. The man was useless. He was given his cards.

"You think I don't know why you're sacking me? It ent on account of a bloody horse! It's because I'm a union man, that's why it is! You bloody farmers is all the same!"

"There's an extra thirty shillings there. That's instead of a week's notice. You can go this minute, without delay."

"I shall see my union about this!"

"Just be sure and tell them the truth!"

"What about my cottage? Are you putting me out in the road?"

"You can stay in the cottage till the end of the month. Then I'll want it for a new man."

In fact Morton George was gone by Easter. He left the district with his wife and three boys and was seen driving a cart towards Capleton. When Stephen went to the empty cottage, he found that the place was no more than a shell. Doors and floorboards had been removed and burnt on a bonfire in the garden. Some of the rafters had been sawn through and the glass had been broken in all the windows. The kitchen range had been smashed; so had the copper in the scullery; and in the overgrown garden behind, fruit trees and lilacs had been cut down.

But there was a worse discovery still, for in the pasture behind the cottage, an in-calf heifer was found dying, and the vet said she had been poisoned by eating yew. There were bits of it still in her mouth, and a yew tree grew in the cottage garden. There was nothing the vet could do. She died while he was examining her.

Chapter 10

At Easter the weather improved for a while. The nights were frosty but the days were fair. There was a bustle on the farm and all possible teams were out, ploughing, harrowing, drilling seed, busy wherever the ground allowed. Chris was in a fever from dawn to dusk. He thought and talked of nothing but work. And Jamesy, home for the holidays, followed his brother everywhere.

Joanna was in the grip of a different fever. Her school-friend, Elaine, was staying at the farm for the Easter week-end, and the two girls were writing a novel. They shut themselves away in the attic and played the gramophone all day, mostly Mozart and Mendelssohn.

"Music enables me to think," said Joanna. "It makes me aware of life and death."

Did Elaine know what she meant?

"I think," said Elaine, her eyes half-closed: "I think Persephone will die when she thinks Julian has forsaken her."

"But Julian, of course, comes back a rich man."

"Having intended all along to marry her . . ."

"He goes to the churchyard and sees her grave . . ."

Mendelssohn had come to an end. Joanna reached out and changed the record. She put on the Mozart Sonata in D.

Emma, attracted by the music, climbed the steep stairs to the attic playroom, but found the door locked against her.

"Go away!" Joanna shouted. "We're very busy. We need to think."

"I want to come in and listen to the gramophone."

"Well, you can't!" Joanna said.

Emma, having rattled the door-knob in vain, turned and went downstairs again. She slipped past aunt Doe and Mrs Bessemer, who were busy swilling out the dairy, and left the house by the side door.

Outside, in the barnyard, Jamesy was helping Chris to load sacks of grain onto a trailer. They were sowing barley in the Goose Ground.

"Can I come with you?" Emma asked.

"Don't be silly," Jamesy said.

"I want to ride behind the drill."

"You run along in, there's a good girl, and aunt Doe will find you something to do."

"No," Emma said. She turned away.

"Where are you off to?" Jamesy asked.

"Nowhere in particular," Emma said.

"Well, whatever you do, don't go down to the bottom yard."

"Why, what's in the bottom yard?"

"Never you mind what's there," said Chris. "Just do as you're told and keep away."

"Is it a surprise?" Emma asked.

"No, it isn't. It's nothing at all. Now mind out of the way or you'll get run over."

When they had gone, with their load of seed, Emma went into the barn and climbed the ladder into the hayloft. There was much to be seen from the hayloft door. Half the farm lay spread below. She could see her father, with Spick and Span, harrowing the green winter wheat on the slopes of the One-and-Twenty. She could see three ploughs at work in the Freelands. She could see the shepherd and his boy, moving about the lambing-pens, and could even see a hint of steam rising from the backs of some of the ewes.

When she climbed down the ladder again the spaniel, Sam, came running to her, wagging his little stump of a tail.

"Rats?" Emma said. "Have you seen any rats? You come with me, I'll find you some rats."

She left the barn, with the dog at her heels, and walked down the track to the bottom yard, a place used for stock in wintertime, on three sides enclosed by shelters and stalls. She opened the gate and went into the yard. The spaniel chose to remain outside.

"Rats? Any rats?" she said to him, but although he wagged his tail again, he made no move to follow her. "Oh, very well, you please yourself."

She pushed the gate and it latched shut. Sam stood peering at her through the bars. Then, with a whimper, he ran off home. Emma stood alone in the empty yard.

Lately, the muck had been carted away, and the concrete ground had been scraped clean. The open-fronted shelters had been mucked out and the cobblestones had been hosed down. There was nothing to see in the shelters or stalls. There was only something in the middle of the yard; something bulky, rounded in shape, covered by a stack-cloth weighted with stones. Emma went closer, two steps at a time. She removed one of the big stones and lifted a corner of the cloth.

The dead cow's eyes were open wide, but were covered by a thick clouded film. Its black tongue hung curling out of its mouth; its lips and nostrils were covered in slime. Emma shrank back with a little cry, letting the stack-cloth fall again.

She ran to the gate and climbed over, tearing her pinafore on a nail. There was a hedge at the side of the track, and when she had pushed her way through the thorns, she ran across the pasture into the coppice. From there she passed into Stoney Lane; ran full pelt past Lilac Cottage; and squeezed through the gate onto Puppet Hill. She couldn't run up the steep track because of the terrible stitch in her side, but once she was over the brow of the hill, she ran like the wind down the other side, scattering sheep in all directions. Her feet went twinkling over the turf. She ran as though she would never stop.

* * * * *

In the old walled garden at Cobbs, Betony was working with her mother, putting in sticks to support the peas.

"We've got company," Beth remarked, and Betony, following her mother's glance, saw the child at the garden gate. "Is it the gipsies as usual?"

"No, it's Emma Wayman from Holland Farm."

"What's she doing, flitting about?"

"I think she's probably looking for me."

The moment Betony opened the gate, Emma turned as though she would flee, but Betony caught her by the arm and drew her inside. The child's dark brown hair, usually so neat, was utterly wild and had lost its ribbon; her dress and pinafore were torn, her face and hands were covered in scratches, and she was muddy from head to foot.

"Whatever's happened to you, my child?"

"Nothing! Nothing!" Emma said. Then, suddenly, she was in tears. Her face was pressed against Betony's apron. "I don't like it at home any more! Can I come and live with you?"

"Poor little girl," Betony murmured. Her hand was on the child's hot head. "Let's go indoors, anyway, and do something about those cuts."

Her mother spoke from across the garden.

"Do you want me to come and help?"

"No, there's no need," Betony said.

Talking cheerfully all the time, she led the child into the kitchen and sat her in a chair under the window. She fetched warm water, iodine, lint, and bathed the bleeding cuts and scratches.

"How do you come to be in this mess?"

"I don't know," Emma said. She squinted down at herself in surprise and tried to brush the mud from her pinafore. "I ran and ran, right down the hill. I couldn't stop and I fell in the mud."

"Why were you running down the hill?"

"I wanted to run away from home."

"Did something happen to you there?"

"Yes, it was horrible," Emma said.

"Won't you tell me what it was?"

"The cow was after me," Emma said.

Betony, smiling, turned away. She busied herself with the iodine.

"Well, it's always as well to keep out of their way, especially if they happen to have calves."

"She didn't have a calf, she was dead," Emma said. "She was all black and slimy and she smelt bad."

"Oh! That *is* horrible!" Betony said. She folded the lint and put it away. "But dead cows don't chase you over the hill."

"I thought she was going to," Emma said.

Soon, with her face and hands washed clean, and her hair put to rights, brushed and combed, she appeared less of a wild wan waif, and Betony, looking into her eyes, saw there was no real terror there. Indeed, Emma sitting by the fire, enjoying biscuits and warm milk, while her muddy boots dried in the hearth, looked on the whole well-pleased with herself, as Beth, coming in from the garden, remarked.

"No bones broken nor nothing like that?"

"Cuts and scratches, mostly, that's all, and a bit of a fright."

"And rather enjoying it, I should say."

"Yes, perhaps," Betony said.

Emma's only tragedy, now, was the state of her clothes. Whenever she glanced down at them and saw the terrible muddy stains, she wrinkled her nose in disgust.

"I need a clean frock and pinafore."

"I can't help you there, I'm afraid. There's nothing in the house small enough."

"Aunt Doe will see to it, when I get home."

"I'll walk back with you," Betony said. "They will be wondering where you've got to."

"Oh, *they* never worry," Emma said.

* * * * *

But the child had been missed for an hour or more, and Stephen was out looking for her. He came across the turnip field as Betony and Emma walked into the yard. He spoke to the child with severity.

"Where have you been, all this time? You promised aunt Doe you'd stay within call." And, to Betony, he said: "Where did you find the wretched child?"

"It was one of those days for running away from home, apparently and Emma got as far as Cobbs."

"It might be one of those days when somebody got a smacked bottom," he said. "It seems to me it's what they deserve."

Emma was quite unmoved by this threat. She showed him

182

the mud and dirt on her clothes.

"I need clean *everything!*" she said.

"Yes, I can see you do, my girl. You'd better go in to your aunt Doe and say you're sorry for causing her so much anxiety."

The child went skipping into the house. Never once did she glance back at them. She was intent on the need for clean clothes. Stephen looked at Betony.

"It seems my children are determined to be a nuisance to you. You'll be sick of us Waymans before long. What's all this about running away from home?"

"It was mostly to do with seeing a dead cow, I believe."

"Damn and blast!" Stephen said. "All the farm to play about in and that child has to choose the bottom yard. I thought the carcass was safe enough there."

"Surely it would have been safer still if it had been buried?" Betony said.

"I can see what you must think of us, Miss Izzard, and of course you're quite right. The cow died two days ago but what with our landwork being behind – "

"And a shortage of labour perhaps?"

"Shortage? No. I wouldn't say that."

"I heard you'd got rid of one of your men."

"Ah. Yes, I see. That was Morton George." Looking at her, he considered her. He knew her well enough by now to guess what was passing in her mind. "I suppose you've heard gossip of some kind. Victimization. Is that it?"

"George was a member of the union, I understand."

"That's not the reason he was dismissed."

"He thought it was," Betony said.

"Did you know him?" Stephen asked.

"Only slightly, I must admit, but one of his boys was in my class."

"Do you know what kind of man he is?"

"Surely no man, whatever his shortcomings, deserves dismissal at such times as these?"

"The times are bad for all of us, not just for those like Morton George."

"You can't deny it's worse for them?"

"That dead cow," Stephen said. "It was Morton George

183

who did that. He poisoned her by giving her yew."

There was a pause. She frowned at him.

"Have you any proof of that?"

"Enough to satisfy myself. I don't have to satisfy anyone else."

He could see from her face what impression his words had made on her. She thought him high-handed, that much was plain.

"Have you got a few minutes to spare?"

"What for?" Betony asked.

"I'd like to show you something," he said.

He took her to Morton George's empty cottage and showed her the damage that had been done there. He showed her the fruit trees and lilacs cut down, lying on the grass in the back garden.

"I know it's no proof that he poisoned my cow, but it's proof of the kind of man he is. And there's the yew by the gable there. The cow couldn't get at it by herself."

"I would never have thought," Betony said, "that a man could stoop to such spitefulness."

"The cottage will take some time to put right. I've been meaning to come along to your place, to ask if your father will do the repairs. I shan't take another man on just yet, but when I do he will want the cottage."

"My father will see to it certainly. I'll ask him to come and call on you." Betony, turning, met Stephen's gaze. "I'd like to apologize," she said. "I was speaking in ignorance, defending Morton George as I did."

"You are a champion of the unemployed, Miss Izzard, and it means the employers get all your blows. But not every farmer is a despot, you know, and I'd like to think I'd convinced you of that."

He looked at her and she smiled at him. Her hair in the sunlight was smooth and bright; her eyes reflected the spring-blue sky. He found he enjoyed looking at her. There was serenity in her face. He stood with his hands in his jacket pockets and watched her move away from him, walking about the overgrown garden, among the fallen apple trees.

"It may seem unfair, bringing you here to see all this,

when George is not here to defend himself, but – I happen to mind what people think of me."

"Will you try and prosecute him?"

"I doubt if he could ever be found. He'll take good care to cover his tracks. And he certainly won't be writing to ask me for a reference!"

Together they walked across the pasture and out through the gate into the lane. In the ten acre field on the other side, Tupper and Hopson were drilling oats, and Tupper's quiet voice could be heard as he spoke to his team. The air was full of the scent of spring.

"Will you come to the house for a cup of coffee?"

"No, thank you," Betony said. "I've got a jumble sale after lunch. It's high time I was getting home."

"Then you'd better take the right of way. It'll save you half a mile from here. I'll come with you as far as Blake's Wood."

* * * * *

The right of way lay across part of Challoner's land, crossing two pastures and skirting a coppice. Betony had not been there since childhood.

"I thought Mr Challoner had closed this path."

"He's tried to close it a couple of times. He doesn't like people crossing his fields. But the parish council directed him to take his barbed wire down."

John Challoner, however, determined to discourage "trespassers", had allowed his hedges to overgrow the stiles, and Stephen, with a stick, had to beat aside the brambles and briars before he and Betony could climb over. Even so, a sharp briar caught her face and a spot of bright blood squeezed from the scratch, like a glistening red jewel on her cheek. Stephen watched her brush it away.

"I'm sorry about this," he said. "It wasn't such a good idea after all, taking the short cut, was it? I must speak to my neighbour about his thorns. If he doesn't cut them back, the parish council will do it for him, and he won't like *them* trampling over his land."

Betony laughed.

185

"It must be useful, having practised the law. Do you ever miss it at all?"

"No, not really. I always wanted to farm. I went in for the law to please my father."

The second field they had to cross was steeply humped in the middle. Once they were over the top of the hump, they were walking beside a fenced coppice, which ran down to the foot of the slope and filled the whole of the hollow below. There were horses in this field: Challoner's hunters, his pride and joy; and as Stephen and Betony walked down the path skirting the coppice, two of these horses, a black and a roan, came thundering down the slope behind them.

Stephen knew the black horse: he had a bad name for tormenting his fellows; and today his victim was the roan. Both horses were highly excited, the black with devilment, the roan with fear, and they came careering down the slope, ears back and eyes rolling and the breath coming in visible spirts out of their widely dilated nostrils.

Stephen and Betony turned to face them. Caught as they were in the angle formed by the fenced-off coppice, they had no room to step aside. The horses bore down on them at a gallop, sweat and foam splattering off them and bits of turf flying up from their heels. Betony stood, paralysed, sure that she and the man beside her were going to be trampled under the hooves. But Stephen stepped forward a pace or two and spread his arms in front of the horses. He spoke to them in a loud voice.

"Whoa, there! Steady, now! Get over, you brutes! Whoa! Whoa!"

His last words were lost in the thundering of hooves. Then, a miracle, the horses were past, veering away at the last instant. They passed so close in their headlong career that as Stephen stepped back a pace, one flying hoof snicked the shin of his boot, and the roan's tail caught him full in the face. Drawing breath, he watched them go. They gradually slowed as they circled back up the slope again and in a moment they had stopped, leaning over the fence of the coppice to pull at the leaves on the hazel trees. The roan kept a watchful eye on the black but otherwise, as they browsed together, they looked the picture of peacefulness.

"Whew! That was close!" Stephen said. He wiped away the dirt that had spattered his face and turned towards Betony. "Are you all right?"

"Yes, I'm all right. Or I *think* I am!" She gave a little tremulous laugh. Her voice was not quite under control. "But I really thought . . . just for an instant . . . that we were both going to be killed."

"No thanks to Challoner that we're not!" Stephen said angrily. "He's no right to keep such mischievous brutes on this public right of way. I must certainly see him and warn him about it." Pausing, he looked more closely at her. "Are you sure you're all right?" He put out a hand and touched her arm.

"Except that my bones seem to have melted, yes, thanks, I'm fine," Betony said.

Her voice was perfectly steady now, and she gave another self-mocking laugh. She had passed from a moment when violent death seemed inevitable to a moment when she was immortal again. But only the pallor in her face showed what that moment had done to her. Otherwise she was herself. Her eyes were steady, calm, amused. Stephen admired her self-control.

He opened the gate and they passed through it into the wood. There were primroses growing under the trees, and the pathway was starred with celandines. The wood smelt of moss and new green growth, and the sunlight, finding its way through the scrub oak and ash and the hazel boughs, lit the greenness on the ground.

"This business of Emma running away from home . . ."

"I don't think it's very serious."

"Not another example of my neglect?"

"I retracted that charge, if you remember."

"I'm not sure that it wasn't deserved. The child does wander about a lot. I must keep a closer watch on her."

"Remembering my own childhood, I know how difficult that can be. I was always running away from home. I never got any further than Emma did today, but it must have been very worrying for my parents, all the same."

They glanced at each other, silent a while, and the sunlight, shining through the straight ash poles, flickered on their faces as they walked. They came out at the end of the wood and leant together over the gate, looking down on the straggling village.

"You're no longer given to running away from home, Miss Izzard? You seem pretty settled nowadays."

"Too much so," Betony said. "I've hardly been away from home since the war ended. I've been at the school for four years."

"Is that such a bad thing?"

"Sometimes I feel perhaps it's wrong to be settled so comfortably into one's rut."

"I hope you're not a puritan, Miss Izzard, courting discomfort for the good of your soul."

"You make it sound reprehensible."

"I don't see why life should not be enjoyed."

He opened the gate and she passed through. He closed it again, remaining inside. This was as far as he meant to go.

"I'll call at Outlands on my way back and see Challoner about those horses. I'll make it quite clear that they gave us a fright. Thank you for bringing Emma back. It was kind of you to take so much trouble."

"I enjoyed the walk," Betony said.

He watched her until she had gone from sight.

* * * * *

In the schoolroom, when Betony arrived after lunch, the stalls had already been set up and money was already changing hands. Her sister Janie, selling produce from her own dairy, was doing the briskest trade of all.

"Thank goodness you've come! I really can't manage both stalls at once. You're nearly twenty minutes late."

Betony had a rummage stall. Everything on it was priced at twopence. The coppers rattled into the tin, and she was kept busy until four o'clock. The afternoon's sale raised four pounds seventeen shillings and sixpence.

"Ah, well, every little helps!" said one of the stall-holders cheerfully. "We shall have our parish hall by the time I'm eighty!"

Afterwards tea was served from a big copper urn. Betony

and Janie sat together, drinking out of enamelled mugs. Janie looked at Betony's hair.

"Isn't it time you had it cut?"

"Whatever for?" Betony said.

"Nobody wears it long these days."

"Oh, yes, they do," Betony said, looking around her at the other women in the room. "I can see five or six at least."

"So old-fashioned you are still!"

"Am I? Yes, perhaps I am." Betony, although the elder of the two, was used to Janie's criticisms. She listened to them and laughed them off. "I certainly can't compete with you."

Betony was not much interested in fashion. She took trouble with her clothes, but once they were on she forgot about them. As for her thick straight flaxen hair: her mother had coiled it into a bun for her on the day she had left school, and she had worn it like that ever since.

"That was ages ago," Janie said. "Aren't you ever going to change it?"

Janie herself was passionately interested in fashion. "I may be a farmer's wife but I don't have to look like one!" she would say. "Besides, Martin likes me to look nice." Janie had been married for ten years. She felt sorry for Betony.

"It's high time you found yourself a husband. *He'd* soon make you mend your ways."

"Would he indeed!" Betony said.

"Haven't you ever thought of it?"

"Not in so many words, no. Not since breaking with Michael, that is."

"Then it's high time you did!"

"I'm perfectly happy as I am."

"You certainly look it, I must admit."

It was something Janie could not understand. Her husband and children were everything to her. To be twenty-eight, as Betony was, and not yet married! – How could she bear such a wasted life?

"Mother once said to dad that you'd find it difficult to give yourself heart and soul to a man."

"How do you know she said such a thing?"

"Because dad mentioned it to me, that's how." Janie drank the last of her tea. "I've often wondered if it's true."

189

"I don't know. I haven't thought." Whether it was true or not, Betony was reluctant to discuss it with her sister, close in affection though they were. "Mother says a lot of things."

"Surely you *want* to get married some time? You'll leave it too late if you don't watch out."

"When you've found someone suitable, I promise to give it my consideration."

"I wish you'd be serious once in a while."

"I'm getting myself another cup of tea. Shall I get you one as well?"

Janie, with a look that admitted defeat, handed Betony her empty mug.

* * * * *

The school reopened on April the twenty-fifth. The weather had turned bad again, and every morning the two rooms were filled with the smell of wet boots and overcoats drying around the two stoves. The sky was so dark that the lamps were kept burning all through the day. It was just like wintertime. Emma, coming down the lane through the rainy darkness, liked to see the lights shining out from the schoolroom windows, and would run the last two hundred yards, drawn by the brightness and bustle within.

"No one is to sit down in their places until they have shed their wet boots or shoes," Miss Vernon would say every morning, and there was always much jostling and noise before her order had been obeyed.

"Whew! What a smell!" said Florrie Ricks, holding her nose between finger and thumb, and the other children all did the same.

But Emma, although she held her nose with the rest, rather enjoyed the smell of hot wet wool and mackintosh and leather drying by the stove. She liked the bustle and noise of the wet mornings; the flickering of the lamps and the smell of the oil; the red glow of coals in the iron stove and the mugs of cocoa, steaming hot, handed out by Miss Vernon.

It was difficult for the children to settle down after these preliminaries. They were restless; excited; full of naughty

190

glee. Three little boys, in the dinner-hour, hid Miss Vernon's pinafore behind the stove-pipe, where she discovered it, black with soot. They were sent to Miss Izzard, who kept them in for ten minutes of their playtime, sitting with their hands on their heads.

The next day, Miss Vernon's galoshes were filled with mud, and the two culprits, Emma Wayman and Winnie Aston, received the same punishment. And, on yet another day, in the middle of a scripture lesson, Emma leant across to Betty Trennam and yanked her hair-ribbon undone. Miss Vernon witnessed this incident, and Emma spent the afternoon break sitting under Miss Izzard's eye, writing out twenty times. "I must behave better in class." The following morning, Emma threw a lump of plasticine at Festubert Wilkes, and was sent to Miss Izzard yet again.

Betony looked at the dark-eyed child standing before her and wondered at this burst of naughtiness.

"Well, Emma? You're always in trouble nowadays. Why is that?"

"I don't know," Emma said. She stared at the watch on Betony's bosom.

"This is the third time you've been sent to me in a week. Aren't you ashamed?"

Emma dutifully hung her head.

"Well, run along, then!" Betony said. "Go back to Miss Vernon and be a good girl."

Emma's head came up at once.

"Aren't you going to keep me in?"

"No, not today. It's stopped raining for once in a while and you will be better taking your playtime out of doors."

Emma went off, out to the playground, and stood with her feet in a dirty puddle. Nobody came to scold her for it. After a while she moved away.

* * * * *

May was almost as wet as April. Landwork was halted everywhere. Rootseed rotted in the waterlogged ground and young cabbages, yellow-leaved, were washed out into the furrows, which ran like rillets continuously. The

191

derrent brook broke its banks again and many people's homes were flooded; part of the road at Slings Dip had been washed away; and, at the little village school, fires were still being lit in the mornings, six weeks after they had usually stopped.

On May the twenty-sixth, the school celebrated Empire Day, and the morning began without rain. In Miss Vernon's room, after prayers, each child in Standard I was given a sheet of paper and told to paint a union jack, copying the flag draped over the blackboard.

"Don't try to hurry. There's plenty of time. Be sure to let each colour dry before commencing with another."

In spite of the warning, Emma's colours ran together, and the more she tried to put matters right, the worse mess she made on her paper. The smaller children were using crayons. Even their work was better than hers. She hid her flag inside her desk.

Miss Vernon stood before the class.

"Is your paint dry, Standard I? Then take the two pins I've given you and pin your union jacks to your chests. When you've all done that, you can help the little ones with theirs."

The children became extremely busy; all except Emma, who sat quite still.

"What's the matter?" Miss Vernon asked, coming and standing beside the desk. "Why aren't you wearing your union jack?"

"It's gone all runny," Emma said.

"And whose fault is that, if I might ask?"

"It's her own silly fault," said Florrie Ricks.

"Show it to me, Emma, please."

Emma took her painting from the desk and laid it on top. She could not bear to see it. She looked away.

"Stand up, Emma. I'll pin it on."

Emma stood up, her face hot and red. Miss Vernon pinned the flag to her chest. The other children were looking at her.

"There! It's not so bad as all that. Now get into line, everyone, and march out of the school in an orderly fashion."

192

But Emma, looking down at her union jack, knew it was very bad indeed, and as she marched out in her line, she removed the odious thing from her chest and tore it into pieces. She dropped them into the wastepaper basket as she passed.

Miss Vernon was cross. Emma was taken before the head and asked to give an account of herself, while the rest of the school marked time in the playground, under a sky that threatened rain.

"Why did you tear up your union jack?"

"It had gone all runny," Emma said. "It's a silly idea, anyway. Who wants to wear a union jack?"

The upper standards were wearing rosettes. They were beautiful, Emma thought.

"Well, get into line," Betony said, "and when we all get to the green, I shall expect to hear you singing all the more heartily, to make up for not wearing your red white and blue."

Thus the school, as always on Empire Day, marched out to the green and assembled there. They heard the vicar's brief address and sang "O God, our help in ages past." They then saluted the union jack, hanging bedraggled on its pole, and marched back into school again, just in time to escape the rain.

Afterwards, when the children had all gone home, Sue Vernon discussed Emma's behaviour with Betony.

"All this naughtiness!" she said. "It's only to gain attention, you know. *Your* attention, to be precise. It will be better in future, I think, if I deal with her bad behaviour myself instead of sending her to you."

Betony, however, disagreed.

"I think it's time she came into my class. She's forward enough for Standard II. She'd be moving up anyway next term."

"But that's exactly what she wants. It's most unwise to give in to her."

"Sometimes children are much improved by getting what they want," Betony said.

"Well, it's your decision, of course," Sue said. "You are the head."

Privately, she thought her own thoughts. Was Miss Izzard a bit of a snob, favouring this gentleman farmer's daughter? Or were her motives more personal? She seemed on good terms with Stephen Wayman. Perhaps there was something brewing there.

The following morning, when school began, Emma had a place in the big room, with the four boys and seven girls of Standard II. She shared a desk with Hilary Slewton. Hilary helped her to do her sums.

At home, when Emma announced her news, the family made a great fuss of her.

"Why have you been moved up? Is it because you're a good scholar?"

"No, it's because I was naughty," Emma said.

Joanna and the boys laughed at her.

"It must be a jolly funny school!"

"Trust our Emma to be the opposite of everyone else!"

"Our little Emma naughty?" said Chris. "I don't believe a word of it!"

"I *was* naughty," Emma said. "I did all sorts of naughty things."

"Then I'm sorry to hear it," Stephen said. He frowned at this youngest child of his. "I shall have to speak to Miss Izzard about you."

But, meeting Betony soon afterwards, he heard that Emma was now a model pupil.

"She gives me no trouble," Betony said.

* * * * *

Although promoted to the big room, Emma did not forget Robert Mercybright, left behind in the infants' class. Sometimes she sought him out in the playground and gave him a sweet or a piece of chocolate or half the banana she had brought for her elevenses. One day, as they sat together on the toolshed step, she gave him a share of the small blue-black berries she had taken from a bush in the garden at home. Robert, on chewing them, made a face. He gave a shudder and spat them out.

"Aren't they nice?" Emma said. She tried one herself and

found it bitter. It made a roughness on her tongue. She too spat it out. "Oh, they're nasty, horrid things! Here, have a peppermint instead, and that'll take away the taste."

That afternoon Robert was sick. His mother was sent for, from Mrs Frail's, and came at once to take him home. By then his lips were swollen inside, and he complained that his tongue was sore.

"What have you been eating?" Linn demanded.

Robert was silent, looking at her. His face was pale and miserable.

"Did you eat anything?" Betony asked. She knew that Emma gave him sweets. "Don't be afraid to tell us, Rob."

They were standing together in the school porch. The boy was reluctant to answer them, but the story of the berries came out at last, and Betony went to fetch Emma.

"What sort of berries were they that you gave Robert to eat?"

"They came off a jumper bush," Emma said.

"Jumper bush? What is that?"

"It's just a bush in the garden at home. I picked them on the way to school."

"What did they look like?" Betony asked.

Emma put her hand into her pinafore pocket and took out the berries remaining there. She dropped them into Betony's palm.

"Juniper berries! Thank goodness for that!" Betony showed them in her palm to Linn. "You've nothing to worry about," she said. "They're perfectly harmless. Just bitter, that's all."

"How can you be so sure of that?"

"For one thing, they're used in flavouring gin. For another, I've chewed them up myself – long ago, when I was a child. They taste nasty but they do no harm."

"I wouldn't say they were harmless, myself. Look at the state of Robert's mouth. *And* you say he was sick as well." Linn, in her anxiety for her son, rounded angrily on Emma. "How dare you make him eat things like that? You're a very wicked, naughty girl!" She disliked the child's remote, calm gaze. She wanted to see some fear in her; some awareness of her own wrongdoing. "His lips are all swollen and sore

195

inside. You should be ashamed, a girl of your age, forcing a little boy like Robert to eat bad things that make him ill."

"*I* wasn't sick," Emma said. "*My* lips aren't swollen inside."

"Perhaps if they were," Linn replied, "you might be a bit more sorry, child!"

Emma looked at the little boy, leaning against his mother's side. Then she looked up at Betony.

"Is he going to die?" she asked.

"No, of course not," Betony said. "Juniper berries aren't poisonous. You've just heard me say they're not. But I want you to promise me, faithfully, that you won't ever eat strange berries again or give them to other children, either."

"We didn't eat them. We spat them out."

"Will you promise me, anyway?"

"Yes, I promise," Emma said.

Betony sent her back to the classroom.

"She doesn't care twopence, does she?" Linn said. "Doesn't she realize the harm she could have done?"

"She's only a child," Betony said.

Linn was now preparing to leave. She laid a hand on Robert's forehead.

"I shall take him to the doctor before I go home. I'd sooner be on the safe side. I don't like the look of his mouth at all."

"Yes, I should do that," Betony said. "It will set your mind at rest. But I'm sure there's nothing to worry about. He's beginning to look better already."

She was sufficiently anxious, however, to walk over to Lilac Cottage that evening and find out how the little boy was. She found him in the garden, watching his grandfather Mercybright, who was up on a ladder, repairing the roof. The soreness and swelling had gone from his mouth; he had eaten his tea without being sick; and there was some colour in his cheeks. The doctor had said there was no reason for concern.

"Well, Robert!" Betony said. "I'm glad to see you're yourself again."

"Linn fusses too much," Jack Mercybright said. "She wraps the boy in cotton wool. If he comes to no worse harm than that, he'll be a lot more lucky than most."

Linn herself appeared in the doorway.

"Will you come in for a cup of tea?"

"No, thank you, I'll be on my way."

But Betony paused long enough to gaze up at the sunken roof, where four or five of the tiles were missing, leaving a gap some two feet wide. Jack was inserting a piece of tin, edging it under the upper tiles, spreading it over the lower ones. Elsewhere the roof was similarly patched.

"Won't Mr Challoner do those repairs?"

"I've been asking him since the year dot."

"At least he could let you have some tiles."

"The laths is gone under this tin. The whole roof's as daddocky as a sponge. We shall have it in on us one of these days. Challoner's got no money to spare for roofs. It goes on his hunters and his motor cars and paying his tailor to make him look thin."

"Yes, I know," Betony said.

And she walked away from the damp, dilapidated cottage, angry at the truth of what Jack said.

Next she went to Holland Farm. Aunt Doe answered the door and Betony told her about the berries.

"I thought I ought to warn you," she said, "in case Emma suffers some ill-effects."

"Silly child! She ought to know better!" aunt Doe said. "She certainly hasn't been sick so far. Is the little boy all right?"

"Right as rain now," Betony said.

"It's very kind of you to come. Emma's gone with her brothers up to the woods. Will you come in for a little while?"

"No, thank you, I'm on my way home."

"Stephen's over in the barn there. He's doctoring a sick cow. Won't you wait while I fetch him in?"

"No, please, don't call him away. I really must be getting home."

On her way back across the yard, she heard a rustling in the straw in the barn, and the quick loud snorting of a cow in distress. She heard Stephen's voice as he spoke to it; soothing it; calming it down. For a moment she paused,

197

listening to him, thinking that perhaps she would look in on him after all. Then some strange shyness came over her. She had second thoughts and went on her way.

Chapter 11

That summer was the wettest for thirty-six years. In Chepsworth, in June, the three rivers overflowed and the town was flooded. Swans swam down the High Street and people went to and fro in punts. Many roads were badly damaged, and part of the railway embankment collapsed. The agricultural show had to be cancelled, for the first time in its history. On every farm throughout the district there was deep gloom. Haymaking was held back for weeks on end. Corn crops were beaten down and lodged.

"You were a lot wiser than me, cutting back on your corn crops so hard as you did," John Challoner said to Stephen. "The wet won't harm you the way it will me. I shall damn well go bankrupt if this goes on. I'll be coming to ask you for a loan!"

This was his refrain all through the summer. Stephen grew somewhat irritated. Once he said something sharp in reply.

"You could always send your new billiard table back!"

"Ah, you think that's extravagant, I suppose? But damn it, man, you wouldn't deny me a bit of fun?"

Stephen said nothing more. It was none of his business, obviously. But Challoner, spending up to the hilt, was a worried man, and he took it out on his labourers. The bad weather made loafers of them. Why should he pay them a full wage just to watch the rain from inside his barn?

"They've got to live, whether it rains or not," Stephen said.

"So have I!" Challoner said.

He reduced his men's wages yet again. He paid them twenty-four-and-six. In this he was ignoring the recommendations of the local Conciliation Committee, but he knew they had no power as a body. He scarcely gave them a passing thought.

"Another flaming cut in our pay?" said Bill Mayle, when pay-day came.

There was a seething among the men. They crowded close against Challoner's desk.

"You ent playing fair with us, master. It ent our fault the weather's bad."

"Twenty-four-and-six! Hell! How'm I going to feed six kids?"

"It ent even enough to starve on, by God!"

"I've got a sick wife at home. It'll just about kill her when she hears about this!"

"If you cut our wages much more, Mr Challoner, you'll soon be paying us in threepenny bits!"

There was a double barb in this, for Challoner carried a collection of silver threepenny pieces in his waistcoat pocket, and would dole them out, when the mood took him, to any children he happened to meet. He made himself popular in this way. There was always someone to speak well of him.

"That's enough of your lip, Cox!" he said. "If you don't like it, you know what to do. There's plenty of men only too willing to step into your shoes for that wage."

"How are we supposed to live?"

"You'll have to cut down a bit, that's all."

"Ah, we'll have to cut down on the luxuries, such as food and drink!" said Jack Mercybright, witheringly.

"That'll be the day!" Challoner said. "*You're* no stranger to a pint pot!"

"I'm a stranger to a decent living wage."

Later that day, when Jack left work, five of his mates were at the farm gate, waiting to have a word with him. Two of these were union men. They were keen for Jack to join.

"I'm reporting this cut in our wages," said Cox. "I'm going along this afternoon to see Harry Davids straight away."

"What good'll that do?" Jack asked.

"If the union was stronger, we'd soon get things done. There's talk of the Wages Board coming back. We shall press for that at the next meeting. Why don't you join us?

We need your sort."

Jack merely shrugged his way through the group.

"I prefer to fight my own battles."

"Ah, fight 'em and lose 'em!" Cox retorted scornfully.

Jack took no notice, but walked on. His bad knee, injured more than forty years before, gave him pain when the weather was wet. His only thought was to get home.

Linn, when she put his supper in front of him, saw at once that something was wrong.

"Another Irishman's rise this week!" He planked his money down on the table. "The way things are going with Challoner, I reckon *we'll* soon be paying *him* for the privilege of slaving on his land!"

Linn sat down wearily. She had her own story to tell, for her work at Tinkerdine, skivvying for Mrs Frail, would come to an end in another week. Mrs Frail had been displeased because Linn had left at two o'clock on the day Robert had eaten the berries. Now that a replacement had been found, Linn had been told that she could go. But the bad news would keep until after supper. Her father, she saw, was in pain with his leg. She leant across to her little son and dropped a knob of margarine into the centre of his mashed potatoes.

The day was already growing dark. It was raining heavily again. Overhead, in the room above, there was a rapid thud, thud, thud, as the rain dripped through the cottage roof, into the bucket placed to receive it.

* * * * *

When, a few weeks later, the Wages Board was reinstated and the minimum wage for a farm labourer was set by law at thirty shillings, Challoner promptly sacked two men. For him the issue was simple enough. "I can't afford you at that wage." His choice of two men was also simple: he sacked those two who belonged to the union, Fred Cox and Johnny Marsh.

Betony, shopping at Jeremy Rye's, met Fred Cox coming away, and they stood talking for a while. Fred was in a bitter mood. It was the day he had been dismissed.

"Funny it's always us union chaps. It was the same at Holland Farm, with the chap that was sacked at Easter time. The only union man on the farm and *he* was the one that got the push. You don't mean to tell me it's just by chance!"

"That wasn't the same," Betony said. "Morton George was a bad lot. He was an idler and a mischief-maker. Mr Wayman had no choice but to dismiss him."

"That's what all the farmers say. No doubt Challoner says it of me! Am I an idler, I'd like to know?" Cox's wrath and bitterness brought a hint of tears to his eyes. "It ent only me. It's Kitty as well." His wife cooked and cleaned for Challoner. – She also was losing her job. "And of course we've got to quit our cottage. We've got a week to find some place else. Jesus, what a bloody life! No job! No home! No bloody dole! Is this what I fought in Gallipoli for?"

"Can't the union do anything?"

"What can they do? They can't make jobs!" Cox took out a newspaper, some days old, and showed it to her, open at an advertisement in bold black type: "There is NO unemployment in Canada. Men and women are wanted here."

"Are you thinking of going?" Betony asked.

"When I got home, after the war, I swore I'd never leave England again. But what is England doing for us? It's treating us as if we was dirt. It can't be no worse in Canada."

"What about Billy John?"

Fred's eldest son, as expected, had won his free place at the Grammar school and was due to take it up in September.

"Where's the sense of his going to a good school if his dad's a pauper begging his bread?" Fred took the paper and pocketed it. "I wonder, if I was to apply to emigrate, whether you'd write me a character?"

"Yes, of course," Betony said. "If it's what you really want."

But it made her sad to think of men like Fred Cox being driven from their own country to seek a living elsewhere.

* * * * *

In a field of oats lying behind Jack Mercybright's cottage, he

202

and the other Outlands men were at work with their scythes, for the corn had been badly lodged by the rain and could not be cut by the reaper-and-binder. Challoner came down to see how the work was going on. He picked up a musty sheaf here and there and threw them from him in disgust.

"Not even fit for the pigs!" he said. "I shall soon be bankrupt at this rate!" He stood beside Jack and watched him at work. "Your leg playing you up?"

"Not so's you'd notice," Jack said.

"How old are you now, Mercybright?"

"Why do you want to know?" Jack asked.

"Strikes me you'll soon be putting in for your pension."

"Well, I ent the only one, come to that."

Challoner glanced at him narrowly, but Jack seemed intent upon his work, and his bearded face gave nothing away. The weather was humid; close and warm; Jack sweated as he worked with his scythe, and the sweat ran down into his beard. The other men worked some way away; they were keeping clear of Challoner.

Linn came out of the back of the cottage, carrying a mug of beer for her father. She faltered when she saw Challoner there, but then she came on, through a gap in the hedge, and so up the field to where Jack stood. Robert followed close behind, dragging a horseshoe on a piece of string. Jack took the beer and drank it half down. He wiped his mouth with the back of his hand.

"Good morning, Mr Challoner," Linn said.

John Challoner gave her a nod.

"You got a holiday from your work?"

"I don't go to Mrs Frail any more."

"Can't say I blame you," he said. "A bit of a Tartar, from what I've heard."

Jack finished his beer and she took his mug. Challoner watched her as she walked down the field. The dress she wore was too big for her; it hung in ugly folds round her hips. Her shoes were badly trodden down and a piece of brown paper, lining one sole, had worked its way up at the back of her heel. Challoner noted all these things. He also noted her shapeliness; the set of her head on her smooth slim neck; the roundness and whiteness of her arms; a certain something in the way she walked. If she had money to spend on clothes. . . . He pictured the stir the girl would cause, arriving, perhaps, at the Hunt Ball. It was a pity she had red hair, and yet it was striking in its way; and he wondered, not for the first time, how Jack Mercybright, a common labourer, had come to produce such a beautiful daughter.

The following morning, when Jack arrived at the farm for work, Challoner met him in the yard.

"I need a woman to come in and cook and clean for me now that Kitty Cox is going. What about that daughter of yours? Would she be willing to come in?"

"You'd better ask her," Jack said.

"Can't you ask her when you get home? It's not too much trouble for you, is it?"

"All right, I'll ask her," Jack said, "but I dunno that she'll want to come."

He was against the idea from the start. He made that plain when he spoke to Linn.

"But why shouldn't I take the job? It would be so convenient, being close at hand."

"You'll have no peace if you go to that house. He's got a bit of a name, you know, and I've seen the way he looks at you."

"Oh, what nonsense!" Linn exclaimed. "Mr Challoner's always treated me very politely. You do exaggerate sometimes."

"You know the man better than I do, no doubt!"

"You want me to turn down a pound a week when we are as hard up as we are nowadays?"

"Whose fault is it that we're hard up? It's Challoner's fault and don't you forget it!"

"We need that money," Linn said.

"We can manage without it if we try. At least I'm back to thirty bob."

"No, father, I'm taking the job."

"All right. You suit yourself. But you'll have trouble with that man as sure as God's in Gloucestershire, and then you'll wish you'd listened to me."

Jack's tone was so earnest that Linn for a while experienced some fear. But later that evening, mending her small son's shabby clothes, she thought of the things she needed to buy, and the fear receded to the back of her mind. She went to the farmhouse on Sunday morning and told Mr Challoner she wanted the job.

"There is just one thing, however," she said. "I shall have to bring my little boy."

"Isn't there someone you could leave him with?"

"I'd sooner have him with me, Mr Challoner, at least until he goes back to school."

"My house is not a nursery, you know," Challoner said, in his jocular way. "I'll be paying you to cook and clean for my son and me, not to be coddling that boy of yours."

"The work will be done, I promise you, and I'll see that Robert gives no trouble."

"Very well. You bring him along. We'll fit in together, I daresay."

It was agreed. Challoner shook hands with her and saw her to the door. Linn looked at his good-humoured face and was sure that her father must be mistaken.

"I wonder if I might ask you something, Mr Challoner?"

"Ask away! I'm all ears!"

"It's the roof of our cottage," Linn said. "I know you're a very busy man, but it is in rather a bad condition, and what with the weather we're having now – "

"Leaking, is it? Well, that won't do. I'll get a man to come along and see what wants doing as soon as possible."

"Oh, if you could! I'd be ever so grateful, I really would."

Linn felt rather pleased with herself. She went home to her father and repeated Mr Challoner's promise

"'As soon as possible'?" Jack said. "And when is that, I'd like to know? The roof's been leaking for nearly three years. I've asked him and asked him a hundred times but it ent made no difference that I can see."

"Perhaps you went the wrong way about it. You can be very surly sometimes."

"And *you* went the right way, I suppose?" Jack raised his newspaper and shut her out. His anger rose with the smoke from his pipe. After a while he spoke again. "Is it all fixed up, then, that you're going there to molly for him?"

"Yes, father, it's all arranged. I start tomorrow at seven o'clock."

Thus Linn went to work at Outlands Farm, and Robert went with her every day. She thought her father's fears were groundless, but if by any chance he was right, Robert would be her best protection.

"So this is young Master Mercybright?" Challoner said, on the first morning. "He's a solemn little chap, isn't he? And dark as dark! I can't see that he's much like you, so I take it he favours his father, eh?"

Challoner knew, as everyone in Huntlip did, that Linn had not been married to Robert's father. She glanced at him, suspecting some slyness in the remark, but he was still looking at the little boy, and was pressing a coin into his hand.

"Robert's father is dead," she said.

"I know that," Challoner said. "Chap called Tom Maddox, wasn't it? A carpenter down at old man Tewke's? But *does* the boy take after him?"

"Yes, there's a likeness," Linn said. She was shedding her mackintosh. "Where would you like me to start work?"

* * * * *

Within a week, Linn knew she had made a mistake. Challoner was in and out of the house all day. He hung about while she cooked the meals. Sometimes he came and stood by her, looking over her shoulder, into the pans, as she stirred a thickening into the stew or prodded the potatoes to see if they were done. He would lean against her, thigh to thigh, his body pressing hard against hers. He would take the wooden spoon from her, and would taste the broth, looking at her through the rising steam.

"A bit more salt!" he would say to her, and when she was putting the salt in, his big hand would clamp down over hers, squeezing her fingers very hard till the salt-lump was crushed and sprinkled in. "Don't be afraid to bung it in! We're both salt-herrings, my son and me. Let's try it again and see if it's right. Here, you have a taste and see what you think."

Sometimes, when she was down on her knees, scrubbing the flagstones, he would stand in the doorway, watching her, eyeing the shape of her bent body. Although Robert was in the room, his presence was no protection to her, for the man made remarks to the little boy, playing upon his innocence.

"She's got a fine figure, this mother of yours. She's worth better things than scrubbing floors, don't you think so, young Mercybright?"

More than once, as he made these remarks, he stooped over Linn and touched her body, his hands going over the curve of her hip or tracing the slender course of her spine as she stooped to her work. And each time, when she squirmed away, pushing at his hand with her scrubbing-brush, he would step back, laughing deep in his throat, and would stand for a while in front of her, watching the colour that rose like a fire in her fair-skinned face. Once when he laid his hand on her, Robert ran forward and pushed at him, looking up at his face with a dark-eyed frown.

"Don't do that, my mother don't like it!" the little boy said.

"How do you know what your mother likes? You don't know everything, young fella-me-lad!"

He was always trying to catch Linn's eye. His admiring glances were meant to please. But Linn found it hard to look at him. In the past she had thought him a handsome man, but now his big face and easy smile and the meaningful softness in his eyes had become disgusting and loathsome to her. She knew that if she met his gaze her loathing would be betrayed at once.

Challoner's admiration for Linn was not confined to her looks alone. She was a cut above the rest of her kind. Her speech was less broad and her voice itself was pleasant to hear. Her work in the house was full of little touches that took him by surprise. When laying the table for a meal, she put out the cruets and serving-spoons that had long lain idle in their black bags, and when serving the meals, she made use of the gravy-boats and soup-tureens and saw to it that they were hot. The meals themselves were excellent. She took trouble in making savoury sauces to go with the carrots, the marrow, the swedes; and her light fluffy pancakes delighted him.

"Where did you learn to do these things?"

"I was in service at Meynell Hall."

"Seems to me we're in clover, my boy," Challoner said to his son Gerald. "We haven't been so well looked after since your mother was alive."

Gerald agreed. The house was a pleasant place these days. It was clean, comfortable, cheerful, and bright. There were fresh sheets on the bed every week; there were beautifully ironed shirts to put on; clothes were mended, boots were cleaned, and messages were got from the shop. There were even flowers in a bowl on the hall table.

"Why not ask her to come full-time?" Gerald suggested to his father one evening.

"What, come and live in?" Challoner said. "I doubt if she'd leaver that father of hers."

"She might if you made it worth her while."

"I'm not sure that I know what you mean."

"If you were to marry her," Gerald said, "that would make it worth her while."

"You're jumping the gun a bit, aren't you, my boy? She's only been here a couple of weeks!" But the thought was not new in Challoner's mind, and he saw that Gerald suspected as much. Casually, yet choosing his words, he said: "What would you really say, I wonder, at having a stepmother in the house?"

"I'd say good luck to you," Gerald said. He was already courting a girl at Blagg and hoped to marry her in the spring. As he was only nineteen, he was bent on winning his father's goodwill. "You could do a lot worse than marry the Mercybright girl, I reckon, though the boy'd be a nuisance, I suppose."

"I wouldn't say that. He's a nice little chap in his funny way. I've taken quite a fancy to him."

"Well, so long as you don't go and leave him the farm!"

"What, another man's child, and a bastard at that? Don't talk rubbish!" Challoner said.

But the thought of marriage, endorsed as it had been by his son, began to take firmer root in his mind. He began to watch Linn in a different way; weighing her up; all the pros and cons. He would be marrying beneath him, of course. He could hear what some of his neighbours would say. "One of his own labourers' daughters, and with an illegitimate child at that!" But he had no taste for marrying a woman of his own class, for that meant some widow, nearer his age. He would prefer a young wife like Linn; someone he could cosset and spoil; someone who would be grateful to him for lifting her up out of poverty; someone he could dote on and enjoy.

Linn was a very beautiful girl. He saw her, in his mind's eye, dressed in good clothes and some jewellery, presiding at his table when friends came to dine. He saw her accompanying him to whist drives and dances and the N.F.U. social evenings. He saw her wearing smart little hats, coming to him from the hairdresser's in town, smelling of scent and face-powder, her golden-red hair set in rippling waves.

One morning he woke with his mind made up. He would soon be sixty-two. He had been a widower for eight years. Where was the sense in hanging back?

* * * * *

The harvest weather was terrible. Most of the corn had to be cut by hand. And all day, across the fields at Outlands, came the tseep-tsawp-tseep-tsawp of the mowers sharpening the blades of their scythes.

Linn, when she took her father's dinner up to him in the Big Piece, found him wearing sacks tied like gaiters round his legs, and some of the other men the same. The corn as they cut it was sodden and heavy; the grain was sprouting in the ear; the straw was blackened and smelt of mould. There was no harvest jollity in the field. Jack took the basket with scarcely a word. She noticed that he was limping badly.

"Is granddad cross with us?" Robert asked, returning with her to the farmhouse.

"His leg is hurting him," Linn said.

One day when she had been picking beans in the garden at Outlands, she suddenly found that Robert was missing.

209

She went into the house, calling him, but only Challoner was there. He stood in front of the kitchen range, booted feet wide apart, hands deep in his breeches pockets.

"The boy's not here," he said to her. "I sent him to the village to buy some sweets."

"But he never goes to the village alone! And I don't like you giving him money to spend, Mr Challoner. I mentioned it to you once before."

"Don't be a spoilsport. He'll come to no harm. I wanted the chance of a word with you, without little pitchers listening, all ears."

"I'd rather you didn't, Mr Challoner."

"You haven't heard what I've got to say."

"I don't think I want to hear it," she said.

"You'll soon change your mind when you know what it is."

Challoner was deeply amused. He watched the movement of colour in her face and wished she would look him straight in the eye. He had arranged things pretty well; he meant to savour this courtship of his. The girl's show of modesty did her credit; it was only what he expected of her; and he would enjoy breaking it down. He was going to be very gentlemanly. He meant to treat her with perfect respect. He was going to show her, in fact, what marriage to a man of his sort would mean for a woman such as she.

But Linn, alone in the house with him, was filled with a sudden choking fear. The way he stood seemed to threaten her. His broad bulky body filled the hearth. She set down her basket and turned towards the door. Challoner quickly followed her. He took her by the shoulders and swung her round and when, more by chance than by design, one of his hands caught the front of her blouse, he thrust it inside to cover her breasts, squeezing her flesh most painfully between his big fingers, rough-skinned and hard. It was not what he had intended, but, once having touched her, he was inflamed. He spoke to her in a thickened voice.

"What're you running away for? Why don't you stop and give me a chance?"

"No, let me go, for pity's sake!"

As Linn writhed away from him, freeing herself, her fear

210

and disgust were so extreme that they blazed out of her, uncontrolled.

"Don't touch me!" she cried in a shrill voice. "Don't touch me with your big ugly hands!"

Challoner stared. He became very still. He saw the loathing in her eyes.

"My God," he said, incredulously, "I wonder what you think you are?"

"I may be your servant but I'm not your whore!"

"You can't always have been nice! That boy of yours is proof of that!"

"Oh, I knew very well enough what was in your mind!"

"You lived with Tom Maddox, didn't you? Brazenly, for all to see? You made yourself the talk of the place! – Do you think I don't remember it? And what were you then, living with him? Were you his servant or his whore?"

"I loved him," Linn said. "You'll never make me ashamed of that."

"You were never his wife, though, were you, by God? You were never any man's wife so far. Well, let me tell you something, madam! You with your talk about being a whore! If you hadn't been so quick off the mark – if you hadn't jumped to the wrong conclusion – if you hadn't shown yourself up for what you are – I was going to ask you to be *my* wife! Yes, madam, you can stare! That's brought you up short a bit, I can see."

"Your wife? You must be mad!" Linn said. At another time she would not have believed him. Now she hardly knew what she said. Her physical revulsion against the man gave her tongue a cruel edge. "Did you really think I would marry you? A man of your age with grown up sons? Did you think I was yours just for the asking, because I'm a servant in your house?"

"I hope you've finished now!" he exclaimed. "I hope you've said all you've got to say."

Challoner's face was an ugly red. His rage brought a wetness to his eyes. But Linn, as she recovered herself, saw that he was deeply hurt. She saw him as a foolish, self-deceived man, and fleetingly she was sorry for him. She wished she could call back some of the things she had said to him. But it was too late; she knew he would never forgive her now; and a new terror arose in her for, having offended him like this, her own job and her father's would be at stake.

"Mr Challoner," she began. "Mr Challoner, I'm sorry it's all turned out as it has."

"Sorry, are you? I can well believe that!"

"Do you want me to leave the house?"

"It's up to you. You can please yourself."

"I don't want to lose my job."

"No, nor lose your father his!" Watching her, he became sly. He knew what fears tormented her. There was a sneer in his voice. "You need the money, I daresay, and I shouldn't like to see you starve. You've got your boy to think about. Your little love-child. Your little mistake."

Abruptly he made towards the door.

"You can stay on by all means, and when you're doing your bits and bobs of chores about the place, you can be thinking this to yourself. – You could have been mistress of this house if only you'd played your cards the right way. Your little boy could have had my name. I could have done a lot for him and sent him to a good school. You just think what you've thrown away!"

The door slammed, and he was gone. Linn sat down, trembling, in a chair and rested her elbows on the table, but before she could yield to the threatening tears, Robert returned from the village shop. He had not spent his threepence on liquorice laces; he had bought a small tortoishell comb for his mother to wear clipped in her hair.

* * * * *

Challoner never touched her now, but he kept a close watch on her just the same, and whereas before he had been full of praise, now he found fault with everything.

"Do you call these clean?" he said, flinging his boots down in front of her. "You'll have to do better than that, by God, before they're fit for market wear."

There was far more washing to do now. Challoner changed his shirt every day. And whereas before, on washday mornings, the young lad Godwin had brought in the coal, now she had to do it herself. She had to pump all the water and carry it in, and chop her own sticks to light the fire. Gerald soon noticed the change in his father's manner to her. He wanted to know what was wrong.

"Never you mind!" Challoner said. "The girl is a bitch, I can tell you that. I was never so taken-in in my life."

"She can't be as bad as all that, surely?" It was easy enough for Gerald to guess what lay behind the change. "You'll drive her away if you treat her like this."

"Hah! Not her! She wants the money too much for that. She said so herself."

Out in the fields, as wet as ever, harvest progressed with dreadful slowness. The sight of the sprouting, smut-blackened corn, mouldering as it stood in the shocks, did nothing to improve Challoner's temper. Once he came into the farmyard when Linn was carrying buckets of kitchen-waste to the boiler-house next to the piggery.

"Kitty Cox always used to give a hand out in the harvest-field," he said. "I suppose you're too refined for that?"

"I can't do everything," Linn said.

She bore his treatment as best she could. He would surely not keep it up for long. But his spite was not so easily assuaged; instead of lessening, it grew; he was determined to have his revenge. One day he took her out to the barn and set her to pluck two dozen fowls. They had to be ready by seven o'clock, he said, and it was then just after two. It took her till eight to pluck them all, and her hands by that time were red and raw, the finger-tips bleeding, too sore to touch. Robert played outside in the yard. He came into the barn when she was trussing up the fowls. Her hands were so sore she could hardly bear to handle the string. Robert helped her to tie the knots.

At home that evening, preparing supper, she wore a pair of cotton gloves.

"What's wrong with your hands?" Jack asked.

"It's some kind of rash," she said, shrugging, and to her relief he asked no more.

He took little interest, apparently, in the work she did for Challoner. He never asked her how she got on. He rarely

213

mentioned it at all. But once he said sarcastically: "When's he sending someone to fix up the roof? I thought you'd arranged it, you and him."

Whatever Challoner told her to do, she did without a word of complaint. But what caused her anguish, secretly, was that Robert should witness the humiliations heaped upon her. It was nothing that he saw her scrubbing floors, but that he should see her emptying the latrine, struggling to carry the big slopping bucket across the yard and down the track, to tip it into the piggery midden: she hated Challoner for this. That in front of the little wide-eyed boy the man should fling his gaiters at her and send a tin of saddle-soap rattling across the table to her, and should say in his loud contemptuous voice, "You won't take all day at that job, I hope? – I'm going out at ten sharp!": she hated Challoner for these things.

The depth of the hatred she felt for him sometimes shocked her and made her afraid. Following him out to his motor car once, carrying a hamper filled with game, she was shocked at the picture that filled her mind, of the motor car skidding on the wet road and the man lying dead across the wheel. What sort of woman had she become, that she could wish someone dead? she thought. But her greatest fear of all was that Jack should learn of the way Challoner treated her.

"Don't tell your granddad that I empty the privy up at the farm," she said to Robert one day. "It's better for him if he doesn't know. Promise mummy you won't tell?"

Robert nodded, giving his promise. She knew she could trust him, young as he was.

* * * * *

But it so happened, the following day, that as she was carrying the latrine bucket across the yard, her father came through the gate from the pasture, leading a horse that had gone lame.

"What's this?" he said, coming to her, and she set down the bucket to ease her arm. "Where's the lad that does these jobs?"

"I don't know," Linn said. She looked round the yard in a vague way, as though expecting Godwin to come.

"How long have you been doing jobs like this?"

"Father, don't make a fuss!" she cried, for the look in his face was frightening, and she knew that Challoner was in the barn. "It's no concern of yours what I do. Just leave me to manage my own affairs."

"That bastard's been putting on you, by God! D'you think I ent seen it in your eyes? D'you think I ent seen you dwindling away to a nottomy streak these past few weeks? D'you think I'm going to let it pass?"

"Dad, do be quiet!" Linn said. "Get back to your work and leave me to mine."

"That's no work for you!" Jack said. "Not after today, it's not, by God! Where's the swine hiding hisself? I'd like to have a few words with him!"

Challoner came out of the barn and stood with his hands in his breeches pockets. His voice rang out across the yard.

"You asking for *me* by any chance?"

"I'm glad you know which swine I meant!"

"You must be drunk, Mercybright, if you think you can talk to me like that!"

"What do you think my daughter is, that you get her to empty your stinking slops? Slavery's been done away with this good long time since! Are you aiming to bring it back?"

"If she doesn't like it, she knows what to do! She can clear off and leave the job to someone else!"

"She's going, don't worry! I'll see to that!"

"You can take yourself off at the same time! You think because you're an old man – "

"Old man be buggered!" Jack said. "At least I know what age I am! I don't make a fool of myself trying to get young women half my age to warm my bed for me and then turning nasty cos I don't get my way!"

"Have you finished, Mercybright?"

"I'll have finished when I get to the end!"

News of the quarrel had gone round the farm. The harvesters had come from the nearby field and were loitering about the yard. The two cowmen had come from the sheds. Gerald Challoner now appeared and stood with a spanner in his hand, having come from repairing one of the tractors. His handsome round face was darkly flushed. He raised his spanner in a threatening way.

"We've heard about enough from you, Mercybright! You can come to the office and get your cards!"

"Lead the way!" Jack said. "I've been on this farm for ten years. That's ten years too long, so let's not waste time!"

Ten minutes later Jack and Linn and little Robert walked away from the farmhouse. Challoner's voice followed them.

"I want you out of your cottage by the end of next week! I'll serve an eviction on you, else! Do you hear me, man?"

Jack made no answer. He merely walked on. He was trying hard to disguise his limp.

"I knew this would happen!" Linn said. "Why, oh why, couldn't you leave me be?"

Again Jack said nothing, but walked on. His bearded face was grimly set. His mouth was a single tight-closed line. Robert, walking with one hand in Linn's, looked up at her anguished tear-stained face. She began to sob uncontrollably.

"I knew it would end like this!" she said. "If only people would leave me alone!"

Chapter 12

There was more heavy rain again in September. The Derrent burst its banks again and the roads were flooded for days on end. When the waters at last went down, Jesse Izzard with his son Dicky and three of the other carpenters from Cobbs were out working for eighteen hours, repairing the ruined sluice-gates. Then there were more thunderstorms and the Derrent was in flood again. But at least the sluice-gates were working now. The floods could to some extent be controlled.

"Them sluice-gates should hold till domesday now," Jesse said to Beth, his wife, "with all the good timber we've put into them."

Jesse was very important these days, now that great-grumpa Tewke had gone. Although his wife and son had more say than he in how the carpenter's shop was run, it was nevertheless a great thing for him to go to the sawmill at Capleton Wick and order timber in huge supplies. He had a little notebook for it. He talked of "invoices" and "delivery notes" and "credit charges". His lips were stained blue from sucking the tip of his indelible pencil. "All this paper-work!" he would say. "Seems there's no end to it, don't it, eh?" But he enjoyed it all the same.

"Dad's never happier," Dicky said, "than when he's walking to and from with a bit of paper in his hand."

There were other things, too, on Jesse's mind. The little Pikehouse, which he owned, out on the lonely Norton Road, was about to become empty again. Horace Nash was giving it up and going to live with his son at Blagg. Jesse, as landlord, had much to do.

"There's one or two been after me, to let them have the Pikehouse," he said, "and I reckon there'll be more as well."

"You can only let it to one," said Beth, with a glance

217

towards Dicky and Betony.

"That's what I said to them. My very words! 'I can only let it to one,' I said, 'and I need time to decide just who.' "

Betony and Dicky exchanged a smile. Their mother pretended to frown at them, over her spectacles, which were new.

"It's a great responsibility, being a landlord," she said to them. "You should treat your father with respect."

"They don't seem to realize," Jesse said, "that that little house will be theirs one day."

"That'll be useful," Dicky said, "when we need a kennel to keep a dog in!"

Jesse's face showed that he was hurt.

"I was born at the Pikehouse," he said. "Your two sisters was born there too. It ent just a matter of bricks and mortar and a bit of thatch. Your mother and me was married from there. We lived there two years of our married life."

"Sorry, dad! It was only a joke!"

Jesse looked at Betony, who was counting money on the kitchen table.

"Do you want me to take you in to the station, blossom?"

"No, I'm getting a lift with Jeremy Rye."

Although September was well advanced, the village school had not yet reopened, due in part to the late harvest, in part to the flooding of so many roads. Betony had decided to go away for a week, to see an old school-friend, Nancy Sposs, who now lived in Birmingham.

She left the house at eleven o'clock. That afternoon, at about three, Jack Mercybright called at Cobbs, having heard that the Pikehouse was falling empty. Jesse, as landlord, saw him alone. He led him into the best room.

"So you've come about the Pikehouse, then? The news soon gets round, my word, it does!"

"Is it right that Nash is going?"

"Moving out on Friday next."

"Then what about it?" Jack said.

"That needs some repairs doing first," Jesse said. "I was out there the other day and –"

"Never mind that," Jack said. "I don't mind doing a bit of repairs. The Pikehouse will just about suit us fine."

218

"It's the landlord's job to do the repairs."

"Ah, I know," Jack said. "I've seen 'em scrambling to get it done!"

"You won't find *me* neglecting the place. As soon as there's anything leastlike wrong –"

"Then you'll let us have it, Friday next?"

"Glory be, you're in a hurry!" Jesse said. He took out his pipe and began to light up. It was a thing that took some time. "How come you're looking for a house all of a sudden?"

"I've lost my job, that's how," Jack said, "and that means I'm losing my cottage too."

"Laws! You as well! Wherever will it end? There's any event of men out of work, coming to ask me for jobs and that –"

"D'you think I don't know it? I ent blind!"

"The same with the Pikehouse," Jesse said. "There's two or three been after me, wanting me to let them have it, and that's none too easy to decide."

"It's easy enough, I should've thought. Just a plain yes or no."

"Then there's the question of the rent."

"I can't pay no rent for a week or two. Not until I've found some work."

"Laws!" Jesse said. "As bad as that? Now Bert Smith was here on Monday night and offered me two shillings a week. That's sixpence more than the mason paid, and sixpence is sixpence, after all."

"So you're letting him have it, is that what you mean?"

"I never said so. Not in so many words."

"Well, I reckon my need it greater than his, so how about it?" Jack said.

"That's what they all say," Jesse said. "Please one and offend another – that's how it is when you're letting a house."

"Can I bloody well have it or not?" Jack said. "All I want is a straight yes or no."

"There's no need to swear," Jesse said. "It ent so simple as all that. You've got to give me time to think –"

Suddenly Jack could stand no more. He swung on his

heel and left the house. Jesse followed him as far as the kitchen and stood staring at the outer door, still vibrating on its hinges. Beth came in from the scullery, wiping her hands on her pinafore.

"What did he want to see you about?"

"He wanted me to let him have the Pikehouse."

"You surely didn't refuse him, I hope?"

"Of course I didn't!" Jesse said. "He gave me no time to think myself out."

"Then you'd better go after him, hadn't you?"

"Laws!" Jesse said. "He *is* a queer chap! Fancy flying off the handle like that, before I had time to say a word!"

"Are you going after him or am I?"

"All right, all right, I'm on my way."

But when Jesse caught up with him, Jack refused to stop and talk.

"You can keep your Pikehouse and be damned to you!" he said, brushing Jesse aside. "All I wish is I'd never asked!"

"Don't be a fool," Jesse said. "It's yours for the asking. You should know that."

"I ent asking! Not any more!"

"Then what'll you do?" Jesse said, calling after him anxiously.

"I'll do what I've always done!" Jack replied. "I'll fend for myself!"

Jesse returned home to his wife.

"Laws! But he *is* a funny chap! He threw my offer in my face."

"You should've stuck out," Beth said. "You must go to his cottage and try again."

"It won't do no good. You know what he is. He looked as though he could murder me."

"I don't blame him. I could do it myself."

"Oh, it's bound to be *my* fault, I know that!"

"What about Linn and the little boy? Didn't you ever think of them?"

"It's Jack's place to think of them. I said he could have the Pikehouse, didn't I? If he don't take it, that's his fault, not mine."

"I'll go and see him myself," Beth said. She took her coat

from the back of the door. "It's the only way to get things done."

But when she went to Lilac Cottage, neither Jack nor Linn was at home. And although she went twice the next day, each time there was nobody there. She pushed a note under the door and hoped for the best.

"I don't know what Betony will say to you when she gets home," she said to Jesse afterwards. "Such a mess you make of things!"

* * * * *

Betony returned from Birmingham on Friday night. It was after ten and the family were in bed. The next morning, as soon as she heard the news about Jack, she drove to the cottage in Stoney Lane. She found him and Linn in the act of moving out. He had borrowed an old hand-cart and was loading their furniture onto it. Linn was carrying out the bedding. Robert sat on a wooden hutch. He had a tame rabbit in his arms.

Betony tried to reason with Jack. She offered him the Pikehouse and work at Cobbs. But Jack, grim-faced, would have none of it.

"I've already got myself a job."

"On a farm?" Betony said.

"No. Sweeping the roads for the council at Springs."

"You'd sooner do that than work at Cobbs?"

"I'd sooner do *anything*," he said, "than be beholden for what I do."

"What about a place to live?"

"We've got the loan of a couple of rooms."

"Springs is a long way away from here."

"The further the better, where I'm concerned."

He lifted the bedding Linn had brought out and piled it on top of the furniture. Betony turned and took Linn's arm.

"What about you, do you feel the same? Can't I persuade you to change your minds?"

"I reckon dad's right," Linn said. "It's better for us if we fend for ourselves." She drew away from Betony's grasp. "I must get on. There's a lot to do."

221

"Yes. Very well. I'll give you a hand."

"No, there's no need," Linn said. "We can manage by ourselves."

Betony watched them helplessly.

"All this stuff on a hand-cart!" she said. "You'll kill yourselves, pushing that to Springs. Why not borrow our horse and cart?"

"No favours, thanks," Jack said. He hoisted a clothes-basket onto the load. "I asked one favour. I'll ask no more."

"You know my father meant no harm. It's just that he's so slow in his ways. He's very upset that you slammed out like that. He'd far rather *you* had the Pikehouse than anyone else in the world. Surely you must know that?"

"I don't know nothing of the kind."

"Won't you give him another chance?"

"I've just told you. We've got fixed up."

"At least let me take Linn and Robert in the trap. It's nearly fourteen miles to Springs."

"Robert can ride on the hand-cart," said Linn. "I shall be helping dad to push."

"Good God, but you're obstinate!" Betony said. "You'll kill yourselves, the pair of you!"

Neither Jack nor Linn answered her. They busied themselves, loading the cart. She saw that further argument was useless.

"You'll let me come over sometimes and see my godson?"

"Yes, of course," Linn said; but there was no hint of warmth in her tone, nor in the brief glance of her eyes.

"Can you tell me the address?"

"We're not quite sure where it is ourselves. We have to enquire when we get to Springs. The council foreman will take us there."

"Then I hope you'll write to me later on."

"Yes, of course," Linn said again.

Betony turned to the little boy. She stroked the white doe rabbit he held in his arms. He looked at her with deep, dark eyes.

"You won't forget your auntie Betony?" she said.

The little boy nodded, but she knew he meant "no". She laughed at him and touched his face.

"You *will* forget me? What a shame!"

"No," he said. He shook his head.

"I'll be over to see you as soon as I can. As soon as your mummy sends your address. If she forgets, remind her for me. Otherwise how shall I know where to find you when the Whitsun Fair comes round again?"

Reluctantly she left them and drove away. She was filled with anger at their plight, but she knew there was nothing she could do.

"Don't blame *me*!" her father said, meeting her when she got home.

"I *do* blame you!" Betony said. But, seeing the stricken look in his eyes, she relented at once. "No, I don't blame *you*. – I blame the world."

* * * * *

The world was growing old, she said to herself, and God was beginning to feel his years. In ancient times, or so we were told, whenever disorder came to his people, God put out a hand and pointed a finger accusingly, and men were brought to their senses again. Now, it seemed, he no longer cared.

On the third Sunday in September, the vicar of Huntlip, in his sermon, touched on the chaos in the world and took his text from the Book of Judges: "In those days there was no king in Israel: every man did that which was right in his own eyes."

People liked to hear Mr Netherton preach. His eloquence stirred them and woke them up. They felt cleansed and scoured after hearing him. And his sermon this Sunday touched on matters that were near home for many of the members of his congregation. Men had lost sight of those things in life that had the most value, he said. In agriculture, in industry, indeed throughout the world of commerce, there was a breakdown in hope and trust. On the land, especially, those who lived by the sweat of their brow were filled with sullenness and resentment. Who could have faith, who had been so betrayed? Was it any wonder that the faces of men and women everywhere were empty of hope, who had looked for guidance and found it not? Our politics, our economy, our morals and our religious feeling, were in disorder throughout the country, and there was no one to point the way. . . .

Outside the church, after the service, Betony stopped for a word with Stephen Wayman. He was there with Joanna and aunt Doe.

"Were you suitably chastened by the vicar's sermon, Miss Izzard?" he asked. "We none of us escaped his lash this time. Employers and employed, rich men and poor! – We were all treated roughly here today!"

"The only one who escaped was God himself," Betony said. "Yet I think perhaps it is he who really needs to be taken to task."

Joanna, looking at her, was shocked. She had recently been confirmed and had entered into a pious phase. Aunt Doe merely smiled. But Stephen gave a little laugh.

"I'm inclined to agree with you, Miss Izzard, and I can think of no one better fitted for the job!"

He caught the quickening of her glance and saw her expression alter a little. He realized how uncouth his joke had sounded. But before he could say anything more, Betony's sister came up with her children, and she was surrounded by nieces and nephews. They were all going back to Cobbs for lunch; Stephen saw her borne away; and he swore to himself, under his breath. Why was he always so inept whenever he met her and talked to her?

Walking through the village with Janie and the children, and listening to their chatter, Betony forgot his remark. She remembered it only when she got home, and then it lodged like a burr in her mind. She looked at herself in the hall mirror as she hung up her coat and hat on the stand. Was that how he saw her? she asked herself. Officious? Admonitory? Self-satisfied? The quintessential school-marm ready to scold even God himself? She laughed at herself, because it hurt.

"There is no king in Israel," she said, speaking to the face in the hall mirror. "Only a handful of schoolmarms like me!"

There was a restlessness in her these days. Janie

remarked on it that afternoon.

"Are you busy hatching something?"

"What sort of something?" Betony asked.

"That's exactly what I want to know."

"I was only thinking, that's all. Perhaps it's not God that's set in his ways. Perhaps it's me after all."

"What do you think you're talking about?"

"I think I'm settling into a rut. I feel it's time I shuffled out."

"Then you are hatching something? I knew you were!"

"No. No, I'm not. It's only a thought. I've got no plans of any kind. At least not yet."

But it so happened that the very next day a letter came to her by post from her old school-friend in Birmingham. Nancy was working in politics. She was chairman of the local Women's Socialist Group. "You seemed interested when you were here, and I thought you might like to know that we shall soon be needing a new assistant secretary. Not much money but plenty of work. The job is yours if you care to take it." Betony wrote asking for details, and a fat package came by return. There was plenty in it for her to read. It occupied her mind for three days.

* * * * *

The weather continued very wet. At Holland Farm, as elsewhere, the harvest dragged on eternally. Although Stephen was growing less corn these days, it seemed it would never be gathered in. They worked in the fields wearing gumboots and macks, so wet was the corn as they handled it.

Betony, driving in the trap down Holland Lane, found her way blocked by a loaded waggon, its front axle lodged on the hump of ground between the deep ruts. There were three or four men gathered about the front of the waggon, and from the field higher up on the left, where barley was being cut and stooked, aunt Doe, helping the harvesters, was calling out unheeded advice.

Stephen came to Betony and raised his cap. He wore a brown tweed jacket, much patched with leather at the elbows and cuffs, and tied round the waist with a piece of string. His gumboots and breeches were coated in mud.

"I'm sorry to hold you up like this. Tupper's gone to fetch a spade. You haven't got an appointment anywhere, I hope?"

"Luckily, no," Betony said. She would not have been able to turn in the lane, because of the terrible depth of the ruts. "The pony is wanting her manger, that's all. Otherwise there's no hurry."

"I'll give her something to stay the pangs."

He groped in the pocket of his shapeless jacket and gave the pony a couple of knobs of cow-cake. Rosie ate them and blew through her nose. She nuzzled his jacket in search of more, her lips exploring the knotted string. She then leant her forehead against his chest, and Stephen, stroking the smooth dappled neck, looked at Betony with a smile. His angular face, with its strong cheekbones and long jaw, looked somewhat drawn and tired, she thought. This was a worrying time for farmers. It had been the worst harvest for forty-six years. But his slow smile was cheerful enough; there was humour in his eyes when he looked at her; and when he came to the side of the trap, to stand with one hand resting on the ledge, he seemed at ease, unhurried, relaxed.

"A dry day for a change, thank God. Overhead at least, though not underfoot."

"Is your harvest very much spoilt?"

"I'm a lot luckier than some. I've increased my stock in the past year or two and most of this – " He pointed to the heavy load of corn towering up from the rut-bound waggon " – will be fed to the cattle in the sheaf."

"What about the years to come?"

"We hold tight and hope for the best."

"You are preparing for a siege?"

"It's what it amounts to, yes," he agreed. "Only a miracle can stop the recession getting worse, and I don't hold out much hope for miracles."

"You don't seem too desperately worried," she said.

Stephen gave the matter some thought.

"For myself and my family, no, I'm not. I paid off my mortgage a month ago. – We've got no debts of any kind now. So I think we shall live to tell the tale. But for many others it will be worse. Some poor devils are going bust. A farmer near Kitchinghampton last week went and hanged himself in his barn. The rest of the breed are frightened men and fear makes them hard on those they employ."

"Your neighbour, Mr Challoner, for one."

"Yes," Stephen said, "I'm afraid that's true."

While he and Betony were talking together, Hopson, Starling, and Billy Rye were talking together on the far side of the waggon, and now, as Bob Tupper came up, bringing mattocks and spades, there was some teasing and laughter among them. Stephen went to see how the work was getting on. He returned and stood by the trap as before and his right hand, with its twisted fingers, rested on the narrow ledge.

"Shouldn't be long before we get it moving now. We'll pull into that gateway lower down so that you can get past without more delay."

"There's no hurry," Betony said. "I'm perfectly happy sitting here."

As soon as these few simple words were spoken, their implication came home to her and she wished them unsaid. She felt a hotness in her face and she stared, frowning, at the pony's ears. She knew that Stephen was looking at her. She turned her head and their glances held. With an effort she spoke again.

"I think perhaps you're right," she said. "It would be better after all."

Stephen stared at her absently.

"What would be better?" he asked. For a moment his mind had gone quite blank. "Oh, you mean if we pulled off into the field?"

"If it's not too much trouble," Betony said.

"None whatever. Certainly not. We've got to take a bit off this load, anyway. We've overdone it, I'm afraid. – We'll never get it home stacked up like this."

The axle was got free at last. The patient horses leant to their task. The wheels began to roll in the ruts and the waggon began to move down the lane. Creaking and swaying, it was driven left through the next gateway, onto an empty field of stubble. The way was now open and Betony, raising her whip in thanks, drove past the gateway and down the lane. Stephen raised his cap to her. He watched her until she had gone from sight.

When he turned to go into the field, he found that aunt Doe was watching him. She had come down the lane from the field above to share her flask of tea with him.

"Was that Miss Izzard you were talking to?"

"Yes. I'm afraid we held her up."

"Did she say when the school would be opening again?"

"No, and I didn't think to ask."

That evening at home, when he and aunt Doe were alone together, he found her thoughtfully studying him.

"Is there something on your mind?"

"When the day comes that you think of getting married again, just say the word and I'll be off. I'll get a little cottage somewhere. You needn't think I'll be in the way."

"Have you someone in mind for me?"

"Goodness, no! I leave that to you."

"Thanks a lot. You're very kind. I'm glad I'm to have same say in the matter."

Stephen was amused, and yet not amused. Had his thoughts been going that way? Well, yes, perhaps they had. But only as an exercise of the imagination. He had been a widower for three years. The thought of Gwen still brought him pain. But for some little time now, he had to admit, he had been looking at Betony Izzard as any unattached man looks at an unattached and pretty woman: with pleasure; curiosity; speculation; sometimes even with a certain longing. But marriage as a serious proposition? That was something else again. He was ten years older than she was; he was set in his ways; and she would not be a docile wife by any means. There were also his children to be considered.

And what about Betony herself? What was her attitude to him? She was aware of him certainly: her blush that day had shown him that; but how deep did her interest go? She appeared self-sufficient; self-complete. She seemed to have arranged her own life to her own perfect satisfaction.

He would have to give the matter some thought; dwell on it and give it time; see how his feelings worked themselves out. Did he want to fall in love? He, a man nearly thirty-nine? He remembered the wonderful singing pain of falling in love as a young man and he answered firmly, No, he did not. He remembered the blinding horror of loss and he felt a dreadful shrinking inside. No, not again. Still, the longing was there, and he recognized it. He would have to give it some thought. Dwell on it, and then decide.

But he was busy on the farm, getting the last of the harvest in. There were a good many things on his mind. Emma, starting her new school term, caught measles and had to be put to bed. Chris fell from a cornstack and twisted a ligament in his foot, and Hopson had jaundice for a couple of weeks, which meant more work for everyone.

He did not have a great deal of time for thought, but Betony had a place in his mind, and her presence there, constantly, was like a gentle kind of warmth: pleasurable, but as yet unexplored; so that now and then he would say to himself: "Yes, oh yes, I know you're there. But do you know you're in my mind and would you care twopence if you did?"

One Saturday morning when the weather was bad and there was a lull in the work of the farm, he walked out to the carpenter's shop to pay for the repairs that had been done on Morton George's cottage. He spent twenty minutes with Jesse and Dicky, chatting with them about this and that, and when he left he stood for a while at the workshop gate, gazing across at the old house. Had he come in the hope of seeing her? No, not really, he told himself. Yet he went away home feeling disappointed.

"You should have called if you felt like that," said a scoffing voice at the back of his mind. "No, I haven't had time to decide how I feel," said another, more cautious, voice in reply.

* * * * *

Purely by chance, Betony had seen him from her bedroom window, where she sat with her portable desk on her lap, writing a letter to Nancy Sposs. She had seen him looking up at the house; she had even begun to rise from her chair,

229

thinking that she would go down to him; but then he had suddenly turned away, and she had gone back to writing her letter.

Later that day, between the showers, she thought she would venture out to the post. Her father was just coming in from the fold.

"Mr Wayman was here earlier on. He paid for the work we done on that cottage."

"Yes, I saw him," Betony said.

"He seems a nice gentleman," Jesse said. "He pays his bills on the nail, anyway, and there ent so many that does that these days." He noticed the letter in her hand. "Have you decided, then?" he asked.

"Yes, I've written to Nancy to say I want the job."

"Gadding about again?" he said. "I thought last time you was home for good."

Betony laughed. What nonsense he talked!

"It's nearly eleven years," she said, "since I went away from home before."

"Is it, by golly?" Jesse said. "Don't the years go flying by?"

"Yes, they go much too fast," Betony said.

She went out to the village to post her letter.

Afterwards she called on the vicar to say that she was resigning her post as mistress-in-charge of the village school. He was much incensed.

"May I ask why you wish to leave?"

"I've decided it's time I had a change."

"Well, really, Miss Izzard, I *am* surprised! Why, only last year, let me remind you, when we had that disgraceful incident at the school, you came very close to losing your job. You were far from happy at the prospect of leaving then."

"That was nearly a year ago," Betony said, "and being dismissed is a different thing from deciding to resign for personal reasons."

"Very different indeed! And in view of the managers' lenience on that occasion, I consider it most ungrateful of you to throw our kindness back at us, after such a short interval."

"Must I stay at the school for ever, then, to pay off my

debt of gratitude?"

"Oh, you're perfectly within your rights, Miss Izzard, I don't dispute that. But I'm bound to admit that I am extremely disappointed in you and I'm sure the other managers will feel the same. You would almost certainly have been dismissed if it hadn't been for Mr Wayman speaking so strongly in your defence. Why, he even threatened to resign from the board, and he went to a great deal of trouble on your behalf, persuading the other managers that you should be allowed to stay."

"Did he do that? I didn't know."

"Had he known then that in less than a year you would be resigning your post so capriciously, I doubt if he would have been so zealous on your behalf."

"No, perhaps not," Betony said.

"You realize that your notice should have been given in before the beginning of term?"

"Yes, and I'm sorry about the delay, but it should be easy enough to find a replacement, I think. Teachers are two a penny these days."

"I don't know what the Education Secretary will say about this, but speaking for myself and the managers, Miss Izzard, I am extremely displeased and disappointed."

"I'm very sorry," Betony said.

* * * * *

She had heard nothing of Linn and Jack and little Robert; no letter had come, telling her of their address; so she drove in the trap to Springs one day in the hope of finding out where they lived. She enquired at the Scopton council offices but no one could tell her anything. A man named Mercybright *had* been employed by them for a while, sweeping the roads, but now he had left and nobody knew where he had gone. Betony returned home, feeling depressed. She thought of Linn and the little boy, shunted about from place to place, and she feared she would never see them again. She felt she had failed them in their time of need.

On nearing Huntlip, she decided to call at Holland Farm.

She had a duty to fulfil, and it had been weighing on her mind. Today she felt a certain detachment; nothing seemed to matter much; she was facing up to the prospect of change. When she drove into the farmyard, Stephen came out of the barn to her. He was dressed in his shabby working-clothes and the pony, knowing him at once, nuzzled the string that tied his jacket. He gave her a handful of cow-cake and stroked her nose.

"Your pony regards me as a friend."

"Mr Wayman," Betony said. "It appears that when the school board came close to dismissing me last autumn, you were responsible for changing their minds. I didn't know till a week ago. The vicar happened to mention it."

"The managers' threat was ridiculous. I'm sure they'd have realized that themselves. But, seeing that my son was one of those who caused the trouble, whatever I did was little enough."

"I'd like to thank you all the same."

"Did you come especially? It was kind of you to take the trouble. But I've earnt no thanks, I assure you."

"There is one other thing," she said. "I wanted to tell you – the news will be pretty general soon – that I'm leaving Huntlip at the end of the term."

"Leaving?" he said. "What do you mean?"

"I'm giving up teaching, at least for a while. A friend has offered me a job, helping the Women's Socialist Group, and I have decided to accept."

Stephen stared at her, feeling afraid. Her news had hit him like a blow and the shock of it, coming so casually, had told him something about himself. It had woken him out of a timeless dream.

"But you can't!" he said in a harsh voice, and they stared at each other, silent, shocked.

He had given himself away completely. He knew it and he no longer cared. Betony sat, very straight and still. His expression and tone had shaken her, and she found herself unable to speak. He saw the confusion in her face, and it brought him some degree of calm. He went to her and put up his hands.

"For God's sake get down from there!" he said. "We've

got to talk."

He helped her down out of the trap, and they walked together across the yard. He opened a gate and they passed through, into a narrow grass-grown lane, lined on each side with sycamores. It was not raining that morning, but the trees dripped moisture onto them, and they had to walk carefully, skirting the puddles.

"What are you trying to do to me?"

"I'm not sure that I know what you mean."

"Dropping by so casually! 'Oh, by the way, I nearly forgot! – I'm going away in a couple of months!' And where to, I should like to know? – The end of the world?"

"Only to Birmingham, actually."

"Don't joke with me! I'm not in the mood. As a matter of fact I'm seething mad."

"Yes, I can see you are," she said.

"Can you?" he said, his voice still harsh. "Then no doubt you can see something else? I've given myself away plainly enough!"

He came to a halt, confronting her. He knew they were hidden from the house. Betony met his accusing gaze.

"Well?" he demanded. "And what do you see?"

"I don't know. I can't be sure."

"Then you must be a fool, that's all I can say!"

The way he looked at her held her fast. It frightened her, yet she wanted him.

"Stephen –"

"Yes?"

"You have only to ask."

"For God's sake, I'm asking, aren't I?" he said, and took her angrily into his arms, holding her in a burning stillness, a terrible weakness in his flesh as he thought how easily he might have lost her. He hid his face against her hair. "I'm the one that's a fool," he said.

So much for those calm deliberations of his! He *might* just consider marrying her or he might just put her out of his mind. . . . As though he had had any real choice in the matter! His body had known better than he, and now it ached against her unbearably, recognizing that she was his. His eyes had known, ages ago, dwelling on her as they had done at every opportunity; taking pleasure in her looks. His hands had known, certainly, and had found excuses for touching her. Only his mind had held aloof and even that had yielded now. Capitulation was complete.

After a moment he looked at her. Being in love at thirty-nine was not so very different, he found, from being in love at twenty-two. He wanted assurance. He wanted some pledge.

"Do you love me, Betony?"

"I think I do," Betony said.

"Only think? Aren't you sure?"

"Yes. I love you. Are you satisfied?"

But there was no answering smile from him, and when he kissed her she understood why: his longing for her was too intense: although he had only now yielded to it, his surrender was swift, free of doubts, complete. And, being a man and unreasonable, he demanded the same surrender from her. She had much to learn of what it meant to be loved and desired. His lips gave her warning of what to expect and she was almost overwhelmed. She withdrew a little, breathlessly, and looked at him, touching his face. They walked together along the lane, and the sycamores dripped on either side, splashing into the dark puddles.

It was a strange thing, this relationship between a man and a woman. They could circle around each other in thought, each aware of the other's interest, sometimes admitting it in a glance; sometimes even going so far as to laugh together in a certain way. But, being unspoken, lacking a sign, it could all be erased in the fraction of a second. Each or both could decide to draw back: the glance would grow cool, the laughter be withheld; and that would be the end of it. But perhaps, instead, came the overt sign: the word was spoken and the secret out; and once this had happened, it could not be recalled. There was a sense of inevitableness in it. Every glance and every word became charged with significance, and when the two people touched each other, there was a new confession in each caress.

"Betony."

"Yes?"

"You're certainly not going to Birmingham."

"Aren't I? No. Perhaps I'm not."

She was almost twenty-nine. She was used to making her own decisions. Could she give herself up to this man? Once again their glances held. The choice was not hers, any more than his. They had need of each other, in their bones.

* * * * *

One of the first things Betony did was to send a telegram to Nancy Sposs: "Sorry. Changed my mind. Getting married instead." And back by return came Nancy's reply: "Treachery! But good luck all the same!"

Betony's family were well pleased, especially her father. "You'll be staying in Huntlip after all." And Janie, her sister, somehow managed to take the credit for it all. "That you should marry a farmer too! I must have talked some sense into you!" Her mother said little, but welcomed Stephen into the house by reaching up and kissing his cheek, a thing which he took to be natural in her but which Betony found astonishing. Dicky was pleased, but had a little worry, too, which he divulged to her in private. "Four kids you're taking on! Have you thought what that'll be like?" he said. "I daresay I'll manage," Betony said.

Stephen's children were filled with dismay when first he broke the news to them. They stared at him in numbed silence. But then Joanna, who prided herself on her quick perception, said: "I knew there was something in the wind!" and somehow the ice was broken with them all.

"I knew it too!" Jamesy claimed.

"So did I," Emma said.

"I'm hanged it *I* did!" Chris said, and there was a bleak, precarious moment when he hung between anger, disapproval, and disbelief, all of which could be seen in his face. "I'm hanged if *I* did!" he said again.

"Well, now that you do know," Stephen said, "I'm hoping you will give me your blessing and wish me well."

He made it clear to his eldest son that the blessing was very important to him, and when he offered Chris his hand, the boy remembered that he was a man. The difficult moment passed away.

"I *do* wish you well! I wish you all the luck in the world!" He clasped Stephen's hand with a son's loyal warmth. "Both of you! I should think I just do!"

When Betony met the children for the first time after they had heard the news, there was shyness on both sides. But Joanna, who was nearly fifteen, had been reading a great many books lately, and she knew the mature way to behave. It was her duty to make Betony feel at ease, and, encouraged by aunt Doe, she made herself spokesman for the rest.

"The main thing as far as we are concerned is that you should make our father happy."

"I will do my best," Betony said.

"It's a great comfort to all of us, to know that when we begin leaving home, dad will not be left alone."

"I hope that won't be for a long while yet. I'd like a chance to get to know you first."

"Well! I'm the clever one of the family!" Jamesy declared, and in the laughter that greeted this sally, there was an easing of constraint.

"Will you still be my teacher?" Emma asked.

"Only till Easter," Betony said. "Then, when your daddy and I are married, I shall be your stepmother instead."

"Will you be coming to live with us?"

"Of course she will, silly!" Jamesy said. "What did you think?"

Emma fell silent, and while her sister and two brothers vied with each other for Betony's attention, she wandered out to the garden alone. At tea-time, when Betony took her place at the table, there was a marigold on her plate, and Emma, slipping into the chair opposite, was watching her with steady eyes.

"My favourite flower," Betony said. She took it and held it to her nose. "How did you know it was my favourite flower?"

Emma merely looked away, almost as though she hadn't heard. She reached for a piece of bread and butter and was scolded for it by aunt Doe.

"Visitors first, Emma. *You* know that."

236

Chris offered the plate to Betony, and Jamesy passed her a dish of jam. Stephen, in his place at the head of the table, watched with relief and some amusement as his children put themselves out to please. Once he met Betony's glance, and a smile passed between them, out of their eyes. "My God! I do love her most damnably!" he thought, and looked away hastily for fear of betraying his feelings too much, under the watchful eyes of his children.

Joanna was talking about the wedding. She was already picturing it, at the church, with herself and Emma as bridesmaids.

"It's a long time to wait, until Easter, isn't it?"

"The time will soon pass," said aunt Doe.

Chapter 13

They were married on Easter Monday and spent their honeymoon in Wales. When they returned to Holland Farm aunt Doe, true to her word, took herself off bag and baggage to the cottage she had bought in Holland Lane.

"We shall be better friends this way," she said to Betony. "The children are your responsibility now. You don't want a watcher in the house."

But always, during the busy times on the farm, or when some domestic crisis occurred, she would come without fail, rattling into the yard on her old ramshackle bicycle, scattering the poultry in all directions and shouting at them in Hindustani.

"Here comes aunt Doe!" Chris would say. "Trying to see how many chickens she can run over before she gets to the back door!"

At shearing-time she would be there, helping to prepare the shearing-feast; at harvest-time she would be there, working tirelessly in the fields; and always, on any family occasion, she would come to lunch or tea and join in the family celebration. When Chris won first prize in a ploughing-match; when Joanna was made head girl of her school; when Jamesy's design for a village hall was accepted by the Huntlip parish council, earning him the sum of twenty guineas; when Emma had a poem called "Autumn Leaves" published in *The Chepsworth Gazette:* these were landmarks in their lives, and the celebration was not complete until aunt Doe was in the house, to add her word of encouragement and praise. Christmas, birthdays, anniversaries, brought her to them laden with gifts, bought as always at church bazaars and rummage sales.

She enjoyed having a home of her own. She called her cottage "Ranjiloor". It stood next to that of her old enemy, the retired schoolmaster, Mr Quelch, and she delighted in vexing him. Her garden was full of docks and nettles, tall purple thistles and willow-herb, and the seeds, floating into his well-kept plot, would bring him storming to the hedge.

"I will *not* get rid of my nettles! – The butterflies like them!" aunt Doe said. "As for the thistles and willow-herb, did you ever see anything so beautiful?"

"Wretched woman!" the old man would say. "You only came to live here to be a plague to me!"

Although her garden was a wilderness – she had sown the willow-herb there herself – she was able to grow all sorts of things merely by clearing a small space and sticking a cutting in the ground.

"You'll never get a clematis to grow like that, not in a month of Sundays!" Mr Quelch said scornfully, but the clematis flourished and so did everything else she grew.

Often she broke off bits of his shrubs, where they overhung his wall in the lane, and these in due course became small bushes, flowering among the nettles and docks.

"I've no idea what it's called," she would say, when her visitors admired some unusual shrub. "You'd better ask Mr Quelch next door. He knows the name of everything."

She could grow better carrots and onions than he did and to add insult to injury would leave great bunches outside his door. He never got the better of her, but he sometimes took her by surprise. One evening she played her violin and the next morning, over the hedge, asked if the noise had disturbed him.

"Yes, it did!" he said to her. "You need to tune up on your middle G!"

"I can't tune it up. The peg's got loose."

"Let me have it," the old man said, "and I'll see what I can do for you."

Aunt Doe gave him the violin and he fashioned a new peg for her. He cut short her thanks with a wave of his hand.

"I couldn't stand that faulty G! But now you can do your worst!" he said.

* * * * *

Emma's poem, "Autumn Leaves", came as a surprise to everyone but Betony. It was she who had prompted the child to write it, and it was she who had suggested sending it to the children's page of *The Chepsworth Gazette*. It had all begun during a walk, when Emma, treading the dead leaves, suddenly said to Betony: "I love the autumn, don't you?"

"Why do you love it particularly?"

"I don't know. I just do."

Betony waited patiently. The child sometimes talked when they were alone, but she needed time.

"It's because of the smell," Emma said. "And because of the berries everywhere. All that colour on the trees!" Then, having glanced behind her as though afraid of being overheard, she said: "I've got a poem in my head."

"Say it to me," Betony said.

"Oh, no, I couldn't do that. I haven't thought of the words yet. Only the feeling, that's all."

"Well, write it down when you get home."

"I expect it will have gone by then."

But that night at bed-time, when Betony went in to say goodnight, Emma produced the poem, neatly written on ruled paper, from under her pillow.

Joanna was just a little put out by Emma's success with this poem of hers. After all, she had once made a serious study of the subject of writing, and she could have given Emma some very valuable advice, if only Emma had bothered to ask.

"I didn't want your advice," Emma said.

"No, that's just it. You always think you know best, my girl."

"The writing of a poem," Betony said, "is rather a private affair, I think."

But Joanna knew all about such things.

"I thought of being a writer myself once, only I grew out of that some time ago." She wrinkled her nose at Betony. "Well, everyone does, don't they?" she said.

"Not quite everyone," Betony said, "otherwise we should have no books."

"With Emma, though, it's just a phase."

"Hark who's talking!" Jamesy said.

Joanna was very grown up these days. She knew there were more important things in life than writing novels and poetry. She had earnest discussions with Betony on the subject of God and religious vocation.

All the children called her Betony, though Emma, in the early days, sometimes called her "Miss Izzard" by mistake, and once made the family laugh by putting up her hand, as in the classroom, when she wanted to gain Betony's attention. The village school had a man in charge now. He was thin and pale and sandy-haired and his name was Mr Toogood.

"Toogood for what?" Chris asked.

"Toogood to be true!" Jamesy said.

"Toogood for this world!" Joanna capped.

The headmaster's name was a huge joke to them. Emma could never mention school without their laughter breaking over her. Once she suddenly burst into tears, struck at Jamesy with her fists, and ran from the room.

"Whatever's the matter with our little Emma, getting into a paddy like that?" asked Chris.

"You tease her too much," Betony said. "You should try listening to her for a change, instead of jeering at everything she says."

"She ought to be used to us by now. She ought to know we mean no harm."

Betony saw, as aunt Doe had seen, that Emma was being held back.

"You should give her a chance to grow up."

But she knew all too well that she wasted her breath. Emma was the baby of the family. She always would be, all her life, and everything she said would always be met with teasing laughter.

Betony got on with all the children. They saw that her interest in them was genuine, and they brought all their troubles to her, as well as their joys. Chris liked to argue with her about politics; the state of the world in general and of agriculture in particular; and the running of the farm.

"If we were to invest in a single tractor –"

"It would mean a man thrown out of work."

"I might have known you'd side with dad!"

"Of course," said Stephen, joining in. "It's a wife's duty to side with her husband. Isn't it in the marriage vows?" And, alone with Betony, he said once: "Am I an old stick-in-the-mud?"

"Sometimes you are," Betony said.

"When?" he asked, somewhat piqued.

"Over this business of the wireless, for instance."

"Let's not have *that* all over again!"

"Well, you did ask me," Betony said.

"I should have known better," he said with a smile.

He was against the wireless. "Noisy spluttering things!" he said. "Why should we want to hear signals from the North Pole?" Yet when the wireless came into the house at last, he would stand transfixed, listening to it, and make himself late feeding the cows.

"You may as well sit down to it, dad."

"No, no, I'm just off," he would say, and would still be there ten minutes later.

The news coming over the wireless was not too good at that time. Everywhere there was grave unrest. The General Strike was in the offing. There was even fear of civil war.

"I'm not surprised!" Betony said. "What does the government expect?"

"It seems as though they expect the worst, judging by the preparations that are going forward."

"Then I hope they get it, that's all."

"You don't mean you hope for civil war?"

"I hope for something that will make the powers-that-be see sense."

"The solutions to our problems don't grow on trees, I'm afraid."

"No, I know," Betony said. "But the government – and, as Bob Tupper says, there's not much to choose between one and another – is not looking for solutions in the right place. They are not *trying* hard enough. That's why there is so little trust among the working-people of our country."

And when the General Strike was over, broken by government strategy, she felt that hope and trust among the working-people would not be revived for many a long

242

and bitter day.

* * * * *

One Sunday in May, 1926, aunt Doe fell off her bicycle, on her way home from church. Mr Quelch found her lying in the road and she was taken to hospital.

"The fuss that man makes, you'd never believe! No doubt he hopes I shall be laid up. But there's nothing whatever the matter with me. Not so much as a scratch anywhere."

But there *was* something wrong with aunt Doe. She had thrombosis in both legs. The doctors advised amputation.

Sitting up in her hospital bed, she told Betony how she had overheard the two specialists talking, only a couple of paces away.

" 'That right leg will have to come off,' I heard one of the so-and-so's say. 'Probably the other as well.' So I drew my curtain and said to him: 'That's *my* leg you're talking about, young man, and *I'll* say whether it's to come off or not!' "

Betony was deeply moved by the old lady's fortitude. It was a moment before she could speak and even then she could not match aunt Doe's composure.

"Will you take their advice?"

"I haven't decided yet. I'm keeping the blighters in suspense!"

In the end, a few days later, she decided against the amputation.

"I think I prefer to take my chance."

While she was still in hospital, she received a visit from Mr Quelch. He sat on the edge of the visitors' chair and tried to make her change her mind.

"A wheelchair wouldn't be so bad. I could easily wheel you about."

"Up and down that steep hill? Don't be ridiculous, Mr Quelch!"

"You'll die if you don't let them amputate."

"I shall die anyway," aunt Doe said. "The only difference between you and me is that I have an inkling of when I shall go. But dead or alive, I'm keeping my legs!"

So she went home to her little cottage and lived a

perfectly normal life. She rode her bicycle to church; dug her garden and mowed her grass; and sowed her rows of wallflower seeds, for filling her borders the following year. Then one day she collapsed and died. Mr Quelch went in, and she lay on the floor. He fetched Stephen immediately.

"Stubborn to the last, that cousin of yours! Why couldn't she listen to good advice? I'd have looked after her, silly old trout!"

There were tears in the old man's eyes, and after the funeral, when the grave had been filled in, he planted a few "slips" from her favourite rose. It was the wrong time of year of course.

"But I daresay they'll grow – for her," he said.

That was the middle of July. Soon the oats were ripening palely in the Freelands at Holland Farm and the men were heard sharpening their scythes. They missed aunt Doe at harvest-time, leading the way out to the field, with her long mannish stride and her heavy shoes and her dark blue straw hat tied over her head. They missed her at every family gathering, and remembered her always, at every turn, even when her name was not actually mentioned. If anyone left a morsel of food on a plate, someone else was sure to say: "The people in Calcutta would be glad of that!" and if anyone expressed too nice a fastidiousness, someone else was sure to say: "I've seen worse that that in Ranjiloor!"

Among the treasures aunt Doe left, there was a dressing-box, which went to Emma, a Ghurka's knife, which went to Chris, and a piece of ivory scrimshaw, which went to Jamesy. She left Joanna her violin. And each of the children received a hundred and fifty pounds.

Joanna was almost seventeen. She would soon be leaving school, but had not yet decided on a career. Having flirted in the past with music, writing, medicine, and religious work, she had now discarded them all and so far nothing had taken their place. She talked about it to the family.

"I want to do something – Oh I don't know –" And, in despair at expressing herself, Joanna flung her arms out wide. "Something *different*!" she exclaimed.

"You could be a lady balloonist," said Chris.

"Or go as a missionary to the Isle of Wight," said Jamesy.

"What about charming snakes in the market-place at Chepsworth?"

"Or deep-sea diving for pearls at Land's End?"

The boys were full of frivolous suggestions. They came up with something new every day. But when Joanna knew about aunt Doe's legacy, she decided to spend it in travelling through Europe for three months with her school-friend, Elaine. Elaine was going with her parents and they had invited Joanna to join them.

"You don't mind if I spend aunt Doe's money like that?"

"Of course I don't," Stephen said. "You can spend it as you please."

"When I come back," Joanna said, "I shall know what work I want to do."

The older children were growing up. Only Emma remained a child. She was doing well at the village school and would probably win a scholarship to the girls' grammar school in Chepsworth in due course.

"You'll be going to Lock's," Betony said. "I went there, after leaving Huntlip. You'll like it, I'm sure."

"What shall I do afterwards?"

"What do you think you want to do?"

"Wanting's no use," Emma said. "That doesn't get you anywhere."

Emma wanted a great many things. She wanted passionately to be able to draw, like Jamesy; to play the piano, like Joanna; to have fair hair like Betony's; to save Mr Toogood from a terrible fire. Often she wished she were somebody else: Flora Macdonald or Edith Cavell; St Teresa or Joan of Arc; Maggie Tulliver or Becky Sharp. She would practise being cold and impassive, denying herself her favourite foods. Then she would switch to the opposite, saying clever, wounding things and snatching the best cake from the dish. She would change her character every few days, almost as often as she changed her frock. She would try something new and cast it aside.

"Emma, my child, just be yourself!" Stephen said once, in exasperation.

But Betony knew that for some children, and Emma was one, it was difficult to know what that "self" was. She had to find it. She had to explore.

"I wonder," she said to Betony once: "I wonder what it's like to be really wicked."

"I hope you're not going to try it out."

"No, I'm putting it into a poem instead."

* * * * *

Sometimes the whole family spent a Sunday at Cobbs. The two boys enjoyed the carpenter's shop. Sometimes Betony went alone, on a week-day, perhaps; but however frequently she went, her father's greeting was always the same.

"Hello, my blossom. You're quite a stranger nowadays."

She had always been his favourite child, and although he was happy to see her married, he missed her sorely at every turn.

"I seen Jack Mercybright last week. He was driving some sheep along the road, out not far from Capleton Wick."

"Where are they living? Did he say?"

"Somewhere near Oakshott, seemingly."

"Nothing more precise than that?"

"I *did* ask him where, but you know what he is. Strikes me he don't never want us to know."

Betony felt that this was true. She had tried often to track them down, but always, by the time she had word of them, they had moved to another place. She worried about Linn and the little boy. She thought of her dead foster brother, Tom Maddox, whose child Robert was, and she felt that she had let him down.

"But what can we do," her father said, "when they make it so plain that they don't want no help from none of us?"

"We can go on trying," Betony said.

The recession was worsening with each year that passed, and the signs of it were everywhere. A great many men, tramping the roads, travelling from one "spike" to the next, called at the farm in search of work. Betony always gave them food and a shilling, perhaps, to set them on their way, just as aunt Doe had always done, and she listened to what they had to say. Once Stephen came into the house just as a man was walking away.

"That man went right through the war," she said. "He's a skilled toolmaker out of a job. He hasn't worked for nearly three years. A land fit for heroes? It makes me ashamed!"

The children of the village itself: sometimes she saw them in the fields, pulling a few turnip-tops or a few leaves of kale, on their way home from school: ragged, ill-shod, all skin and bone, especially those whose fathers had no work. She was on good terms with Mr Toogood, the headmaster, and sometimes she called on him and his wife.

"Some of these children come to school without any breakfast but a cup of tea. They have a slice of bread and margarine at dinner-time and they go home to God-knows-what in the way of supper."

"Yes, I know," Betony said.

She still sent baskets of apples to the school every autumn, and whenever the weather was hard in wintertime, she sent a copper can full of hot baked potatoes every day till the weather improved. Mr Toogood gave them out the moment they arrived, and the children devoured them, skins and all. But one angry mother stormed into the school and railed at him for giving her Ernie "charity".

"What did you say to her?" Betony asked.

"I said this was one decision Ernie was entitled to make for himself."

One evening in the spring of 1928, Betony and Stephen walked in the fields above the farmhouse. From the top of the holl, as they looked down over their own land and that of their neighbours round about: on bright green corn and darker pasture; cattle and pigs and flocks of sheep; with plum orchards in blossom here and there: England looked a land of plenty.

"And so it should be," Betony said, "if only things were properly run."

"I don't see much change in the offing yet. Not for a year or two anyway. Perhaps the thirties will be better."

"Perhaps we need to do something to try and *make* them better."

"What can we do?"

"I don't know. I wish I did."

Stephen gave a little laugh. He drew her arm into his.

"You want to take the whole world and turn it upside down," he said.

"I want to turn it the right way up."

The evening was fine. The air smelt of greenness and freshness and life. There was a gentleness in the wind. They walked together, arm in arm, enjoying the softness of the evening. In the home pasture, next to the house, the mare, Thisbe, was showing off with her new foal. In the meadow known as Long Gains, the shepherd was going the round of his flocks, for lambing time was close at hand. Life at Holland Farm was fair. Of the world beyond – what of that? It would be easy, Betony felt, to shut it out and forget about it.

"There ought to be *something* we can do."

* * * * *

One Saturday morning in May, Challoner called in his motor car, on his way in to town. He returned a shotgun he had borrowed. He and Stephen stood in the yard, and all the time as Challoner talked his gaze was following Betony as she went to and fro, feeding the hens. When she went indoors, he spoke of her.

"You did a good thing when you married that girl. It's given her something to do with herself, instead of poking her nose into men's affairs and stirring things up, as she used to do. A woman's place is in the home."

As Challoner drove away, a boy on a bicycle rode into the yard, bringing the morning's newspaper. Stephen, on his way into the house, glanced inside it, at the back page. There was an advertisement for a debate to be held in the Shire Hall in Chepsworth on Friday, May the twenty-first. Among the speakers would be Mrs Betony Wayman of Holland Farm, Huntlip, who would open the debate with this question: "Unemployment in our land: Is the government doing enough?"

Stephen Wayman smiled to himself. He went indoors in search of his wife.